THE SOULSTEALER WAR

BOOK ONE:
THE FIRST MOTHER'S FIRE

A Novel by

W. L. Hoffman

First published by Dog Ear Publishing
4010 W. 86th Street, Ste H
Indianapolis, IN 46268
www.dogearpublishing.net

ISBN: 978-159858-539-1

This book is printed on acid-free paper.

Printed in the United States of America

DEDICATION

The Soulstealer War is dedicated with love and gratitude to the entire Hoffman Clan, and especially my personal crew—Stephanie, Hallie B, Hannah and Quigley—for their ongoing support and willingness to journey into my worlds....

Finally, with the utmost respect, in memoriam to Roger, whose insight and enthusiasm have inspired so many.

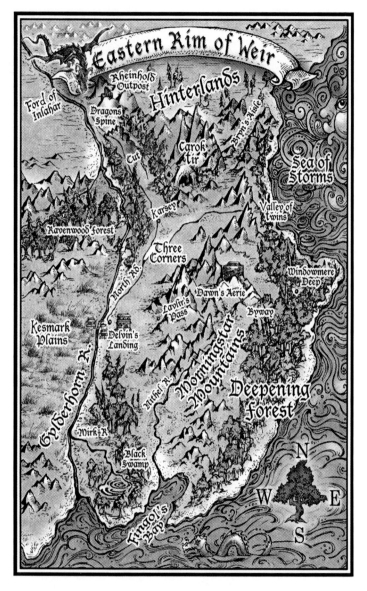

Eastern Rim of Weir

PROLOGUE

F ire, death, and the dust of lives forever extinguished. Black smoke blotted out the sky, an artificial night shrouding pitiful scenes being played on a world drawing its last tortured gasp.

Qualin waited at the Gateway for the inevitable confrontation. Here they would come, at the end of all things. He looked at the two trees, growing side by side, and the magical doorway bridging the gap between their soot-covered trunks. Even now, it wouldn't be too late.

Escape... he thought.

He leaned toward the portal, longing for its saving embrace.

No.

He wrenched away at the last second.

It must stop here. No other world must suffer our fate.

He had been a fool and now bore the guilt for thousands upon thousands of souls. He threw himself down, seeking a hole in which to hide, or maybe a place in which to pray. Finding neither safety nor salvation, Qualin cried hysterically. After a while, his crying subsided.

Then the anger replaced the emptiness; revenge became an oasis for his sanity. They had lied, tricked him into destroying his race. They would pay. Qualin rose from the lifeless soil.

Wait. Can it be?

Beautiful color interrupted the formless gray of destruction. A lone flower had blossomed in the cradling roots of one of the Gate's trees. He marveled that anything so fragile could thrive so magnificently. The air was poison now. The sun was naught but a faded memory. Yet this flower survived.

Then a petal fell.

And another. And another.

They disintegrated before touching soil.

Qualin screamed and then lapsed into a moan. The stem, verdant and healthy, sickened into a moldy hue. It curled earthward, becoming one with the putrid ash burying his world.

They had arrived.

Turning to confront his doom, Qualin could barely see them. Their images were blurred with those of the ghosts screaming in his consciousness. Just as had been foretold, he was the Ruler of all.

Sire of this emptiness, this place of the dead.

The deception was complete. But he had power yet, and it might be sufficient for redemption. So he lingered, dwelling on the only task left to the forsaken.

As the group neared, Qualin returned the blank stare of his once mentor. He bore witness to a sinister visage that ere now had taken refuge from the light of day within an encompassing cloak. Midnight in color, the cloak's uniquely opaque fabric had been much sought after by the ladies of fashion. Little did they fancy that such would be their funeral garments.

Nekros grinned. His mottled yellow skin was bloated, glutted after the feast. It alone gleamed in the ubiquitous dismal haze, a symptom of the pestilence ingesting Qualin's world. The light no longer existed to do Nekros injury.

Qualin brushed his fear aside and then said, "I will not allow you to enter the Gate. Your dark god must look elsewhere for souls to swallow. He may even find pleasure in your worm-ridden half heart."

"Dost thou intend to stop us?" The amused whisper vibrated through the languid air.

"Yes." Qualin regained his former arrogance. "I can and will."

They had given him the tools and the training. He was a master in his own right. Qualin focused his will upon the Gate, seeking, one last time, to command the planet's consciousness to forever seal the doorway.

A laugh echoed, resembling the keening of women, the howling of dogs, and the raving of the insane. Nekros had enjoyed the game and savored this final move. "What was thine is now ours. The Gate heeds our bidding. Did thou think we would share our purpose and the fullness of our powers with thee?"

The full extent of their duplicity crashed inward upon Qualin. In desperation, he wheeled around to the Gate. Before he could leap, the pain piercing his skull brought him to his knees. Nekros had breached his defenses with ease.

"Now the master truly teaches the pupil," said Nekros in a cold, dispassionate voice.

Qualin fell to the ground, writhing. The agony would last long. He knew. He had drained many himself. As Qualin thrashed about, feeling his life force being ripped away, his last vision was of the Nosferu, one by one disappearing into the Gate.

CHAPTER 1
A GIFT IN THE WOODS

Ken McNary walked assuredly along the rugged and often illusory forest path that he had chosen to pursue. For the last week, he had been traveling the Appalachian Trail, roving the more secluded parts along the southern Blue Ridge Mountains. He had set aside two months. A graduation present, he told his friends from law school. A chance to commune with nature before the real world intruded. Well, that part was at least true. He had always been drawn to nature when he needed to do serious thinking. Its scenic highways and unspoiled solitude agreed with his pensive moods, and there were far more of those lately than he cared to admit.

Who would have thought that after surviving three years of law school I'd be searching for options at graduation? An Ivy League law degree and over a hundred thousand of debt...where does that...

His thought was interrupted. Less than one stride away, a mature coral snake, a rare occurrence in the upper Appalachians, bobbed in agitation. It had been basking trailside in the late spring sun. The cold-blooded creatures in this cool mountain climate required a heat infusion to begin their foraging.

Ken was sympathetic, but not overly so. Although unlikely to strike without provocation, the eastern coral is one of the most venomous snakes in North America.

Your fangs may be small, but they pack one heck of a punch. Talk about a loss of focus...it would be a toss-up whether I could reach antivenom before a serious bite put me down.

The toe of his boot was about ten inches from the snake's head. At that distance, there was a remote chance of sampling its potentially fatal brew.

"My luck's holding," said Ken, using calming monotones. "I know that you can hear my voice...at least the vibrations. If you were a cottonmouth, I'd be prying you off my leg. But you don't want to hurt me, and I don't want to hurt you. Take care now; I'm relying on your good reputation. I'm not going to squash you, just easing my foot out of your turf."

Ken retracted his leg slowly while keeping his eyes locked on the snake's coiled form. In so doing, he couldn't help but admire the intricate beauty of its banded markings. He remembered an old rhyme to help novice hikers distinguish the eastern coral from harmless snakes mimicking its colors. *Red touches yellow, kill a fellow.* The mnemonic also reminded Ken of a snake named Jack and of his fifth-grade biology teacher. Mr. Hankol had encouraged Ken's aptitude for the life sciences, even so far as appointing him as that year's caretaker for the biology lab residents. Jack had been a scarlet kingsnake, a coral mimic. Jack's name came from his color rhyme: *Red touches black, friend of Jack.* Although nonvenomous to humans, Jack's periodic feeding had still demonstrated the "circle of life" in no uncertain terms, and while Ken's upbringing had prepared him more than most of the class, there was a whitewash to that phrase that had bothered him even then. *Circle of life...it says nothing of higher purpose, no guarantee of fairness or of living in a world without pain.* He remembered his distaste as each frantic mouse had been dropped into Jack's terrarium. Did their tiny rodent brains guess their impending fate? Why did he care? Millions of mice were consumed each year by private labs, academic institutions, and zoos. He conceded the necessity of their role, but that realization did little to cure his unease. Was it the manner of their death? Had the desperate squeaks of the hopelessly outmatched touched upon a buried thread of commonality? After all, on the geologic timeline, modern humanity was mere centimeters from its ape-like ancestors, who had first risen up on their hind legs only to flee the most terrifying predators in history. Whatever the link, Ken's tenure as zookeeper had been short-lived.

Fifteen years ago, long time.... I bet Jack is eating juicy rats by now if he's still slithering along.

While maintaining a vantage on his venomous friend, Ken detoured sideways from the trail. He hoped the snake would return unmolested to its reptilian daydreams.

The scrub hedging the trail made for rough going, but it was the right choice. Ken was the intruder. It was his responsibility to walk with care. To do otherwise was plain reckless, but that didn't stop anyone these days. He had seen them—the unwary—in every national park that he'd ever visited, and over the years, he had rescued his share.

The unwary, blissfully strolling into harm's way, never imagining that something as simple as poorly fitted shoes, an unbalanced pack, or a compass left in the car could put life at risk and, once in a while, cause a tragedy. Maybe it's the disconnect with today's challenges.... Urban survival is a hodgepodge of knowing when the market opens for fresh bagels, which cell phone carrier has the best coverage, and how to download the latest antivirus definitions. You can't really blame people for the occasional leap from that merry-go-round, but it would be nice if they carried proper equipment and read the instructions before landing. People seem to think that technology has tamed the world. We aren't there yet. Out here, in what's left of the green frontier, the old rules hold sway. You can die just as easily with a portable GPS in hand as not.

As Ken nudged through a patch of mountain laurel and found his feet back on the trail, his thoughts again wandered to less deadly equations in his life. This trip was supposed to be as much of an inner journey as it was an exploration of the Appalachians.

The Clean Air Act... the Environmental Protection Agency... what good is this law degree and the years of sweating out finals if the only people hiring environmental lawyers are the corporations and gas companies who want to know how to avoid everything except the bare letter of the law? I could work for the grassroots environmentalists, but with no money and no resources, not much potential for changing people's views. And if I take that road, how the heck will I ever repay my school loans?

He sought answers as he progressed. The moss and lichens covering the forest floor silently accepted his passage. Occasionally, Ken paused in his journey, acknowledging his only witnesses: the wildlife.

As he stopped to adjust his backpack harness, he glanced at his watch compass.

Due west...surprising, but should be nothing to worry about. Though the Park Service map had shown this trail leading southeast, it would not be out of character for them to neglect a few details.

He scanned the neighboring trees, checking for the two white-paint rectangular blazes used on the Appalachian Trail that would signal an obscure turn or route change. All the trees were clean, and no stone cairn markers were to be seen.

It's been about a mile since the last white blaze. That's probably about as good as I can expect for this offshoot....It's not mainstream Appalachian Trail. There's also bound to be errors when you're mapping this much country. I can always do the yo-yo hike... find my way in, find my way out.

Tightening the shoulder strap of his pack, Ken was ready to resume. A gust of wind ruffled the trees. He looked skyward.

Fresh moisture in the air... pressure is dropping... rainstorm sliding up from the south. As long as there's no lightning, it won't be more than a nuisance in these mountains.

He threw on his wet weather parka and moved on.

The rain caught him a few minutes later, a windy cloudburst at first, then thinning to a light drizzle. In the time it took to cover half a mile, the rain ceased. Ken stuffed his parka in the side netting of his pack.

The muddy path slowed the journey, but not nearly as much as the foliage did. With each bend, more and more branches meandered across his way. It was a gradual build-up; a less seasoned hiker might have stopped.

Ken considered the possibility that the map was right and that he had made a wrong turn.

If this is the trail, the Park Service hasn't done much to maintain it... branches hanging all over the place and nature's brand of barbed wire at my feet. That vine is greenbrier, shiny heart-shaped leaves, and those spikes... cat's claws, as Grandma Gwen would say. She flavors one of her jellies with your crushed pith. And look at your stout cousin there—thistle...waist high and chock full of prickly wings and little daggers... bane of the Danes. According to legend, you stopped a Norse invasion on the coast of Scotland long ago. The Vikings landed at night and removed their boots, hoping for a stealth raid on the sleeping Clansmen. How could they have predicted, until the first painful yelps warned the Scots, that defeat lay underfoot? To this day, the Scots often wear thistle as a charm against evil. You two are a bothersome pair, but I don't see that there's a way around. Well, I'll give it another few miles or so—never know what treasures are waiting on the path less traveled... nesting birds, black bear encounters, weird mushroom outcrops. I've seen great stuff before, and that eastern coral snake will be a contender for this adventure....Most people go their entire lives without meeting one. Maybe the path will clear ahead.

He pressed onward.

Twenty minutes later, Ken regretted his stubbornness. The undergrowth seemed to have a will of its own. Ken's legs were in a constant tangle. As he swept aside the thorny creepers, he couldn't help but nick his hands. The scratches on his fingers were too shallow to be of any worry, but when he bumped into the sturdier thorns at just the right angle, they pricked clean through his jeans, and he felt it.

"Ouch!"

This time he pulled a nasty cat's claw from deep in his palm. He held his sleeve against the cut while a clot formed. His hands were a mess.

If this was an earlier age and I returned from the woods with these wounds, there would be talk of the forest folk and their mischievous ways.

Ken cupped his hands around his mouth and playfully called, "Faeries, Faeries, come out, come out wherever you are."

Of course, there was no reply. Once he had called out, though, Ken regretted his foolishness. One does not casually invoke the legends of Faerie.

He thought about his pragmatic father.

Faeries and the old gods.... Dad would be in hysterics over the notion. All those years immersed in the sterility of the hospital—white walls, beeping monitors, pile after pile of patients' charts—he never stood a chance. Modern medicine doesn't leave time for much else. It's ironic when you consider just how far Grandma Gwen leans in the other direction. The tales of the trooping and solitary Sidhe from her days in old Erin are the gospel truth to her. Not a Midsummer's Eve could pass without a bowl of milk waiting on the windowsill. As much as she and I might wish it, the Sidhe are pure fantasy. Seems a shame.... The world would be brighter with such magical folk.

With his free hand, Ken removed the Park Service map from his vest pocket.

"I don't see how, but I must have lost the trail back at that bend to the west. Well, this isn't the first blind alley that I've taken, and it won't be my last." He sighed. "There's a lesson in humility here. All these years back country, and I can still blow it."

He laughed to himself and said, "Too much thinking on jobs and money. It serves me right."

He folded the map and stuck it inside his vest. As he turned to begin the outbound trek of the yo-yo hike, his foot snagged a rock. His pack weight clinched the awkward tumble.

Though he tucked his arms in to cushion the impact, he hit unexpectedly hard for such a short fall.

Rolling over, Ken saw that his uncomfortable landing was compliments of a broom-handle–thick stub. It jutted a finger's length aboveground, a bull's-eye for pain.

After getting to his feet, he removed his vest and raised his shirt. An ugly black and blue mark was forming, but the skin was unbroken. Flexing, Ken felt a generalized dull ache in the ribs nearest the bruise, but no sharpness or acuity that would signal a more serious injury. He exhaled in relief.

"Whew. The damage could have been a lot worse. Some expert hiker I am; this definitely isn't my best day. Where is that stub? There you are."

He pushed down with the base of his boot. "You won't be bothering anyone else that's crazy enough to follow in my footsteps. Now let's see to your accomplice."

He reached down and gripped the rock that he'd tripped over. It took a few seconds to pry loose. His palm started to bleed again as he tore the rock from the earth. To his utter surprise, when he heaved the rock through the abundant greenery, Ken heard a resounding splash... not the slight *plop* of an object hitting a puddle, but an onerous *thud* suggesting depth.

"There aren't any ponds on the map."

Curiosity impelled him. A curtain of leafy shrubs and hanging branches obscured his vision, but Ken knew the rock had not traveled very far. With a last determined effort, he forged ahead.

A dark pond lay in front of him, serene and still, but by no means stagnant. It formed a perfect circle, but there was no overt indication of human construction. The sole interruption in the pond's glassy smoothness was a diamond-like pattern of mossy rocks that rested an arm's length from the bank nearest him. They, too, had a strangely regular shape. Then he realized that each point of the diamond was aligned with the cardinal directions—north, east, south, and west.

"What are the odds of this grouping occurring naturally? Way too slim."

He refined his observations. The pond was roughly twenty yards across. Except for the exact spot he occupied, it was encircled by old-growth trees. One might even say concealed. Plus, unlike the surrounding forest of mixed northern hardwood, these trees were all white oaks. The Park Service literature said nothing of this rare formation.

He gazed upward, and upward, and upward, along the winter-gray bark of the nearest trunk.

"Definitely old-growth. What are you doing here, and in such a tight cluster? Between the high elevation, wildfires, and early logging, your presence is nothing short of a miracle. White oaks are long-lived, maybe as much as a thousand years. I wonder who planted you and to what end? Circle of trees, water, stone markers…." He drew in a deep breath and stood dumbstruck in admiration and wonder.

I'm in a temple, a sacred site of some sort. That doesn't make sense. I don't know of any Native American shrines like this, and it sure as heck wasn't European explorers. Let me think… one thousand years ago or more… the Early Middle Ages, the days of Charlemagne, and the last gasp of the Druids—tree worshippers. Could be, but nothing that I have read has ever put the Druids here at that time. Talk about discovering treasure on the path less traveled. This is unbelievable! How can this have remained hidden until now? Seems impossible, but if it's true, I'd love to see what artifacts a proper archeological dig would uncover, especially in that pond.

His eyes fell upon the water, and his bedraggled image in its mirrored surface snapped him back from his idle. "Speaking of strange sights, you're looking a bit wild yourself."

After several days of hiking without a shower, Ken saw, the humidity had caused his normally wavy brown hair to curl, and, for lack of a razor, a permanent five o'clock shadow had taken up residence on his jaw. Well, not entirely—he felt the smooth, hairless skin of the four-inch scar that extended downward from his right cheek. It had been almost six weeks since the incident at school. One of the locals at Johnny's Royal Pub had taken the quarters reserving Ken's turn on the pool table. Ken had already waited for more than two hours to play, and the night wasn't getting any younger. Granted, the delay had passed while he shared one-dollar pitchers of beer with his buddy Steve, but a pool game had never failed to relieve stress during finals. Steve had been ambivalent.... They needed decent shut-eye before the following morning's law exam anyway. But Ken couldn't just walk away. The infraction against barroom pool etiquette was annoying, and the continuing saga of the locals resenting students was infuriating. He had tolerated that attitude for too long; it had been a necessary sacrifice if one wished to stay in the good graces of the powers that be at school. With only a few weeks before graduation, the line could be drawn in the sand; they were going to shoot their game. When he had grabbed the guy to tell him so, Ken knew it had been a mistake. Events had been set in motion...cause and effect. The best he could do was to shift his head back. Had he not, the knife slashing upward would have found its intended target. As it was, it had sliced Ken's lower jaw to the bone rather than slicing his neck, and while instincts had preserved Ken's life on the first cut, it was Steve's prompt intervention that had prevented a second swipe. Ken couldn't have asked for a more dependable friend in a tight corner. He had met Steve at the school's flag football team's first game….Steve had been the star offensive lineman, and Ken had been the hot-hands receiver. Steve had also been the only team member other than Ken who had stood more than six feet tall.

Ken rubbed his pink scar and smiled wolfishly. He now had a permanent reminder of two simple rules: anger is trouble and let the unexpected be your guide.

Focusing again on his shimmering reflection, Ken knew that one positive fact was evident: His eyes were no longer stunt doubles for any of Hollywood's famous Dracula stares. It had taken a week of solid sleep and fresh air, but the perpetual red haze that had appeared during finals each semester had departed without a trace. He had known that it would clear in short order, but he wasn't nearly as confident about the other stress factors in his life. Going directly from college to law school had been an expedient path. It also had the semblance of purpose. With law degree in hand and hard debt accruing, however, Ken could no longer ride the academic train. He had never really stopped to think about that day until it was upon him. That was the reason for this trip.

Ken inhaled and was greeted with a full dose of his body odor.

"Whew, sacred site or not, I'm long overdue for a dip. These jeans could sure use a bath, too."

He unclipped his pack and let it slide to the ground. His back felt surprisingly good. He had expected worse after a semester without any real distance hiking. He tossed his vest and shirt nearby and then bent down to unlace his boots. He stopped abruptly as a shiver that had nothing to do with his body temperature crept down his spine.

Doesn't surprise me the way this day's been going. What is it now?

His last such warning had been on a Spring Break climbing excursion to the Pacific Northwest. There, he had been traversing a granite ledge above the timberline, a short runway to his next vertical ascent, when a similar feeling had caused him to hesitate and execute a visual check on his gear. As he scrutinized harness, carabiners, knots, and anchors, the earthquake had hit. He lost his grip, but the lines held. As he rode out the shock wave, however, the granite ramp that he had targeted for his upcoming ascent had sheered off and crashed below with a thunderous boom. Had his guardian angel not halted him when it did, Ken would have plunged to his death. Ken hadn't been able to explain it then or for any of the previous occurrences. He simply had a knack for sensing trouble, and it had no regard for time of day.

Indeed, he had been pried from sleep so often that he had affectionately dubbed it his night-light. It wasn't extra sensory perception as far as he knew, but it wasn't coincidence, either. Grandma Gwen had been the same way. She had once told him that there are those people who move through this life carrying space that's personal to them. It might be as fine as the hair on their skin or extend greater than a country mile. Whatever the scope, within those unseen bounds, those people could perceive things hidden from others. It hadn't exactly been a textbook definition for extra sensory perception, but not too shabby, considering that Grandma Gwen had spent her childhood slogging in the farm fields of County Cork. Apart from Grandma Gwen's folk wisdom, the best scientific interpretation of his night-light had come from a psychology major in his law school class—Barb. Barb liked to party with his crew, enjoying the spur-of-the-moment adventures and late-night discussions in the college-town bars. Her sex kitten look, matched with an insatiable curiosity, had a way of softening your defenses. She was going to be hell on any cross-examination, but you'd get there with a smile. Although Ken rarely spoke about his sixth sense, as it wouldn't mesh with the propriety necessary for a corporate legal career, it wasn't long before he had elicited Barb's opinion during one of the crew's midnight sessions. In her classic psych way, between a cigarette puff and a sip of gin, she had summed it up as fleeting microcapsules when his subconscious tapped a high awareness state, collated information strands from the surroundings into bundled inference, and then manifested the resulting cues to his conscious self as a motor response. It was a comfortingly mundane explanation for something that for so long had seemed so baffling.

Returning to the present, Ken found himself motionless on the pond's tilted fringe. For all he knew, his life depended on holding his position. But he might also have to run for the hills. It was maddening. When a person sees a threat, he reacts. Smell smoke, and there is a fire nearby. Hear thunder rumble in the distance, seek shelter. He had learned to pay attention to the night-light's signal, but his intellect was not capable of translating it. He could only wait for his normal senses to converge. Action would follow.

I don't see anything threatening here. Sky's clear and it's peaceful. Give it time, though.

After a while, when nothing dire happened, Ken exhaled and released the tension in his body. Soon, the feeling subsided; his night-light was dark again.

He was suspicious, though. He wasn't able to dismiss the prior sensation; there had never been a false alarm before. He slowly rose. Using his six-foot four frame to the fullest advantage, he again assayed the area.

Nothing seemed amiss.

Ken's view shifted to the edgewater at his feet—white pebbly sand formed a featureless bottom that rapidly fell into murky blackness. He had bathed in much worse, including an abandoned quarry famous for its water moccasin population. When he bent for a closer inspection of the water, what he saw, or, more accurately, what he didn't see, gave him reason to pause.

No fish, no tadpoles, no insect life... whirligigs, mosqui-toes, dragonflies. Where is everything? Ponds like this should be teeming. Then again, this isn't your typical watering hole. The surrounding flora is all wrong... no cattails, water lilies, or reeds. No dead branches in the sediment, and it's deep like a lake. It could be a limestone sinkhole filled in by rainwater, or an underground stream, but why would the water be so dark and lifeless?

His arm dipped to stir the water. Just as his fingers were about to break the surface tension, a sharp *crack* caused him to whirl around to face the woods. The sound had resembled a branch splitting underfoot. Removing his knife—a United States Marine Corp Ka-Bar, seven inches of high-test carbon steel—from its hip sheath, Ken eased away from the grassy bank toward the noise's origin. The oiled leather grip of his knife was reassuring. Over the years, he had bumped into fellow hikers who had given him no end of grief for carrying the Ka-Bar's extra weight. They would proudly show him their ultralights, the one-and-a-half–ounce polymer folding knives made by some company with a history shorter than his last hair cut. Those knives were for convenience; the Ka-Bar was designed for survival.

Short of the tree line, he stopped and listened. Peering through the oncoming dusk, he felt wary. Something wasn't right, but he couldn't put his finger on it. He almost called it quits, but then he perceived the discrepancy. It was like those pictures in the newspaper comic section where they change miniscule details in two otherwise-identical scenes: Only the trained eye will discern the differences.

Those two oak trees, growing on top of each other... there's a shadow across the trunks where there should be no shadow.

Try as he might, he couldn't determine the shadow's source.

What could be casting it?

In answer to his query, the shadow vanished. It didn't just move, but disappeared: One moment it was there, interrupting the blended tint of the pale gray bark, and the next, nothing. Ken waited a while longer but saw no further change.

Could be a reflection filtering into the forest…. Light can create odd shadows by refracting off naturally occurring mediums such as water and mineral deposits. Heck, maybe it was just an animal…. No, don't kid yourself. You would have seen or heard something beyond the shadow. Damn. Since I walked into this grove, things have gone peculiar. The question is, do I stay here for the night despite this bull or take the long haul back through the needles for a manageable campsite?

He glanced at the declining sunset. The horizon was already purplish-red, and the darkening blue of the upper sky heralded evening's impending arrival. A decision had to be made.

An evening traipse is possible…but it won't be fun. There will be risks, and if I do that, leaving that shadow and this site unexplored are going to nag me. I know it. Guess I'm bedding down here for the night. It's too late to explore effectively anyway. It would be easy to miss a print or spore trace. Whatever clues are there will keep until morning.

He backed away from the trees. When he reached the pond's edge, he put on his shirt and unloaded his gear. There would be no swimming tonight. In fifteen minutes, his lightweight, two-person tent was fully assembled near a bright fire. He didn't need the fire for cooking; if he wanted a hot meal, his camping stove was fine. Nor did the fire serve for warmth. Like the Ka-Bar on his hip, the fire was a reassuring companion, a link to civilization. Ken watched the flames perform their magic.

So basic in nature and yet so complex.…Putting simulations aside, we still haven't created a computer program that can replicate fire; the mathematics are just too intense. Let's hope it stays that way.... Some secrets should be outside of technology's reach.

His view shifted back to the pond and the surrounding trees. *What secrets do you hold? How many other fires have been kindled here on your thousand-year watch, and who else bore witness to them? Was the blood of innocents spilled here as a sacrifice?*

The idea was unnerving, and quite suddenly, Ken felt alone. It wasn't a feeling to which he was accustomed—hiking alone and feeling alone are vastly different states to the seasoned explorer. Ken's eyes wandered, searching for life.

Apart from that rogue shadow, I haven't seen animal or insect since finding this pond. It goes against my grain, but maybe I should try a food teaser to bring out the natives. I could use a bite before bed anyhow.

He removed his chosen ration from the backpack along with his cookware. He reached for his canteen.

Three fingers from the brim and it won't take much more for this meal. I can filter pond water in the morning.

He unscrewed the cap and poured the required fluid into his meal. As the contents warmed over his fire, he checked for critters. His quest was in vain.

Ken ate fast...too fast. A gloomy disquiet propelled the food at an unnatural pace. He finished in near record time and dashed through the necessary camp chores before returning to his seat by the fire. He stared outward. Then he shot a glance right, then behind, then across the dark water, then to the high branches.

That's about enough!

He recognized the self-induced trap that was dangerously close to springing. Experience kicked in full gear. He shut his eyes and renewed his trust.

You're no tenderfoot, so stop acting like one. There's a rational explanation. No need to get spooked. Just listen and absorb. There. In the distance, cricket song and cicada buzz.

Might not be within this circle of old growth, and that could be because of my presence, but the forest is talking nearby as it should. Now get your head on track and save the investigation for the morning.

Having settled his nervous energy, he once again began to sort his post-graduation options.

With all those years of bio and physical science classes, why didn't I go medicine? Dumb question; you know the answer. Dad worked for years taking care of people. One of the few humanitarians I've known. Between Medicare and Medicaid cutting fees and malpractice insurance to cover lawsuits brought every time a stitch was put in too tight, he just wore out. I thought the other side would be different. Mom was always encouraging me to go environmental law. She would look at her garden that was nursed more than most children in the neighborhood and dream of a planet without concrete or pollution....

His thoughts were broken by the wind.

It's blowing steady now, out of the west.

As the wind rushed through the white oaks, bending limbs created eerie groans. They gave the impression of a conversation, one tree issuing a staccato burst followed by a responding pattern from another. The crackling no doubt resulted from the wind, but still, Ken's eyes sought to confirm that fact.

Soon, however, he relaxed his vigil. He finally decided to pull his sleeping bag from the tent and bed on the spongy grass.

For a short time, he stayed awake while his imagination sought to escape the mundane, building shapes in the dark and words in the air. As he drifted into sleep, Ken's gaze turned to the water. Had he not been so wiped out from the day, he might have wondered more at the aberration. The pond's surface was unaffected by the wind. No ripples at all. It was a pristine sheet of glass reflecting the mysterious white oaks and the dancing flames of his fire.

Ken slipped into dreams. He found himself within a library room; its fine wooden craftsmanship harkened to Europe's master woodsmiths. Books of all sizes, leather-bound and dusty, lined the walls. A trestle table, flanked by fur-lined chairs, dominated the center of the chamber. Various maps were stretched across the table's polished wood. Two men, both very tall, sat at the table. Their attention was focused on the map. They spoke of wisdom and war.

Ken approached the men, who were rapidly assuming giant-like stature. Either he was shrinking or they were growing. He stopped directly opposite them and waved, but they took no notice. He said, "Excuse me."

Neither of the men showed any reaction.

He shouted, "Hello!"

At this, one of the men, white-bearded and holding a wooden staff, stopped speaking and gazed upward from the table. His eyes were sky blue. Graying locks of hair matched the finely embroidered acorn pattern on his brown robe. The white-beard let his eyes wander the room and then asked, "Did you sense aught unusual just now?"

His voice was even and strong, belying his apparent age.

The response was thoughtful, if not slow. "Stellrod, much is amiss, my loyal counselor, but gone are the days when I could answer such with certainty."

Ken tried one more time. "Can either of you see me?"

There was no acknowledgment. Apparently, he was undetectable. Then another idea occurred. He reached for the map on the table, and nearly fell. His hand had passed right through it!

Somewhat shocked, he stumbled for words, "Ah, um, what the heck is going on here?"

Stellrod rubbed his whiskers in thought and then continued the conversation. "The Covenant must not be broken."

"I too, would not wish that path."

Ken studied the faces of the men, hoping for the barest acknowledgment. The one asking for advice seemed younger than Stellrod, but not by much. Hints of gray teased the man's sienna brown hair. The most distinguishing feature of his visage was a gleaming silver circlet resting on his forehead. A black jewel was set within the circlet's center. Around the man's neck, on a silver chain, hung a pendant cast in the shape of an acorn.

Fondling the acorn pendant, the man continued in reserved tones, "Evil times are upon us, and great must be the deeds to follow. What guidance would you counsel?"

"Only this: Trust in the ways of the First Mother. She has guided the Elder Race throughout the Cyclings, and always we have vanquished those who have sought our end."

"You speak of a Cleric's faith, Stellrod, not a King's. My friend, long has She been silent, since before the time of Pelham's Stand at Ravenwood. These Nosferu who have entered our land are dividing the Elder Race. They wield power as of old, not seen among us in untold years, and offer a vision many have dreamed in the silent hours."

Stellrod heard an unfamiliar weariness in the king's voice. He sought to comfort his liege and friend.

"Remeth, take heart. There is yet time. I have bidden Aldren undertake the journey to Windowmere Deep. When he reaches the Grove, the Ancients will surely aid our cause."

Rubbing his hands across the table, King Remeth felt tremors deep in the Heartwood. The macrocosm radiating from its living-wood pulsed erratically. "Let us hope the Elder Race has not declined beyond redemption." Glancing knowingly at Stellrod, he gravely considered his people's future.

The library scene faded from Ken's sight, only to be replaced by a grim spectacle. He walked amidst a forest of death. Black were the trees, and bare of leaves; their charred skeletons lay twisted in deformity. He wandered aimlessly, and yet, as only a dreamer may know, with purpose.

He came upon stone ruins. They wore a shroud of dying vegetation. The pungent odors of decay and fungus seeped into his pores. As his gaze darted among the broken edifices, Ken spied a granite doorway set against the hillside.

He approached cautiously.

The portal columns were riddled with cracks, as if straining to contain that which lay beyond.

He crossed their threshold, forsaking the daylight. His nostrils wrinkled in distaste. He'd once stumbled upon day old bear kill that had been broiling in the summer heat of California's High Sierra. That stench had been pleasant by comparison.

The walls on either side of him were fashioned from stone blocks and in the same decrepit condition as the portal. He stood within a vast chamber that sloped farther and farther earthward until darkness claimed dominion. At the point where Ken's sight failed to discern the cavern's detail, the inky blackness suddenly seemed to move. *That's impossible.* He blinked. The void expanded, consuming every speck of light as it swelled upward from the depths. Its form was shapeless and yet changing. It made no sound, nor permitted any to emerge from its unearthly vacuum. The moving blackness didn't walk, crawl, scurry, or leap. Its method of locomotion was unknown.

Even before his mind could process the situation, Ken stepped backward toward daylight, but his foot never left the ground.

The hairs on the back of his neck rose.

The void had halted his flight.

Ken's thoughts cascaded, memories of past and present jumbled with future tangents, all overshadowed by a vast *presence.* Ken attempted to exert order. *They say in the moment before death, a person's life flashes before him. Science has been at a loss to explain this phenomenon, but there are those who suggest that the human experience includes cellular*

*memories and subconscious perception far beyond the limited
information gathered by our senses. I'm not dead, but this is
way outside the bounds of human intervention. The void, it's
alive—oh my god....*

Whatever the instrument of his current fate, in that single microsecond, Ken felt his awareness expand with terrible clarity to a place that he sensed few, if any, would ever follow. And although he was able to grasp only at strings, a fragment of the larger design made itself known. Ken understood for the first time in his life that he was facing *evil*. It was neither the garden-variety hatred common to humanity nor the raw instinct of the animal world. Naming it the Devil would have been convenient, for that implied a sentience and purpose that could be clothed in human terms. This presence gave no hint of such familiarity, and its utter wrongness resonated through his being

Adrenaline-powered sensations flooded Ken's system. Every cell that comprised Kenneth McNary screamed in primal unison.

*This is happening, so deal with it. Don't shutdown.
Retreat is not an option when you're already stuck in the spider's web. You can't run, you can't hide. What about defense?
Having your life snuffed out like a candle is no way for a man
to die.*

He focused his energy on a smaller victory. His trembling arm moved an inch, and then another. By sheer force of will he reached his knife. He withdrew it, his chest heaving from the effort. His mind was nearly overwhelmed by the horror that issued forth to devour him. A cold malignance buffeted him as squarely as any physical assault, yet no blow struck by man could ever have achieved such monstrous effect.

Though he had not shared in formal religious practice because of Grandma Gwen's influence, he had contemplated God from an early age. It had started with his appreciation of nature's infinite creations and their workings. In college, he had learned that such observations underlie a classic philosophical argument for God. The teleological theory held that nature's architecture was too perfect to have arisen by chance, that there is intelligence behind the grand scheme. Another angle was Aristotle's Prime Mover concept. Simply stated, something had set the wheels of creation in motion. Then there was St. Thomas Aquinas' eloquent five-point proof of God: motion, causation, necessity, perfection, and design. All of these proofs were intriguing, but their logic ran counter to hard science. As Ken's pre-med curriculum had exposed him to high-level studies, however, he had developed his own theory, leading him to enroll in such electives as astronomy and cosmology. And though his personal view of the universe might be summarized as "the intersection of science and religion," right about now, it wasn't science that filled him with dread…. It was sheer terror for the preservation of that unique quintessence of each person, that elemental force of energy, which, for lack of a better word, albeit one to which he would claim a reluctant association, has been termed the soul.

Fear wrapped an unwelcome embrace around him. His heart pounded dangerously. He fought to steady the tremors in his muscles.

How can such a thing exist?

With each passing second, Ken's mental strain increased. It was reaching beyond skin and blood. If thoughts create energetic waves, as some quantum theorists predict, then he was on the front swell of a building storm. No training could have prepared him to deal with this attack.

It wants more than my death; it wants to consume me, *my life, my energy.*

As Ken struggled to maintain sanity, breath fled from his lungs as if squeezed away by an invisible hand of nightmarish proportions. Hope diminished, but with every last ounce of courage, Ken rejected that which sought the undoing of his spirit.

The infringing darkness was rapidly closing the distance. It wouldn't be long.

Then, out of nowhere and everywhere, a woman's voice severed the strings of fear. The voice said, "You are the one."

He was free. It was as if a shield had been erected between his mind and the blackness. For all he knew, his death might still be imminent, but whatever miraculous power the woman's voice held was sufficient to repulse the onrushing presence; it hovered in the shadows, waiting.

The woman spoke again, "By wind and water, by earth and air, I summon thee before the Ancients of Windowmere Deep."

A screeching blast spewed from the blackness. It was unbearable.

Ken clutched his ears and scrunched his eyes shut. Suddenly, the sound was gone.

Opening his eyes, Ken beheld the circle of white oaks and the enigmatic pond. A middle-aged woman, garbed in a regal gown of leaves and flowers, stood on the water's dark surface in the center of the rocks. She had four reflections, each bending toward a corner of the rocks' diamond pattern.

Trying to process all that he had been shown, Ken asked, "Am I awake, or is this a dream?"

"Who is to say what is or is not reality," the woman replied sharply.

Then, with more gentleness, she softly said, "My child, look within and know that existence surpasses the illusion of physicality."

Still reeling, Ken felt his thoughts leap together. This was a topic that he had grappled with over the years. *Physicality, it's the paradox of flesh. What are we? Some folks will give you the medical breakdown starting from single-celled organisms that reproduced and differentiated over eons to evolve into a community of specialized members... proteins, DNA, cells, organs, bone, the human body. Others might take it to the next level and say we are bags of water. That admits the major component but avoids the detail. When reduced to the molecular level, the physical matter that comprises who we are, and which we take for granted, is mostly empty space. And it's in the emptiness where the real mysteries thrive—the relationships or energies that affect the infinitesimal bits of floating matter. And somewhere in that cauldron of universal forces is born consciousness. I think, therefore I am. Physicality is indeed an illusion, but one that provides a subjective framework for thought.*

The woman nodded and whispered, "That is a beginning, you must see more."

"If that blackness in the cavern is your idea of more, then I don't want to go there. Can you tell me what it was and where it came from, and while we're at it, who are you?"

Wearily, the woman answered, "Those simple questions are layered with unimaginable complexity. Let me share what I may. As to your first, that was a manifestation of the Enemy. It does not yet inhabit my sphere of influence, though its minions prepare the way. As for I...among humanity, there once was a belief in a planetary consciousness. Your ancestors averred that it lived within every part of your world, no matter how insignificant. It remains an apt analogy of an immature creation. You will soon discover that others comprehend my essence as the First Mother."

She commanded, "Behold, Child of Light!"

Tendrils of ethereal energy streamed to embrace Ken, and the colors of the rainbow swirled about like the aurora borealis. His mind translated the barest glimpse of the First Mother—molten fire flowed from the earth, flowers blossomed in the sun, wind traveled across the ocean expanse, rain fell from the sky, birds sang in the trees, mothers of every kind birthed offspring—it was too much.

"Stop!" he cried.

The woman's voice released the vision. "Child of Destiny, to pass within my innermost realm...and more...you must bathe in my power."

Confused, Ken asked, "What do you mean?"

With graceful dignity, the First Mother made a sweeping motion with her arm that encompassed the water.

Imbued with a trust that he'd never before experienced, Ken undressed and dove into the pond. As his hands entered the water, a jolt surged though him. It was electric, and it was something else. Liquid energy danced across his nerves.

The dive's momentum carried Ken to the surface, but swimming was no easy task. The cool water felt as if it were sliding through his body. He was losing ground, sinking below, but fear didn't have the slightest foothold in his heart. The First Mother was with him, around him. The water closed over his head; he felt no compulsion to breathe. The First Mother cradled his being in the now, to do otherwise would have destroyed him.

After a while, the water drew Ken toward the light emanating from the First Mother. She was waiting on the grassy bank.

Ken staggered out of the pond, his skin tingling all over. A hot wind blew, soothing the water's chill and drying his body. There was no embarrassment at standing naked before the First Mother, for all was hers to know. Was this the innocence that biblical scholars decried as lost by Adam and Eve after the Fall?

The wind ceased, but the branches of the great white oaks swayed. Leaves rustled steadily. Ken again sensed that he was listening to a chorus of voices. He put on his clothes and turned to the First Mother for explanation.

She raised her hands, palm outward, and said, "You have received that which I have left to give. Henceforth, my children shall heed your call. Use wisely that which has been granted, for you are our last hope. The world must be cleansed anew and the energy shifted to favor life. Seek out the Enemy and its invaders—these Nosferu, those who would tear at the fabric of reality, those who forever rob others of dreams and desires. Such is the nemesis of all life. They have finally punched a rift into my heart, and the damage threatens to exceed my control. You must seal the breach and stem the tide of corruption that divides the Elder Race. Banish the forces of destruction."

The First Mother sighed. Then she disappeared.

Seconds later, she materialized on the bank, gliding toward the two intertwining oak trees. A last whisper teased Ken's ears: "You are the sword that must be forged for victory. Do not fail."

As the First Mother passed between the oaks, she once again vanished.

Ken tried to follow, seeking answers for endless questions, but sleep overpowered his muscles and will alike.

CHAPTER 2
THE WAY WITHIN

With golden rays of sunlight beaming through the morning haze and birds singing contentedly, Ken awoke near the cooling ashes of last night's fire.

Where were the birds yesterday? Wood thrushes, there's no mistaking their beautiful three-note clusters and vibrating harmonic. What was it Thoreau had said, a bird in whose strain the story is told... whenever a man hears it, there's a new world and the gates of heaven are not shut against him.

He whistled the melody back to his vocal companions.

Finishing his rendition, Ken rose to stretch and take care of the morning's business. After relieving himself, he swiftly broke camp.

Donning his shoulder pack, he decided to search near the two oaks for an explanation as to yesterday's vanishing shadow. Lazily scanning the trees, his view converged on the conjoining oaks. Suddenly, his memory was triggered, and as if on cue, his dreams flooded back overwhelmingly—the two men, the dead ruins, the blackness, and the First Mother.

"She disappeared between those trees. Come on, that had to be a dream. The whole thing is too crazy."

But he wasn't so sure. He shuddered at the thought of the Enemy.

Ken stalked toward the two oaks, unsure of what he might discover. He was unwilling to dismiss such a vivid dream as nonsense. He took a hard look.

"White bark and gray twigs, fingerlike leaves with the glossy green lobes, but where are your acorns? This time of year and at your age, I would expect to see fruit and flower."

His eyes skimmed the loamy ground.

"No acorn hats from past crops, either. It's odd, yet nothing supernatural. Any number of conditions could be the cause, as could animals feeding on the harvest. Your location is of interest, though. You two are misplaced in this localized stand of pine and spruce. Given the oak ring at the pond, your presence can't be coincidence. You were planted with purpose, part of this sacred site, if that's indeed what I've blundered into."

He stepped nearer to the intertwining lower limbs. The branches had sprouted horizontally, shoots reaching toward the other, and then turned upward, each becoming part of the other's canopy.

"It's a wonder that you didn't choke off with thickening growth. You remind me of Ovid's myth of Baucis and Philemon. For showing kindness to strangers, who were actually Jupiter and Hermes in disguise, the couple was granted their wish that they should die together so that neither would live alone on the earth. When that day came, the gods, overly pleased, transmuted the loving couple into connected trees. The people who planted you two had their own myths, and if they were Druids, then they might have honored your uniqueness as divinely inspired."

The talk of gods turned Ken's attention to the woman from his dreams, the First Mother. "She vanished here. Vanished." It lingered in his thoughts and filled him with foreboding.

"If it was all a dream," reasoned Ken, "then no harm, no foul. However, if we are talking reality, there's no sense charging ahead haphazardly."

He walked around the twin oaks and stopped when he had come full circle. "Let's employ a little scientific method."

He lifted his arm and, feeling silly, gingerly slid his hand into their doorway-like plane. The chuckling in his throat was abruptly stifled. His hand had disappeared.

He yanked it back.

"To heck with science; that's more like sorcery."

Ken flexed his fingers. "No ill effects, and the temperature felt the same. But what the heck have I gotten myself into? Last night wasn't nerves, and it wasn't my untamed subconscious. It was the real deal, all of it."

Suddenly, the world was wobbling, and he nearly heaved breakfast. He sat down in silence, staring at the choice of his life and let the implications settle.

The minutes passed unnoticed as Ken considered his options. The deciding factor was the First Mother and the message she had delivered.

He rose and dusted off his jeans.

"No matter what else the First Mother may be, I know she is a friend to life on Earth. She might even be the very fountainhead of our existence. If she's in trouble, humanity won't be far behind. She made darn sure that I saw her disappear between these trees. I have to assume that she had good reason. I'm at least going to take a look at the other side. Now, for a marker, something other than 'Here lies Kenneth Lugh McNary.'"

He gathered up egg-sized stones, mostly granite, and put them down in the shape of an arrow before the opening. After a few tries, he secured a rock soft enough to carve. He etched his initials and put the rock face down in front of the arrow.

"That should do if I don't return and if anyone tracks me this far. Oh man, this is insane on so many levels."

After securing his backpack and glancing at his knife, Ken closed his eyes.

"Well, here goes."

Taking a long deep breath, he walked under the oak trees' branches. As he crossed their threshold, his muscles labored to complete their task. He might have been striding through a sea of molasses. Then, like a rubber band that snaps, he lurched free.

Regaining his balance, Ken was stunned by the other side of magic.

Instead of northern hardwood, the forest had been transformed into what appeared to be immense redwoods. They had the right branch patterns and distinctive cinnamon coloration. He was in awe of their sheer presence. He had once visited Sequoia National Park. One of its more famous sights was an ancient fallen redwood straddling the main access road. It had a tunnel through its base that could accommodate most passenger cars. These titans could digest an eighteen-wheeler with room to spare.

Within the shaded forest understory, lusty ferns prospered. He couldn't identify the species; they were enormous. The air, too, had a more vigorous texture. It was saturated with rich organics and woody resins.

As he stood, captivated by the exotic, a memory of his evidence teacher at law school arose. Professor Norwick was a trip, a sixties hippie who had imported if/then logic theorems and out-of-the-box thinking into a class dominated by rigid procedure. On the first day of class, he had put an empty glass pitcher on the desk, filled it to the brim with half-inch stones, and then asked the class if the pitcher was full. Everyone understood there was probably a catch to the question, but finally, one student had raised his hand and stated that he thought the pitcher was full. Professor Norwick had then reached below his lecture podium and held up a bag of sand. He had then poured it into the pitcher, sealing the space between the stones, and once again asked if it was full. More hands had gone up this time, and Professor Norwick had called on a student who answered in the affirmative with greater confidence. Professor Norwick had leaned down again, produced a tall glass of water, and, to the class's delight, added it to the pitcher of stones and sand. Point made, he had begun his lecture. "As good lawyers, you must all pay due deference to the facts. While you cannot manufacture evidence in organizing your case, you can and must learn to explore every possibility and to formulate logical conclusions from the available data."

Ken put the evidence from his experiences in the past twenty-four hours all together, and one answer, however unreasonable, came to mind. "The facts have spoken. This is not the Earth that I know."

He spun around. From this side of the invisible doorway, the landscape was also dramatically altered. The two oaks through which he had passed and the white oaks hedging the pond were now thrice their previous height and girth. Near the area where he had first pushed through the undergrowth to view the pond, there was a path of inlaid stone; it led to the water's edge, circled its bank, and then split off directly to where he stood. There was also a break in the tree ring opposite his arrival point, with another path. The pond was different, as well. It had been intentionally constructed into a perfect sphere, with heavy white stone blocks forming a retaining wall around its perimeter. The diamond pattern of mossy boulders was now revealed as four obelisks rising several feet above the water. They were composed of semi-clear, crystalline rock with angular planes that tapered to pyramidal points.

"The pertinent question of the moment is, can I get home."

He repositioned himself almost under the oaks' arched branches, searching their unseen event horizon for a hint of the supernatural.

"There's no warning from this aspect, either, not even an 'Abandon hope, all ye who enter.'" Ken chuckled dryly and then thrust his face into the aperture. The disconcerting slow-motion effect happened again. It only took seconds to determine that the terrain had reverted to that of the Blue Ridge Mountains. Feeling a bit like a turtle protruding its head much too far from the shell, he hurriedly pulled back.

"At least the door swings both ways. So, do I take the return ticket from Wonderland or join Alice in tumbling down the well? The First Mother said I was here for a purpose. I have to stop the Nosferu, whoever or whatever they are, and keep this Elder Race together. And then there's the Enemy from the ruins. That's a tall order. How the heck am I supposed to find the cure for all these problems? I can't even straighten out my life. I started this adventure hoping for insight, not to enlist for a tour of duty in the war between… between what? The First Mother and this Enemy are way out of my league."

Ken frowned and swore silently. He didn't appreciate being played like a puppet. Up until now, his version of the universe had included unknowns, but, for the most part, had been his to control. If there was a God, then with one hundred trillion planets in the known cosmos, it surely had more grandiose things to do than keep tabs upon mankind. Yet, the First Mother's intercession argued otherwise, and that possibility disturbed him greatly.

Ken wrestled with his doubts. He had made it this far. Was he prepared to go all the way? This might be his last chance to return to a normal life. Before anything else happened, he could walk through the exit. The memories would fade over time.

The alternative was leaving everyone and everything from home… no fanfare, no goodbyes, and no way of knowing that he would again see Earth. As hard as these conditions seemed, they were only the opening act. The real dilemma lay with the opportunity before him, the potentially once-in-a-lifetime chance to make a contribution to a higher cause. Although meaning can be found in every layer of human existence, whether it's smiling at a passerby or sharing in true love, that meaning remains bound and frequently obscured by the limitations of humanity's terrestrial context, Ken knew. On Earth, matters of the spirit are interpreted by subjective faith, not objective fact. He was now in a place where those boundaries were thinner; god-like entities were vying for dominance, and his actions might affect the outcome. He was unexpectedly standing in the universe's express lane. If he gambled and lost to the Enemy, it might be a death far different than his due.

Ken kept arguing with himself; there could be no regrets hampering his actions, no half effort. Survival in any situation is about willpower and commitment. Far more quickly than Ken had expected, the final decision was made.

"I'll just have to trust that she knows what she's doing. First Mother, or whatever you call yourself, you've got a point man. I'm not making any guarantees on results. All I can give you is my best effort, which might go a lot further if you had supplied more information. Where is this place? What are the dangers? And what do I do next? Damn."

For a moment, frustration had the upper hand. Realizing that his dissatisfaction wouldn't improve the situation, Ken forced himself to calm down.

"One thing's for sure, I can't work under the same assumptions as at home, so until further notice, caution is the watchword of the day."

He started by taking inventory of his water and food. "Even with last night's meal, the canteen is only a few big gulps shy of full. It'll keep until the next watering hole. I'll be damned if I let any part of my body touch this pond again. On food, let's see, between dehydrated meals, energy bars, and my trail mix, figure about a week's worth of pack food left."

He had planned to use nature's pantry during his two-month Appalachian hike. In the unlikely event that he was really hurting, he could have always put aside his pride and bought more provisions. The well-traveled corridors of the

Appalachian Trail sheltered many a country market. "So much for purchasing a meal," he observed. "I'll have to make do. That is, if the rules haven't changed too dramatically."

His attention swung to the stone path on the far side of the pond, and then he glanced at his watch compass. The needle wasn't spinning circles. "I've got north and south needle alignment to use as a reference, but this isn't Earth, might not even be a planet. Feels like one, though—solid ground, vegetation, sunlight. Okay, scrap the heavy existence debate. I am on a planet. That doesn't mean that the geomagnetic fields here correspond to true north-south. For all I know, it might be east-west. Plus, I can't account for magnetic declination. The variation between the location of the magnetic pole and the directional pole could be thousands of miles. Still, there was a pond on Earth, and there's one here. Same ring of trees, albeit changed in character. Four stones, four crystals."

He walked over to the four markers and compared his compass readings. "The directions match. That's good for me. Problem solved. Now, is it Door Number One or Door Number Two? I was heading west when all this started; seems like the right way to continue."

As Ken neared the western opening of the tree ring, he saw that the white stones were replaced with natural terrain outside the ring. He laughed. "I never did like the yellow-brick-road factor."

Before embarking, he created the beginnings of a mental map—a discipline that had saved his life on at least one occasion. After all, the twin oaks could be the only way home. Satisfied that he had their location firmly imbedded in his virtual map, Ken began walking.

After seven hours of hiking due west, Ken decided to establish camp for the night. Although he was overall in good shape from years of exercise, it would be reckless to press his reserves in this strange land… maybe outright dangerous. The nocturnal predators would soon be emerging to feed. As long as he completed suitable preparations, chances were he wouldn't wind up on anyone's menu. Usually, he only took extra precautions in bear country, but who could say what sort of creatures might be on the prowl in this colossal forest? During the day, he had noted one obvious pattern that left him at a disadvantage: Though the animals so far appeared similar to North American wildlife, like the forest itself, they were much larger and more robust than their counterparts. Around noon, he had stopped to snack. The split trunk of a fallen redwood had made an ideal perch. Everything had been fine until he tilted his head to drink from his canteen. There, reflected in its mirror-like metal surface, had been two monstrous eyes and a twitching tail. The Ka-Bar practically materialized into his hand as he jumped up to face his nemesis. Ten feet up the trunk, the dog-sized red squirrel chattered happily. Like most opportunistic squirrels, it had simply been attracted by the food. Ken had laughed aloud and then sheathed his knife, but during the rest of the day, he had observed size differentials in animals far more menacing than squirrels. While slightly unnerved by their appearance, however, he had never truly felt threatened. If anything, he had begun to sense an amused tolerance as creatures paused in their daily foraging to inspect this woodland traveler. The night, however, would be different, Ken knew; it belonged to the deadlier hunters, those that feasted on meat. Whether it was the unknowns of the situation into which he had been thrust or a prophetic sense of destiny, Ken perceived an amorphous threat looming in the advancing darkness. Tonight, he might need all his wilderness training and survival expertise.

It didn't take long to spy the ideal campsite. Just ahead, the ground sloped up to become a rolling hilltop. A lone, but truly huge, redwood resided on the crest.

Ken smiled. "Defendable elevation… tradeoff is that it leaves me exposed. Still, I can use the base to protect my flank."

Ascending toward the old goliath, Ken sidestepped an assortment of branches in various states of decay scattered on the grass-carpeted hillside. Years of storm winds and lightning strikes had barely put a dent in this venerable tree; it was ample stock for his purposes. He viewed it as a good omen.

"That's a nice turn of events, a soft bed for my sleep and firewood to boot." Patting the tree's craggy bark, he said, "Thank you, great one."

Incredibly, as Ken's hand touched the tree, he felt the slightest of vibrations. Ascribing it to the wind, he went about his business. He unclipped his pack and propped it against the tree. Relieved of the weight, he then walked a three-hundred-and-sixty–degree perimeter along the foot of the hill. Land features were identified and filed away; darkness had a funny way of playing tricks with the most innocuous landscape, and Ken couldn't afford such folly in this untested world. Familiarity was the remedy. He also marked the backdoor. Though he couldn't foresee a situation in which he would choose to do other than stand his ground, his training called for at least two predefined paths from camp. In the middle of a crisis, precious seconds would not be sacrificed blundering for clear egress. Ken gathered and stacked wood for the night and dug a fire pit with the Ka-Bar—shallow to avoid the tree's roots, but suitably deep to screen the fire from onlookers. Satisfied, Ken lit the kindling. He quickly heaved on the largest logs, letting them burn high while daylight remained. The smoke would diffuse sufficiently as to be unnoticeable, and the hot coals would last overnight.

Ken sat with the fire between him and the tree. Looking outward from his hilltop perch, he contemplated his audience of plant behemoths. *I'm living a fairytale, and there's no one I can tell about it. Or am I? Will I wake up from this dream only to find that I'm trailside in the Appalachians? Maybe that eastern coral bit me? Its neurotoxin might deliver me into a world of delusion? No! Ken, old man, do not start down that road. Your gut knows the difference. This reality may be fantastical, but reality it remains… at least until you confirm the contrary beyond a doubt.*

As he continued to mull over his situation, every so often, he turned from the arboreal splendor to stare at the aged evergreen at his back. As wild as it sounded, when he had touched its bark, Ken had acquired the distinct impression of having been greeted.

Night arrived, and after a while, he unpacked the camping stove and set about cooking his favorite dehydrated treat—Swedish meatballs with noodles. The water usage was forgivable. The comfort of a tasty meal was more important.

After cleaning his eating gear with dirt, he decided to turn in early. Fresh timber was fed to the fire, but no more than was needed to sustain a gentle flame. With the cool night air descending to the forest floor, warmth was a consideration. There would be no tent tonight… it was too risky. He pulled his sleeping bag over to the tree a few feet from the flames and bedded down fully clothed with his back to the fire. Long ago, he had learned that facing a campfire was an invitation to trouble; the bright flame would leave a person night blind. Closing his eyes, he settled into a light slumber.

In the middle of the night, Ken opened his eyes.

Redwood bark stared back.

Damn, I know this drill only too well.

His night-light had roused him. Before he had a chance to unzip his bag, something pushed against the material near his feet.

Reflexes took over. He rolled sideways, sleeping bag and all. In a flash, he was out and crouching with knife in hand. In his head, he heard Uncle Dale's instructions as if the two of them were camping together like times past: *Son, the only thing that has the luxury of minutes to wake in the forest is meat, dead meat.*

Dale was mom's older brother. While mom had chosen to live by the ocean, Dale had turned inland, preferring lush woods and rolling hills. Uncle Dale had a farm in Virginia, along the edge of the Shenandoah Valley. Ken owed his best woodcraft to summer adventures with Dale. Patient and practical, Dale enjoyed Ken's company on the farm. They had hiked and hunted together for weeks at a spell. It wasn't that Dale didn't have responsibilities…. Aunt Louise and the twins could keep anybody busy, and there was also Grandma Gwen. But it was different for Dale having another man around, and Ken was like a son to him. Aunt Louise seemed to understand Dale's need, and, if anything, encouraged the two to disappear on their camping expeditions. Regretfully, with the pressure of law school, Ken felt it had been too long since his last visit; he would have to take care of that when he got back.

Ken's eyes searched for his evening visitor. It was a gloomy night. There was still no moon as far as he could tell. Even on Earth, the moon was finishing its waning phase on its way to the new moon—it would hardly be visible. Luckily, the dim light of Ken's campfire coals helped his cause. He trained his attention on an undulating movement along the ground.

It's probably a snake cozying up for a warm bed.

As Ken stalked forward, he froze.

A half-buried tree root as thick as his torso was plowing through the topsoil. It extended from the old redwood.

"Unbelievable."

He blinked and wiped his eyes.

No change. It's moving. In fact, the whole tree is shaking.

Then he remembered the swaying oaks from his dream.

"The First Mother said her forces would be at my call. Who could've guessed what that meant? If this is par for the course, I'll have to be ready for anything, whether it's in my realm of the possible or otherwise."

He made a mental note to burn only dead timber in his fires. Then, feeling foolish, he addressed the tree politely. "Excuse me, just what do you want from me?"

Although no spoken answer came, the root shook vigorously and then receded into the hillside.

Awake and fully aware, Ken used his senses to surveil the surroundings.

Silence, not even a wayward chirp. Trouble's afoot, and it can't be far.

Ken dug into his pack and removed his flashlight, a black mini Maglite. The beam was bright and tight. Shined in the eyes, it could effectively deter an incoming critter. He would listen and wait. The forest would hold its breath for only so long. As a kid growing up beachfront on the Jersey Shore, Ken had spent his share of days sitting atop the bulkhead in front of his house staring in endless fascination at the incoming waves. He'd start by picking a wake on the horizon. He'd follow it in. The wake would become a top swell. As it hastened shoreward, the top swell would rise. The shallow bottom would force the crest higher... and higher...and Ken would wait, mesmerized by the process, knowing that the graceful pattern would be lost in the inevitable chaos of the shore break. The present silence in the forest was like that fateful gap that occurs the instant before a wave curls over and replaces the aquamarine blue with foaming white water.

Suddenly, a piercing scream broke the spell.

It's time for action. Whoever screamed needs help. At least now I know there are people here... although a cry in the night is not the meeting I would have preferred.

He glided past shadowy outlines, pushing ferns aside and pointing his flashlight earthward to illuminate each footfall.

Another scream. *That's the sound of pain. No animal vocalizations that I can hear.*

Ken tried to increase his pace, but the light conditions were too poor.

The first rule of any rescue operation is to not become a victim yourself.

Gradually and unerringly, he closed in on the direction from which he guessed the last scream had originated. His adrenaline was pumping.

There's a campfire ahead. I don't like the look of this.

Natural caution took control; Ken shut the flashlight off and quietly dropped to the ground.

Five figures and a group of tethered horses were revealed in the flickering firelight. Three men held a fourth man on his knees, arms pinned behind his back. The fifth man had his back to Ken and was facing the prisoner. Judging from his mannerisms and dress, the fifth man had to be in command. He wore sleek pants and had long black riding boots. An impressive fur cape blew lazily in the shifting wind. The other three men were dressed much less splendidly; their clothes were tattered and filthy.

You guys probably reek worse than the manure from those horses.

Ken spied a glitter of light reflecting from the neck of one of the men holding the captive. Ken studied the scene further, and then the realization struck him.

They have metal collars around their necks, and it doesn't look like jewelry. Criminals? Prisoners? What kind of place has the First Mother dropped me into?

Working for a better vantage, Ken inched along the ground on his belly. The movement took a while…. Every foot closer required his undivided attention. This was serious business; distraction might even be fatal. These men were up to no good, and there wasn't any cavalry to come charging to the rescue if he got his back against the wall.

He stopped in a woody hollow about twenty feet away from the five men. Peering over a nearby tree's gnarled roots, Ken ascertained that the leader was the tallest man he had ever encountered. This was an impressive feat, considering that while Ken lacked the talent for professional ball, he had played against giants on the basketball court during college.

And though the prisoner was on his knees, he too, appeared overly large. The others, however, were normal. In fact, all of them were smaller than Ken. The four horses also reflected this pattern: three were earth-sized, and the last was a huge black roan. It was like a Clydesdale on steroids, without the heavy hoof structure. It could easily support the leader.

So, the size differentials aren't confined to the animals and plants. Well, these guys may be bigger and stronger, but I'm willing to bet I've got them on speed and dexterity. Before I make a move, though, I've got to know more about what they're doing.

As if in response to Ken's thought, the leader nodded to his confederates who tightened their hold. He touched the prisoner's forehead.

An ear-shattering scream erupted from the prisoner.

How can he produce that result from touch alone?

The leader laughed in a sickening tone as he removed his finger from the prisoner and said, "Disciple of Stellrod, how do you like the taste of real power? The High Cleric's teachings cannot protect you from this Nosferu gift. Indeed, I doubt any of the Elder Race could withstand such enchantment."

"You," panted the prisoner, "are upon the path of ruin. Forsake this doom while you may."

The leader's face hardened. "You will tell me now the purpose of your journey. If need be, you will scream until finally you have no voice with which to cry. What counsel does the High Cleric hope to receive from the Ancients? Surely, you must realize Her time is over."

At this point, Ken had sat on sidelines long enough: he was committed to action.

Uncle Dale always said that anyone can pick a fight. It's the thinking man who finishes it.

The three men holding the captive had swords held securely in hip scabbards.

Could it be this world hasn't discovered gunpowder?

No weaponry was visible on the leader. Putting aside thoughts of conventional arms, however, this man still represented a grave threat. Surprisingly, the captive had not been disarmed. A sword pommel poked invitingly from a scabbard at his side.

Overconfidence or carelessness... either way it's a plus. If I can free the captive, it's two against four. Those aren't the best odds, but I don't see that there's any choice. I am not going to watch this atrocity.

Removing the Ka-Bar from its leather sheath, Ken felt his jaw tighten in anticipation. He could never kill in cold blood, but he wasn't so sure if it came to self-defense. The leader still had his back to Ken. Rising to a crouch, Ken waited for the exact alignment. The Ka-Bar rested firmly against his forearm, blade pointing to his elbow. It was a concealed extension waiting for deployment.

Closer...Closer...Now!

Ken sprang from the tree's cover and launched himself feet-first into the leader's back. Justifiably startled, the men holding the prisoner released their grip only to feel the impact of their master as he was propelled over the captive and headlong into them.

Before Ken could say anything, the former captive grabbed his sword and ruthlessly slashed at the tangle of men. In seemingly slow motion, the sword pierced one man's midsection. Ken had never witnessed firsthand such violence among men, but neither was he the least bit squeamish. As his chosen ally ripped the sword free and engaged the other henchmen, the leader rose to confront Ken.

"Little one," he growled, "few have ever gathered the nerve to assault me so. None has lived to tell of the deed."

With that said, a presence sank its voracious claws into Ken's mind. It was like the emanations from the Enemy in his dream, and though puissant in its foul intent, this invasion did not produce the same terror. This enemy had a face.

The man spoke, and yet the voice resounded in Ken's consciousness. "Kneel to me, and perhaps your death may be swift."

Ken lost feeling in his limbs. It felt like the lifeblood in his veins was being stolen. He tried to swing his knife forward, but his muscles refused to obey. He couldn't move. It was more of the same as the black thing from the ruins.

"Kneel!" the man commanded.

The word hit like a sledgehammer. Burning torment raced through Ken's head as pressure built like a tightening vise. He tried to resist the malevolent force twisting his will. Sweat trickled down his neck as he sensed his legs were close to buckling. Once again, however, he would not surrender. He mustered the will to reach for sanctuary, though he knew not where it lay.

Fight…. Find something stronger…. This is only a man; you can beat a man.

As Ken searched within, a picture flashed by of the First Mother waving her hand across the pond. His skin quivered with the same bizarre electric excitation he had experienced in the water

That pond, the water… it was like being adrift in some primeval sea, but not alone, never alone. She was with me then, as…as She is now.

His mind leapt to the water that he knew best, the ocean. Not just any ocean, it was the mighty Atlantic by whose shores he had lived for most of his life. Flat and tranquil on a calm day, the Atlantic was unrivaled omnipotence during a northeaster.

Strangely, the debilitating pain racking Ken's head faded. The pins and needles of returning sensation crawled along his arms and legs.

Ken steadied himself. Then, keenly aware of the earth beneath his boots, he defied the man's fanatical gaze and simply said, "Never."

That single word spoken through gritted teeth had devastating effect. The tall man's countenance registered complete shock. His power waned. Like the snapping of a cord, the invading presence fled Ken's mind.

The man backed away. Darting a glance sidelong from Ken, the man saw his last cohort fall under the former captive's blade. His eyebrows narrowed. "Who are you to bear such power?"

Before Ken could respond, the huge man sped to the horses. He untied the smaller ones and slapped them hard; they took off running. Then he leapt onto the black roan. As he grabbed the reins, he shouted, "I will not be denied. Whoever you are, your time shall come."

He then gave boot to the horse's flank.

As the sound of pounding hooves dwindled in the night, Ken too, made a promise. "When our paths cross again, I'll be ready."

Sheathing his knife, Ken turned to greet his ally only to find a sword point waved menacingly in his direction. Although the man towered over him, Ken spoke in a low voice carrying mild irritation.

"Considering I just risked my neck saving your hide, that's a poor way to show gratitude."

The stranger held fast, his long brown hair dangling in the breeze. Each man evaluated the other. The stranger wore sturdy leather bucks and had a light greenish shirt with lacing near the collar. Opposite the now-empty leather scabbard, a brown satchel was secured to his belt.

Ken guessed that he presented an equally foreign image.

Navy blue vest, red river shirt, jeans... he probably doesn't have a clue what to do with me.

As Ken searched for meaning in the lean face before him, he descried a silvery light shimmering within the man's eyes. It might have been the firelight, but he didn't think so.

They say the eyes are the windows of the soul. I wonder if mine tell a story in this world of magic and giants.

The other man finally opted to lower his weapon to a resting position.

"I am Aldren, son of Eril Dragonsbane, of Hemdall's Line. Declare yourself."

Ken didn't quite know how to digest this greeting.

Dragonsbane? If there's any substance behind that title, life just got a whole lot more complicated.

Seeing that Aldren was waiting tensely, Ken returned the introduction with outstretched hand. "Ken McNary, pleased to meet you."

The sword point leveled to within a foot of Ken's heart.

"Who are you, that family lines are nameless?"

Ken replied with a straight face, "You wouldn't know my folks."

Aldren paused and reexamined the man before him. Then, with new awareness dawning, stated, "I know not how, but you are of the race of man, the Despoiler, as some would have it. I mistakenly thought you one of the Elder Race. Your greeting would have been cause for insult were it not so."

Looking down the edge of his long sword, Aldren commented, "You are large for a human, and there is a feel about you that bespeaks not of humanity."

The poised blade dropped rapidly to the awaiting scabbard.

"Nevertheless, I owe you much, and it will not be forgotten so long as Hemdall's Line walks the forests of Weir. You were brave to have challenged such an Elder Lord."

Ken had taken his fill of Aldren's patronizing tone and interrupted. "The one who escaped?"

Aldren nodded. "He is Corin, son of Creth, of Ciarde's Line. There are those who name him Corin Shadowalker. Ere tonight, I had no reason for using that epithet, yet evermore shall it be so. Even from my vision was he able to conceal the extent of his depravity. Thus, I was captured. He suckles deeply upon the living, and eventually, all that he touches will bear his taint. Now that his true nature is revealed, we may yet forestall this doom. This bane is not unknown to the Elder Race, but until this eve, it lived only in the records of old. Stellrod must be told of this as soon as possible."

Ken absorbed the information.

Stellrod! No coincidence there... probably the white-beard from my dream.... Ah, correction, better make that my experience. And the Elder Race... it's as the First Mother said, but since when are humans the Despoiler? That can't be good; seems like I should tread carefully and hold the questions for now.

Ken extended the olive branch. "My camp is a short distance away. You're welcome to join me for the remainder of the night."

Scanning the dark forest beyond the firelight, Aldren replied, "This place bears the scars of Shadowalker's presence. Your camp would be welcome."

"That's a fairly subtle description of three dead bodies and the aftermath of your sword. Still, they probably would have killed us, given the chance. Other than your report to Stellrod, is there anything like the police or a local sheriff in this place that would need to hear our version of events?"

Aldren repeated slowly "Police or sheriff... these words are strange to me. If you are asking whether there is someone to whom we must justify our actions this night, then the answer is no. Your tally will be read at this journey's end. While others will look from without and see what they may, yours is the vantage that matters."

"Not sure about that last statement," Ken mumbled. "With everything that's happened, I'm relieved to hear that I won't have the local militia chasing my tail. Look, I don't know your customs. You feel any compulsion to bury the dead?"

Aldren frowned distastefully. "Let the forest claim its due."

"Agreed," Ken said reluctantly. His preference would have been a decent burial. That could be perceived as weakness, however, and three bodies would take hours of digging that would only be undone anyway by the forest scavengers.

Ken said, "Hang on a minute." He removed a single flaming brand from the fire and set it aside. Using handfuls of dirt and his boots, he smothered what was left.

Satisfied, he slapped his hands against his jeans. "Force of habit. A wildfire in this forest would be a tragedy."

Aldren thought, *there could be no such fire in these woods. He is ignorant of the forest spirits, but it is rare to find such commendable intentions in a human.*

Grabbing the makeshift torch, Ken led Aldren through the woods in silence. When they reached the hillside and the protective arms of the redwood, he felt safe.

Aldren studied the old redwood. "Your encampment is well chosen. I cannot understand why, but this Elder One favors you, though your race be human."

Ken paused. *That's the second time Aldren's talked about humans as if we were a disease.*

Letting the affront pass, Ken squatted near his sleeping bag and began feeding timber to the fire.

Aldren positioned himself on the opposite side of the fire. He removed his satchel, put his sheathed sword over it, and sat, with his back resting upon one of the redwood burls, staring intently at Ken. Aldren asked, "Why did you intervene on my behalf?"

"I did what my conscience dictated. I didn't spend three years in law school just to stand by and watch you be tortured."

Aldren was confused. *Law school? Where in the realm of Weir has a human been apprenticed to a Cleric? Verily, it must be a great distance from Remeth's court. He could be a way-traveler from beyond the Hinterlands; that would account for his garb and mannerism, but there is an aura remnant about him that only we should possess....*

"How is it," asked Aldren, "that you were able to battle Shadowalker's Souldrinking?"

Ken didn't take kindly to the way Aldren stressed the word *you*. He had heard that insulting tone from people too proud to look beyond the ends of their noses. Nevertheless, he said, "Souldrinking. Well, that's as good a name as any to describe it. As for why he released me, who knows, maybe he saw that his numbers were diminishing and decided to cut his losses."

Ken suspected that the First Mother and the pond were responsible for his narrow victory. However, at this juncture, he was unwilling to talk about it. Even if he didn't understand much about whatever gift the First Mother had bestowed, that ace card would remain up his sleeve until he had a firmer grasp of the situation. He couldn't be sure whether his guest was friend or foe. His instincts said the former, but there were too many pieces missing from the puzzle.

Aldren had listened carefully to the explanation. The only remark he had was, "With his mastery of the spell of Souldrinking, Shadowalker holds fear neither of his kindred nor of the seed of man. He would not flee a human."

Ken winced at the word *human*.

That barb has been ground one time too many. Courtesy has its proper place, but courtesy be damned. This needs to be nipped in the bud right now. I don't intend to travel this land with everyone I meet insulting the entire human race as I go. Let's see what we've done to deserve the nickname Despoiler.

"Aldren, I was hoping this could wait until morning. I'm pretty tired right now... actually, downright exhausted. But I've never been one to suppress my feelings for the sake of personal convenience. Occasionally, I make enemies with the direct approach, and I accept that possibility. More often, talking openly and honestly creates a strong foundation for friendship. I hope that's the case here. If not, we can go our separate ways at daybreak. There's a common theme in your choice of words that concerns me. What's your grudge against humans?"

Aldren rose abruptly, hand reaching toward his sword. "How can you pose such a question? Do you mock the Elder Race?"

Ken used fast diplomacy. "Contrary to what you think, I'm not trying to offend you. Please, sit down."

Aldren complied. Seeing that Ken waited patiently, he said, "Truly, you seek enlightenment?"

"I wouldn't have asked if my intentions were otherwise."

"Very well." Aldren sighed. "Perhaps life in the Hinterlands has sheltered you from the tidings of the realm. The northern reach of Weir is ever a lonely place."

Ken's eyebrow lifted at mention of the Hinterlands and the second reference to Weir, but he offered no interruption while Aldren was in a talkative mood.

"I shall start from the beginning. The Elder Race has been the First Mother's chosen steward of Weir for millennia uncounted. Weir is the First Mother's inner world, while her outer skin is what few of your kind may know as Earth. We have endeavored through time to ward the Boundaries from anything, human or otherwise, that would challenge Her existence. On occasion, we have journeyed from Weir to Earth, observing and acting as necessary to remove corruption. In days long past, the Oaken Corridors permitted the crossing of ways to all those who were gifted to see."

Recalling the twin oak trees, Ken asked, "What do you mean by Oaken Corridors?"

"For those with the Farsight," responded Aldren, "there are living Gateways located across the Kingdoms. They most often manifest as two oaks growing side by side with joining branches. The Gateways guard entry into Weir and permit passage to other worlds and planes of existence. In recent Cyclings, however, their energy has dimmed such that the Gateways will activate only for the Great Scions of the Elder

Race. And even then, the need must be urgent. We believe this power flux corresponds to the unchecked rise of mankind upon Her outer skin. Your race's desecration of Earth has progressed to extremes. Like a festering wound, the infection has spread to the heart of Weir, poisoning the Elder Race and warping the First Mother's creations. Thus, there are those of the Elder Race who would make a final effort to restore Weir by purging humanity from the Kingdoms. Others, such as myself, would embrace a solution that honors the Oath of Life taken by Aarondale, Firstborn of the Elder Race."

Aldren bent his head forward reverently. With arms extended to encompass the surrounding forest, he chanted

Wisdom: to know root and tree, river and mountain;
Power: to defend the realms and preserve the dream;
Love: to temper power and forestall the doom;
All will matter lest Darkness reign supreme.

After finishing his recital, Aldren resumed a normal seated position and continued, "Only so long as we remain true to the Oath can the Elder Race regain its former glory and defend Her Kingdoms from those such as Shadowalker who would consume life."

There was conviction in Aldren's words.

With his environmental law background, Ken was more attuned than most people to the extent of humanity's transgressions against the environment. *Nuclear proliferation, deforestation, global warming, barrier reef scourge, and how many others uncounted? No wonder he's bitter toward humanity.*

"From what you say, it may be that humans have been less than ideal in their stewardship of Earth. But there are a lot of us who are striving for greater harmony with the environment. I've always respected life."

Aldren stood. After spreading his cloak on the ground and sitting down once more, Aldren commented, "A fine speech. What can one well-meaning human in Weir do to change a world of humans on Earth?"

"You may be surprised. Have you ever seen a falling pebble cause an avalanche?"

Aldren grunted.

Ken yawned and then lay on top of his sleeping bag. "I'm going to crash for what's left of the night." He let the conversation end there. There still seemed to be confusion regarding his origin, but he could straighten it out in the morning. He was fighting hard to keep his eyes from closing. *It must be the night's excitement. I'm here for less than a day, and what do I have to show? My brain was almost fried by a magic-wielding sociopath from a race that puts humanity on par with cancer, and I helped three men meet their maker. Yeah, they were bad men but did they deserve death? Maybe, maybe not...it's rough justice under the most generous spin. Probably what the Old West was like before the law tamed the lawless... a man could get shot for anything. No guns to be seen here so far, but who needs them if you can slay your enemy with the touch of a finger...not the most auspicious beginning. Oh well, tomorrow's another day....*

Ken fell into a dreamless slumber.

Dawn found both Ken and Aldren awake and actively breaking camp. After throwing the last handful of dirt over the fire, Ken walked to his backpack, where Aldren had been pacing.

Not all of us travel so lightly as you, my large friend. I have yet to discover what you're sporting in that satchel.

Aldren had secured his long hair into a ponytail. The effect made him look older. Aldren's giant-like stature notwithstanding, Ken figured he was probably in his late twenties.

Rummaging in his vest pocket, Ken removed two energy bars and had them for breakfast. He washed them down with water from the canteen.

Aldren looked on with interest but said nothing.

Ken was not insensitive to Aldren's stoicism. "I've got extra in my pack. Here, hold on a second." He handed a third bar to his large companion.

"I thank you for the sharing."

"You'd better wait to thank me until you taste it."

Aldren cautiously took a bite. A wry smile formed. He continued chewing. "It is flavorful."

Upon finishing the bar, Aldren reached into his satchel and produced a leaf-wrapped package about half the size of his palm. He carefully unfolded the wrapping to reveal what looked like a piece of cornbread.

Aldren broke off a bite-sized piece. The rest was returned to the satchel. Handing it to Ken, Aldren explained, "Hala. It is the traveler's fare and meant to sustain one along the way."

Ken lifted the snack to eye level—it looked like crushed layers of nuts and plants packed in yellowish bread. *I've certainly eaten far worse-looking meals on the trail. I just hope that I don't puke on my shoes. I'm already at a disadvantage in Aldren's eyes.*

Ken popped the bite in and chewed.

Like everything else in this place, the morsel caught him by surprise. The Hala rapidly expanded in his mouth. It had the consistency of overcooked steak and tasted utterly bland.

No wonder Aldren enjoyed the protein bar so much. I might as well be crunching on cardboard.

Soon after swallowing the Hala, however, Ken's stomach was full.

"Thanks," said Ken. "I don't think I'll be hungry for a while."

Aldren nodded.

"So, where to now?" asked Ken.

Aldren responded, "Before my trouble last night, I was traveling to Windowmere Deep. It holds special meaning for the Elder Race. By its blessed water and in the First Mother's presence, Aarondale took the Oath, and though we have lost much, the Deep best preserves what once we were and may become again. Knowing this, Stellrod bade me undertake the journey. It was his belief that we might receive divine guidance in that sacred place.

Ken suspected that Aldren was referring to the pond.

"Would this Deep lie east of our position and happen to be a dark circular pond, stone lined, and roughly twenty yards across, bordered by a ring of oaks?"

With amazement, Aldren answered, "Yes. The Ancients dwell along Windowmere Deep. How does a human from the Hinterlands who professes ignorance of Weir possess this knowledge?"

Keeping his dream secret, Ken said, "I meant to correct you yesterday. You assumed I was from the Hinterlands. Well, I'm not. Two days ago, I was hiking near the Blue Ridge Mountains on Earth. I accidentally stumbled through one of your Gateways and found myself at Windowmere Deep."

Aldren contemplated this information. *So that's why one such as this lacks a servant token. Who is this human that he has passed unaided through the Gateways, when none has done so since before the Kevla Cycling? He has saved my life, and for that I am indebted. Dare I reveal more?*

After hesitating, Aldren said dubiously, "One does not happen through the Gateways. Was there no guidance from a member of the Elder Race?"

"No."

"Unusual. Yet, if there be a last bastion where such might occur, it would be through the might and wisdom of the Ancients of Windowmere Deep. Nevertheless, my former mission must be postponed. Stellrod must be told of the Souldrinking and the Nosferu's malignant role."

"Well, who is Stellrod, and how do we get to him from here?" asked Ken.

"Stellrod serves as High Cleric to King Remeth. Heading westerly, our path will converge upon the finger-slopes of the Morningstar Mountain range. We may journey around the mountains using the Valley of Twins or scale the mountains' heights through Lavlir's Pass; from there, we traverse the flowing waters of the mighty Gylderhorn to the Plains of Kesmark. Westward beyond, through the Forest of Water and upon the high dell of Foggy Bottom Falls, sits our destination—the Oakenhold."

"Remind me not to ask next time," quipped Ken. "Then again, I may as well start learning the lay of the land."

"Indeed. As for our next step, Lavlir's Pass would save much time in reaching Stellrod and may reduce our danger, yet, I will not deceive you. There is reason to be cautious about using the pass. However, I do not believe he would expect us to choose that route, and it is with him that our greater danger lies."

"He? You mean Corin?"

"Quiet!" Aldren chastened sharply. "Forbear from speaking his name aloud so openly. Names have a power of their own in Weir. Last night he was weakened from his defeat. Today is another matter. If you must speak of him, let the name be Shadowalker. It is not nearly as dangerous as uttering the Bloodlink."

"Just so I'm clear, Bloodlink refers to his formal name?" asked Ken

"Yes. Our given names at birth are imbued with the heritage and power of the entire lineage as it originates back to the Firstborn member of that particular Elder Race Line. It is my solemn duty to augment the deeds of Hemdall's Line, as my actions will affect that which has been and that which has yet to be. The Bloodlink is much more than mere words, and its uttering may invoke unintended events."

Ken nodded.

"As to the threat facing us," said Aldren, "it begins with the Nosferu. Let us talk as we proceed."

Clipping his backpack straps around his vest, Ken walked side by side with Aldren through the forest. He listened carefully to Aldren's story but never lost a watchful eye upon the woods.

"The Nosferu are strange beings to the Elder Race. Though they have a long lifespan, they are human sized, with sickly pale skin. They are averse to daylight and will venture under the sun only while protected by their encompassing cloaks. Stellrod has heard human stories that say the Nosferu can change their features at a glance, but he has dismissed such tales as folly, for in the thousand or so of your years that span the Nosferu's presence upon Weir, no member of the Elder Race has ever made such a claim. The Nosferu perform deeds of power—you would say magic or wizardry—that we had once mastered, which are now all but lost. My people have come to depend on them, and, as a result, the Nosferu have garnered much influence among the once mighty. Yet, their counsel has split the Elder Race in twain, for it is the Nosferu who most strongly desire us to rid the Kingdoms of humanity."

Ken recalled Shadowalker's thugs and their metal neckware.

I wonder what my status is around here... prisoner-to-be or just Mister Unpopular? He rubbed his neck reflexively and said equivocally, "When you say get rid of humanity, are we talking about traveling elsewhere, or do you mean 'rid' as in dead and gone?"

"The latter, I'm afraid, but that is not the position that I espouse."

"Thanks," said Ken sarcastically, "I'm relieved to hear that genocide isn't on your list of things to do." To himself, Ken thought, *the more I learn, the worse things appear. Best strategy for the moment is to listen up. Knowledge can equal power in some circles.*

Ken didn't miss a word as Aldren continued, "However, the High Cleric honors Aarondale's Oath. He believes we should strive to guide humanity through its self-destructive beginnings. He has come to suspect that the Nosferu plot against our race; thus, he stands in opposition to their wishes. But it is no trifling feat to sway our people. He offers no justification for distrusting the Nosferu's promises. They service our needs and ask for naught in return, while he succumbs to the Dwindling. Stellrod is part of Hiramana's Line, perhaps our finest wielders of the First Mother's Fire. To see him humbled by this faceless plague is unbearable, for it steals hope from all others. Our race now seeks redemption in the arms of the Nosferu. They perform deeds of magic with no ill effects, nor signs of weakness. Stellrod has sought to find our cure through exploring the Nosferu, with no success. They have effectively disguised their magic source even from the High Cleric. Whenever magic is requested, the Nosferu display shining, crimson-colored crystals. Each varies in its display, whether suspended from a necklace, held in the palm, or otherwise worn on the body. In response to queries about the crystals, the Nosferu simply say that these talismans harbor the essence of their world. No one has ever been permitted to touch these crystals, and their nature resists the distant probings of the High Cleric."

Aldren paused in his tale to navigate a fallen tree limb blocking the way. For one of his size, a leap carried him over the obstacle. Being somewhat smaller, Ken preferred to use a foothold to lever himself up the side and over the top. As he stood on the apex, watching Aldren proceed, he suddenly felt his footing give way. His leg sank thigh-deep into the trunk.

It shouldn't have been this rotten. The bark was normal on the surface.

A noxious odor oozed upward from the crack.

That smell, it reminds me of the ruins from my dream. It's the Enemy's signature, less concentrated, but unmistakable, the fingerprint of death.

Ken yanked his mush-covered leg free and peered at the gooey hole. The wood's decrepit state didn't seem to be the product of any fungus or bacterial action that he could recognize. Ken then scanned above, seeking the wound from which this massive armature had torn loose.

Aldren, who had returned to see what was causing the delay, inspected the damage sadly. "More and more, such vile testaments debase our land. There is no trace that you will detect. It has been sacrificed, severed at the first intrusion to preserve the body. This corruption spreads ever deeper." His eyes rested accusingly on Ken. Then he sighed and continued up the trail.

Vaulting down to the forest floor, Ken murmured, "He acts like it's all my doing." He peeled off a wedge-shaped bark fragment from the rot and used it to expeditiously scrape the mess from his jeans and boot.

It took a few minutes to close the distance between himself and Aldren, and several more before Ken's large guide felt comfortable enough to restart the history lesson.

"After last night," Aldren began in a conspiratorial tone, "I know Stellrod's suspicions are justified. The source of the Nosferu's power revolts against our very nature. In times past, our magic flowed from within, a giving of the energy in each of us. These Nosferu who now vouchsafe our destiny are a desecration. The secret that they enfold within the *essence* of their world is far worse than my people would imagine. They steal power by sucking the life energies of those around them. Such is the magic of death. Had you not come along last eve, the knowledge of their detestable practice would have died with me. He whom we challenged last night has strongly championed the Nosferu's desires. I now understand why. They have poisoned him with their evil. He has succumbed to the lure of power and promise of rebirth for the Elder Race, and I doubt he remains alone."

Ken perceived the danger. "So now that he knows that you understand the source of their magic, he's got to prevent us from making that fact public. Damn, we just made the Most-Wanted List. One way or another, he's going to come after us."

Aldren nodded. "We must reach Stellrod. The High Cleric will finally have cause to challenge the Nosferu, and only he can truly mobilize our people against this menace. Time is not something that usually concerns my people, yet I fear it may be our enemy."

Ken intuitively asked, "You say that the Nosferu arrived a thousand years ago and that they feed on the energy of living creatures. Have you considered the possibility that humanity has nothing to do with Weir's corruption or your people's infirmity? A thousand years ago, we lived in a rudimentary agrarian society. I'm not saying that our civilization didn't spread across the planet, that our tools haven't become more advanced and our impact upon the Earth more significant, but consider that our progress occurred slowly over the intervening centuries. It's only been in the past two hundred years, with industrialization and the age of technology, that humanity has tilted the balance. Heck, a lot of folks would argue that it's our activity over the past fifty years or so that accounts for the bulk of the environmental woes. How long has the corruption on Weir, the lessening of your people's power, been felt? Think about it. It's true that humanity has its demons to confront, but maybe the trouble here is not one of them."

The two proceeded along the path in silence, each considering the other's words.

CHAPTER 3
SHADOWALKER

As the sun dipped below the Morningstars and night's twilight embrace seeped into the Valley of Twins, Corin Shadowalker stirred the coals of his campfire, obsessively reflecting upon his defeat. The wood in his hand silently screamed at the flames. He had torn it asunder from the Heartwood of an Elder One while the Frithlen Spirits watched helplessly. It was a trifling recompense but gave him pleasure nonetheless. Occasionally, as if in protest, the winds of the Gwyned Firl swirled their cold breath, fiercely scouring the valley. Glowing embers were sucked into turbulent maelstroms. Some descended upon his arms. He ignored them; the heat from his anger scorched his extremities far more thoroughly than their fleeting spark.

They said nobody, with the exception of Remeth's dog, could yet harbor sufficient reserves to resist the spell of Souldrinking. Clearly, they are in error. How many other doings have the Nosferu not foreseen? And what of this half-grown meddler?

Ken's visage played over and over in Shadowalker's mind. With each remembrance came the bitter dregs of his link being thrust aside.

Who was he, and from whence did he spring? An Elder Lord of such power should have been revealed by my probings. His skill rivals that of Hiramana's Line, and yet I know not his Tribe... a bad omen that one such as this arises now.

Shadowalker's fist slammed the rocky ground.

My plans must not be thwarted.

Blood ran freely from his knuckles. Shadowalker frowned at the damage. He was losing control. Refocusing, he unleashed a measure of stored energy. His injuries vanished. It was a trivial lessening of his power, and yet, disturbing ripples plagued his ego.

How easy it has become since those first days with the Nosferu, but I shall need evermore if I am to fulfill my destiny.

Closing his eyes, Shadowalker extended his consciousness into the valley. As his dark essence swooped across the land, the living fled. All creatures great and small sought escape. Those who could burrow deeper did so. Those above who could take refuge did so. Others, caught in the open, huddled in fear.

Shadowalker didn't feast on the minutiae; he desired a substantive replenishment. His presence touched a lone stag bounding in the night; the stag bolted with hurtling leaps borne of desperation. Shadowalker tightened his grasp on the panic-stricken animal. Its leg muscles failed. It slammed terra firma with bone-breaking force as life energy poured into a ravenous abyss. Seconds later, seven hundred pounds of rushing deer were replaced by a dried and lifeless husk that even the worms would forgo.

Shadowalker reveled in the infusion. Then, opening his eyes, he steadied his mind for what must come next.

Taking out a teardrop crystal, he concentrated.

Soon, a cloaked image appeared within the crystal's largest facet.

"What dost thou desire?" came the sharp whisper.

Shadowalker had hesitated to call this one, but the situation demanded redress.

"Yesterday, as I sought to question the High Cleric's messenger, an Elder Lord intervened and turned aside my power. You promised no one could resist...."

"Silence."

The word sliced into Shadowalker's throat. He immediately regretted his decision to contact this Nosferu.

"Do not whine. If there was a failing, the fault is thine." Then, impatiently, "Show us this Elder Lord."

Shadowalker transferred a memory fragment with Ken's image and energy to the crystal.

The cloaked Nosferu responded with confusion. "Did we not teach thee to discern each creature's taste? This entity is human and is of no consequence."

Shadowalker blurted out, "Human? No, you are wrong."

The pain lanced into his stomach. The whisper twisted in tone, as if lecturing a child. "He is human, there is no mistaking that energy signature. Could it be that thou fabricates an excuse for thy failure to intercept the High Cleric's cub?"

Shadowalker responded carefully. "I know what I experienced. He wielded true power, the likes of which I have not heretofore encountered."

"More likely thine skills deserted thee. Whether or not thou bespeakest rightly, thy human and the High Cleric's apprentice are now aware of the Souldrinking and must be silenced with the utmost alacrity. We do not yet desire our nature to be unveiled across the length of Weir. Didst thou create sufficient contact to capture a further sampling of thy human's essence?"

Shadowalker nodded.

"Excellent. Then call thee forth the Soul-Chase. Thine next report had best bespeak their death ere thou may fair badly amongst my brethren."

The cloaked figure faded.

Shadowalker despised the off-hand dismissal. Putting away the crystal, he cursed the Nosferu. *For now, I shall endure the insults, but I promise, when I have the might and the knowledge...*

He thought of the desires he would sate. Blood started rushing to his groin.

Oh yes, when my star ascends, and not before, all will beg for mercy... Remeth, the High Cleric, the Nosferu, all souls within my dominion... and no quarter shall be given.

Shadowalker soon ended his reverie. He turned his attention to the task before him. Gazing into the stygian night, he once again sent his spectral aura outward, questing for the proper servants. The Nosferu had not been idle in their wanderings. The seeds of destruction had been sown wherever they had roamed upon Weir.

Within moments, Shadowalker found the human's bane.

There, beyond the valley wall... Ah, my beauties, attend me now.

Shadowalker broke contact and leisurely sat to await their arrival.

Hours later, he awoke. He felt their presence. There was a kinship between them, a bond of evolution. His was voluntary; theirs was engineered. They watched nearby.

His steed whined frantically, and not without good cause. The Nosferu's chaotic progeny were not above feeding on their betters. No weakness could be shown.

Shadowalker rose to check the knotted reins and warned his troubled equine, "Quiet your protest, or they'll be feasting on your sorry hide tonight."

He strode arrogantly into the dark and mentally projected a contemptuous summons hinting at the prospect of reward.

A four-legged predator detached itself from the camouflaging undergrowth, a nightmare come to life. Its eyes glowed unnaturally.

Shadowalker held out his hand. "Taste."

The beast leaned closer. When its hot breath moistened his palm, Shadowalker released a scrap of Ken's life force. A bright ball of energy hovered over his outstretched hand.

The creature inhaled the offering.

He gave the final command. "Kill."

The beast whipped around and leaped into darkness. As the night swallowed the monster's passing, Shadowalker gloated. "Human, look to your back, for death undaunted stalks thee."

CHAPTER 4
TRIAL BY FIRE

*A*fter two days of hiking through Deepening Forest, as Aldren had called it, they were fast approaching the Morningstar Mountains. All day, monolithic boulders had occasionally sprouted above the forest floor, solitary islands rooted in a still green sea. And in those rare instances when the forest canopy parted, blue sky was eclipsed by a towering mountainscape.

Ken worked the Ka-Bar into the ground, carving a modest fire pit. Aldren had gone for wood. Digging a suitable hole with crosshatching for sufficient airflow required more effort than Ken had expected. The soil composition here was packed rock and pebbles.

It shouldn't be more than another day to the mountains, given Aldren's pace. He's the strongest hiker that I've ever met, but he could use a refresher on trailside manners. He was annoyed when I suggested we stop for the night. I don't know if he's running on pride or if he really is a human dynamo... whoops, make that nonhuman or whatever his Elder Race calls itself. Anyway, putting attitude aside, I, for one, will need a decent night's rest. The Morningstars are serious mountains.

Ken finished the fire pit. He sat back on his sleeping bag and then took a measured breath, slowly stretching his aching muscles. While they had daylight, he yanked off his boots to check for blisters. Though Ken was feeling the day's mileage, there were no sores or skin irritations. During his semesters at school, he had walked daily up and down the college town's hilly streets; these boots and his feet were old friends. As Ken laced up his footwear, Aldren strutted into camp carrying a huge armful of dead wood.

Ken shook his head. "How is it that you don't even look tired? Come on, you didn't sleep much last night. You were awake every time I cracked an eyelid."

"I have much to ponder," said Aldren as he dropped the wood, "and that is of more significance than sleep." Aldren laid the branches in the shallow hole. Smoke arose as he withdrew his hands.

Ken did a double take. "Ah, the fire… I don't suppose you used flint or lit a match?"

"No," Aldren said curtly. "With effort, we can yet complete such trifling deeds. It reminds one all the more of that which is lost."

"That's a minor miracle where I come from," replied Ken. "I mean… static electricity can discharge from a person's hands under the right conditions, but to actually create flame at will that can light wood is amazing."

"Did I not say yours is a lesser Kingdom?"

Ken let the jab pass. No good would come of opening that door. Instead, he set about making dinner for two: chicken strips and noodles. He spruced the dish up with dill weed and wild rosemary that he had harvested in the Appalachians before all the craziness began. It was a simple gesture of friendship. Like it or not, he had chosen sides in crossing Shadowalker, and despite Aldren's cold shoulder, Ken's instincts told him that here was someone worth calling friend, but it would take time. There were cultural barriers in place that would handicap his intent.

"Dinner will be in about twenty minutes," said Ken, "though I doubt it will be as filling as your Hala."

"I'm not hungry," said Aldren.

"Your call," Ken replied nonchalantly. "Tomorrow you'll be burning reserves that might better be used elsewhere."

Fifteen minutes later, Ken removed the cookware from the fire. He spooned a hefty portion into a bowl and held it under Aldren's nose.

Aldren wavered. "Perhaps more sustenance would be advisable." He took a mouthful and nodded. "You cook well on the march, but this meat is overly tough."

Ken didn't bother explaining about camp rations. He was busy eating his supper.

They ate without interruption. Daylight receded gradually to a clear night sky, the first since Ken had arrived on Weir.

As Ken forked the last sticky noodles up, he grabbed his canteen and downed a satisfying mouthful of water. He took several more swallows. Screwing the cap tight, he looked over at Aldren, who was also finishing his meal. Ken had not seen a water container, but that did not mean Aldren was low on liquids. Ken had assumed the role of host for this dinner party, however, and felt obligated. He extended his canteen. "If you don't have a cup, you can just pour it in your mouth. My water filter takes a while to pull volume, but its purification system is top notch."

Aldren held up a hand. "No, please keep your water. I am fine. Accept my thanks for the sharing of the food."

Ken shrugged his shoulders and set about cleaning his gear before bed.

Aldren sat in front of the fire.

A short while later, Ken relaxed near the shrinking flames as well. He looked at Aldren, who had wrapped himself in a silk-thin blanket. Its somber green pigments overlay burnt umber earth tones and seemed to shift depending upon the angle of sight. Ken found it tiring to focus on the weave. His view drifted instead to the impenetrable forest. If Uncle

Dale had been sitting next to him instead of Aldren right about now, the two of them would be swapping stories and catching up on life... the usual camping banter.

Uncle Dale always said connections come easy without a roof between you and the heavens....

Ken stared upward, honing in on the sporadic canopy breaks. The weather had held true. It was a cloudless night. In seconds, he nearly burst into laughter. He popped up and jumped from peephole to peephole, taking stock of the night sky.

"Are you well?" asked Aldren.

"Yeah, sorry about that," said Ken distractedly. "I was just admiring the moon and stars. They've been absent these last few days."

Finally, there's a moon to be seen, and it's not just any moon, but my moon. And there are the constellations...Andromeda and Perseus, Pegasus, Orion's Belt, the North Star, Ursa Major and Minor. You're all there. Damn if that doesn't raise a red flag. How is it that Earth and Weir occupy the same position in space at the same time? That can't be. Either time or space or both have changed in some regard. Let's see, the moon is in the same phase as when I left Earth, and the constellations are unaltered...could be that time is constant and space has changed. But how can space have changed when the position of the constellations argue that I'm standing on Earth? Got it... Weir might reside in the same space but a different dimension than Earth. As far as I can remember, scientific theory allows for this possibility. Even proponents of the Big Bang postulate a ten-dimensional reality from the first moment of creation. Weir might fit into that premise. Of course, the Big Bang is only a theory for the creation of the universe. Even so, it keeps gaining popularity as technological innovations in the equipment used to perceive the known universe produce confirming results...might want to check that with the First Mother, though. Where does

She stand? Is She a higher form of life, a minor deity, or the Prime Mover Herself?

Ken shook free of his thoughts, "Aldren, the other day, you mentioned inner and outer Kingdoms when discussing Earth and Weir. Do you know more of how our worlds are linked?"

Aldren thought for a moment. "One does not breathe life into existence without leaving imprints of such power. Earth is a reflection of Weir, but it is not like a mirror image. When you place a straight stick in a river, one part held aloft in your hand and the other submerged, what do you see?"

"The stick appears to bend slightly. It has to do with how water impacts light waves and our vision."

"Indeed," Aldren acknowledged smugly. "The image has been altered as if shown through a distorted lens. It is like that with the Kingdoms. Earth is similar in many respects to Weir, but greatly diminished in others. I would not be surprised to find that Earth has its own subrealm. Such a place, so far removed from the core influence, would be undesirable."

"Does time move the same here as on Earth?"

"Time is a relative phenomenon to all worlds, yet it is not unlike the wind. Most will let it push them where it may; as it swirls, some will move in a circle or move not at all. Finally, there are those few who will soar beyond its touch or turn to face the onrush."

"Your analogy is not lost on me," replied Ken, exasperation showing. "I'm familiar with the concept of time as relative. But what I want to know is whether today is today back home."

"Very well," Aldren relented. "Yes."

Ken sighed. "That means at least my family won't hit the panic button for a while. I had intended to be away for a few months... needed the open space to think about my life."

Aldren said amiably, "To journey within is to choose the path of true wisdom."

"Maybe so," replied Ken, "and sometimes maybe you're running from the truth. Either way, the point is moot now that I'm here. This is a fork in the road that I didn't plan on taking."

Aldren released a gentle laugh.

"What's so funny?" snapped Ken.

"Humans are a young race. Do you not see that that your plans rarely match reality? Certainly, there are choices to be made and goals to be attained, but if you always set your eye on the horizon, you will miss that which lies below it. For the Elder Race, the tale of living one's life is to experience each moment in the present. This is so even when the now occurs in the past, the future, or through the instigation of things not understood."

"Are you saying that there's no free will for us?"

"Not at all," assured Aldren. "It has more to do with perspective. Life can be viewed as a series of infinitesimally small choices. Your race tends to preoccupation with brief decision cusps that you identify as the culmination of a series of choices—your 'plans,' if you will. This fragmented focus fails to acknowledge that this very moment has as its foundation the sum total of every choice that you have ever made. Such an event is wondrous, though you may only deem it to be a conversation of passing interest. If you look beyond the rudimentary foundation of this moment and consider that it is also dependent upon every choice that I have made and those of the uncounted influences within this existence, then the event has indescribable meaning appreciated by perhaps only the First Mother."

"And what of the First Mother?" inquired Ken. "Is she… well, there's no delicate way to ask, so I'll just say it. Is she God?"

Aldren closed his eyes. For several minutes, his only response was silence.

Finally, Aldren spoke, "I understand your question. Unfortunately, the answer is clumsily delivered with words from one such as I. The High Cleric is more suited to respond to your thoughts. I do not wish to ignore your spiritual need, but neither do I wish to give further insult to you as a human."

"I'll consider that an apology in advance. But in this area, I value your opinion regardless of insult. First, if I'm going to successfully interact with more of your people, it's important for me to learn their beliefs and customs. However, the straight shot is that I'd simply like to know what I previously considered the unknowable.... Is She God?"

"I caution you to avoid contact with the Elder Race outside my presence. As I have said, there are many who hold a lesser view of humanity. Returning to your issue, the First Mother is the beginning and the end for our races. Her mark lies on each of us, and that is enough meaning in the scheme of all things. You, as a mere human from Earth, probably cannot understand. Indeed, you may never be able to transcend your inherent limitations. The ties that bind you are elusive. But I am of Weir, the inner Kingdom. My very essence concedes Her majesty. She is the First Mother. That which I hold as self-evident cannot be engendered within you by any power that I possess."

"Interesting perspective," admitted Ken.

The terse response gave little hint to his churning thoughts. *I don't "know" that the First Mother is God, but my experience at the Deep was humbling. Was I touched by God, or merely by that of a presence so high up on the universal food chain as to effectively constitute the human conception of God? What comes after the First Mother? Do I even have the capacity to recognize it, or is that level of existence too foreign to comprehend, too incongruent to be placed within any "human" frame of reference? Would an amoeba living in the microscopic universe ever dream of skyscrapers? While my ego wants to say yes, the answer is no.*

Ken rubbed his tired eyes. There was more to be said, but not tonight.

"On that note, I'm calling it a day."

As Ken fluffed his sleeping bag, Aldren said, "I will keep watch yet a while."

Through closed eyes, Ken said, "This is your back yard. If you think it's needed, then I'll do my part. Wake me in a few hours."

Even had he felt the need for sleep, Aldren, son of Eril Dragonsbane, would have found it elusive. Recent events had disrupted his center of harmony. The First Mother seemed distant.

Is She testing my faith? Have we failed Her?

Seated before the fire, Aldren stared at his perplexing human rescuer. *Kenneth McNary... the Ancients have sent a most puzzling message. Your human line is weak and holds no hope for the Elder Race in such times, yet you have emerged from the Gateway. Would that it had been the Great Scions lost to us, for such strength may be needed where we have none to give. Who is left among the Eclesium to defeat the spell of Souldrinking and the Nosferu? Who indeed?*

His introspection was diverted by the rustlings of the Frithlen Domloch. For a moment, he considered forging the sacred communion, but then dismissed the effort. Some messages were easier than others—the forest cried in agitation.

Perhaps it is my doing. Such despairing thoughts are of no credit. I must regain a measure of equilibrium.

Shifting his position silently, Aldren turned to the east.

I will become the Waiting Seed.

It was the Cleric's meditation for calming the inner spirit.

As the rising sun illuminated the Waiting Seed, Ken awoke and propped himself up. His vision roamed warily around the standing trees. *I was running in my dreams, in the woods back home, but from what? I can't seem to remember exactly, except that I couldn't shake the pursuer. Not the way I would have chosen to begin the day here.*

Ken turned to his companion, who sat stiffly across from smoldering ashes, "Guess I needed the sleep more than I thought. You could have roused me for a turn, though."

Aldren was motionless, eyes wide, staring into the light.

"Aldren?" said Ken.

"Yes, human, I am with you," was the muted reply. Aldren unfolded his legs and gracefully rose. He was fully packed.

"Sorry," Ken offered. "I didn't realize that you were occupied. I'm still shaking the night from my head. Is that a form of meditation?"

"What knowledge do you have on that subject?" asked Aldren.

Ken replied, "Well, back in my world, there's a discipline called yoga, which has a position resembling the pose you were just holding. It never really interested me that much, but my parents seemed to enjoy it when I was younger. For a while, I opted for a slightly more active approach with Tai Chi in the morning. It's a way of stretching the mind and body using prescribed routines of slow, fluid movements."

"Is that how your people worship their god?" asked Aldren.

Ken chuckled. "No, it has nothing to do with religion, just exercise and focus."

"Are you so sure? The Clerics of the Elder Race have long practiced such forms as a means of reaching wholeness with the First Mother. We have other training techniques as well." Aldren patted his sword. "They serve a different purpose."

"Yeah, I caught those moves the other night. You Clerics aren't exactly pacifists."

"Neither are we warmongers," Aldren countered. "We

are the defenders of Her will. With that inviolate duty comes responsibility and the possibility of conflict. In days past, many chose such militant training to supplement our magic, for it proved a necessary skill."

Ken pried further, "And what about now?"

Aldren reflected. *Indeed, human. The Eclesium has lost its way. Our indolence may be the undoing of all. How is it that we did not foresee and act upon such things?*

"Now," whispered Aldren, and then with greater resolution, "Now we must go."

"You know, you remind me of my Uncle Dale... low maintenance and no patience when there's work to be done. All right, we can eat on the fly. Just give me a few minutes for my gear and to relieve some bodily functions."

Ken rummaged in his backpack for the wipes. You could always find leaves that would do an acceptable job, but some personal conveniences had more appeal than others. In less than ten minutes, the two of them were gliding among the massive trees.

With each passing mile, the mountain terrain loomed into sharper focus. Here and there, the canopy breaks revealed several high peaks. Ken hoped that Lavlir's Pass wouldn't be found at extreme elevation. If the Morningstars corresponded to the Blue Ridge Mountains, he would probably be fine. Then again, there was the Weir "factor" to consider. As Aldren had framed it, Earth was a diminished reflection of this world in many aspects, including climate. While it was early summer back home and the Blue Ridge Mountains were bursting with green growth and wildflowers, it might not be the case here. That could be a problem. He had neither expected nor prepared for sustained travel above the snowline. And there was another, more immediate concern. All morning, as Aldren strode tirelessly ahead, Ken couldn't help but look over his shoulder with growing unease. Shadow after shadow snagged his attention as he vainly searched for phantoms among the giant sentinels.

After a while, the west wind rose. Like the white oaks around Windowmere Deep, the swinging limbs of the forest added their tune to nature's symphony: cracks and creaks, rustlings and groans, snaps and flutterings. It was background noise. As an experienced hiker, Ken knew the real value lay in heeding the incongruity. That's where the tale would be told. So it was that just after midmorning, his pace was broken by something odd—a word sounded in his ear. He spun around, expecting to meet another citizen of Weir.

Nobody was there.

Ken called ahead to Aldren, "Did you speak just now?"

Without stopping, Aldren brusquely replied, "No." Yet, after a few more steps, he wavered and turned. Reaching Ken, he paused, earnestly studying this man from Earth who had become enmeshed within his mission. *A human who has passed through the Gateways and bears traces of our aura… could one such as this have lapsed into communion unawares? The Frithlen Domloch are quiet now.*

"Don't give me that look. What's the problem?"

"Why did you ask me if I spoke?"

"I can't really say for sure. With that last wind gust, I thought I heard someone speaking. Not a sentence, just a word. It was drawn and hard to make out."

"Think carefully. Can you identify what was said?" Aldren's tone was serious.

"It might have been 'solace' or maybe just 'chase.' Could also be that I slipped into a daydream." Ken shrugged. "Just forget it, and let's get going."

"Follow me well," Aldren said sternly. "You are not in the outer realm. In Weir, such occurrences are not fanciful, for there are powers abounding of which your race is unaware. The words you have identified have two very different meanings. As we cannot be certain which is relevant, we shall continue on our journey. Should you hear aught else upon the wind, do not hesitate to share such information."

"I can do that." Ken shook off his embarrassment and said, "Now, about our destination, are you sure about heading up to that pass? While I might be dreaming up words in the air, I've had a feeling since waking that's been dragging me down."

Aldren's face reddened. "I have walked among the trees of Deepening Forest since long before you were born. My decision stands. The Morningstars await." With that, Aldren strode away.

Ken thought, *You're not that much older than me, buddy. Still... you're the tour guide until fate decides otherwise.* As he renewed his pace behind Aldren's diminishing figure, Ken boosted his blood sugar with an energy bar.

Hours later, Aldren bade Ken halt.

They stood before an ivy-laden stone archway that marked the beginning of a travel lane. On either side of the abutments, heavier wisteria had spread wildly amidst the walled ruins of what might have once been a watchtower. These were the first overt signs of civilization since the stonework of Windowmere Deep.

Ken checked his watch. He estimated forty minutes until sunset.

"The road is the Rohr-Kargon's Byway," said Aldren. Then, pointing to the broken tower, he added, "We stand at Caer Damadan, gateway to the first rise of the Morningstars."

Ken gazed through the archway's horseshoe-like opening and wished that it might bring them good luck, but he was afraid it wouldn't. The Rohr-Kargon's Byway was no more than a cart path of packed dirt, and the dense network of sprawling trees encroaching on the narrow corridor gave one the eerie impression of entering a gaping maw. Beyond, a tall peak overshadowed the closest mountain slope. A massive walled structure crowned the summit.

Aldren perceived Ken's interest and said, "In the Old Tongue, it is Kargassa Holdenhar—the Kargon's Hold—or some would say Caer Mehathmuir Minach. Most in Weir honor it as Dawn's Aerie, mountain fortress of the Elder Race. It is the hereditary seat of rule for the Tuonim."

"Tuonim?" inquired Ken.

"One of the Tribes of the Elder Race," answered Aldren. "The Tuonim have an affinity for lofty places and strong stone. Of late, they bear scant amity for King Remeth. I do not expect aid, but neither do I foresee them hindering our purpose. I have been to the court of Garondel Rohr-Kargon, leader of the Tuonim, only once before. It was long ago and in the company of the High Cleric, yet, Hemdall's Bloodline will not be so easily forgotten. That tenuous connection with the Rohr-Kargon may speed our journey if trouble arises. We should reach the western gate of Dawn's Aerie by morrow's eve."

Ken raised an eyebrow.

"The western gate leads to Lavlir's Reach and then to Lavlir's Pass, the only navigable path through the Morningstars. Assuming we are granted safe passage, it is much faster than the Valley of Twins. We may overtake Him though he is mounted. At the least, we will avoid His foul emissaries that mayhaps lie in wait. The inner Kingdom has lost much these days."

Aldren sat down and then removed his satchel. "It is best we camp for the night and begin the Byway climb with the morning sun guiding our steps. Even in daylight, the Byway can be treacherous."

Ken remained upright, sensing an ominous change. A familiar tingle sprang along his spine. He once again looked over his shoulder in the direction from which they had come. *In the trees, the wee prowlers hide. The birds are quiet. Even the wind has died.* Ken closed his eyes and pushed his sensitivity harder and was rocked. His perception had always been sharp outdoors, but this was light-years beyond his normal acuity. It was like being plugged into the rhythm of life, an electric sensation of emotional data too intangible to describe; one simply had to feel it. *Fear is racing through the forest. There's a hunter on the loose. Damn if I don't know the prey. How can I do this, and what does it truly mean? What power did the First Mother give me at the Deep?* Unconsciously, he clenched his hand into a fist. They didn't have much time.

"We're being tracked," said Ken with rising confidence, "and whatever's following will shortly be within striking distance. We may not have a choice in whether to fight. However, there is still opportunity to choose our ground if only I could know more about our enemy. I don't like these ruins. Call it a gut feeling; they leave a bad taste in my mouth. Although if there's nothing better around, I'll work with the hand we're dealt. What are our options?"

Aldren, too, glanced behind.

"I espy no threat. What does a human know of Deepening Forest and its dangers?" Then he said firmly, "We will stay here."

Ken was about to reply when a hair-raising howl wailed through the woods. As the cry faded, an unsettling silence filled the vacuum.

Ken put on his best "I told you so" expression.

Aldren stammered, "How could you possibly know?" Then, recovering his composure, he reasserted the lead. "Move quickly, the Byway's narrow confines will serve as a more likely battle site."

The two ran up the Byway, Aldren's stride carrying him to the forefront.

Ken hoped they would find decent cover, but after seeing nothing suitable so far, he began to have doubts about the wisdom of abandoning the watchtower ruins. To make matters more interesting, the Byway now meandered against a steep mountain slope. Granted, immense trees flanked the Byway's borders, but the downhill drop-off was growing perilously steeper with every step.

After twenty minutes, Ken slowed.

Come on, breathe... in through the nose, out through the mouth... in, out... work those lungs....

He swallowed; and again; and then tried to control his oxygen intake by inhaling more deeply. The elevation was affecting his respiration. It would only worsen until his system adjusted. Of course, there were other ingredients in the mix aside from altitude. While he had years of hiking under his belt, he hadn't exactly spent much time practicing a sustained uphill sprint with a loaded backpack. Forty-five pounds of gear might be his epitaph; every pounding footfall cut the pack's nylon straps into his weary muscles.

Short barking snarls sounded from the woods at Ken's back.

Each time nearer, a quarter mile now...they're closing the distance. That howl sounded like a wolf, but the vocalization is weird. And it would never happen at home. The pack is all about stealth when trailing prey...scent and nonverbal cues. They also are smart enough to avoid tangling with adult humans. Even stacked against the pack, we can give as good as we get. Or at least we could on Earth. Maybe having human for dinner is the norm in this world.... Does everything have a bone to pick with us? Well, whatever, I'm keeping my bones where they belong.

He stopped and shucked his backpack in a heartbeat. Opening it, he hurriedly removed the last of his trail bars, the rope, the flashlight, and his canteen. He wanted to salvage more, but every ounce might decrease his chances of surviving. He clipped the canteen onto his belt opposite the Ka-Bar, and slipped the rope—fifty feet of coiled static climbing line—over his head and across his chest. The Maglite and food items were stuffed into his vest pockets before he heaved the backpack into a trailside crevice. If he came by this way again, there might a possibility of recovering his gear.

At least it's out of sight.

Ken ran hard to catch up with Aldren. Shedding the weight had made for a huge improvement. However, darkness was rapidly obscuring the Byway. There was no residual glow from a neighbor's lamp or nearby city, and the canopy filtered all but the thinnest moonlight. He fumbled inside his vest for the flashlight. Finding it, he clicked it on and expanded its beam to the widest setting. The diffuse light was less helpful than he had hoped as he flew through the terrain at breakneck speed. It required all his concentration to avoid tumbling over the Byway's steep edge. In this respect, Aldren's decision to flee up the Byway had been correct. There were advantages to such dangers. The near-vertical uphill and downhill topography made attack from those quarters impossible.

Rounding a bend, momentum and lack of vision almost sealed Ken's doom. A brush-strewn sinkhole had eaten two-thirds of the Byway. Sidestepping the hazard, Ken chided himself, "If this goes on for much longer, the wolves won't kill me, I'll have done the deed myself. We'll have to make a stand soon. Where the heck is Aldren?"

As he spoke, a torch ignited ahead. "Well, speak of the devil."

He put his flashlight back inside his vest and rapidly crossed the terrain.

Aldren held a flaming brand before a cave on the Byway's uphill face. The cave appeared to extend well into the mountain.

Aldren had stacked branches to form a waist-high barrier across the cave's entrance.

Ken understood immediately. A fire blockade would illuminate the area and serve as a formidable deterrent. He walked to the black opening, from which a light breeze emanated outward.

Two bonuses...the smoke from the fire won't funnel into the cave, and there has to be a back door. Solid strategy, so long as something deadlier than the wolves doesn't call this place home.

Ken strained his eyes in the torchlight to penetrate the cavern's recesses.

Aldren didn't hesitate. "Come." Aldren held the torch against the wall. A faint symbol resembling two trees separated by a small rectangle was etched on the rock; below it, a few runic letters. It was meaningless to Ken.

"The image is the royal symbol of the Tuonim. The script is the Old Tongue of the Elder Race. It is a calendar reference. As a Cleric, my studies have included knowledge on the history of the Elder Race. I cannot say exactly when this occurred, but the chronology predates any of which I am aware. We may stand within a shaft delved into the mountain during the early days of the Firstborn. I have never heard tell of such an aperture upon the Byway. It must have lain hidden until recently. The Dwindling has been accompanied by many unexplained quakes in the firmament. The Heartwood, too, signals of unrest."

"Heartwood?" asked Ken.

"The Oakenhold's root bundle. All events, great and small, leave their imprint upon its sentience. Indeed, the tale of the world may be found there for those who choose to listen. Such is the idleness of lifetimes."

"Got it," said Ken. "Now, about this cave?"

Slightly exasperated, Aldren said, "Irrespective of its origin, it is an inhospitable dwelling-place for any creature of significance. The Tuonim do more than live within the fortifications of Dawn's Aerie. They abide in the heart of the Morningstars and have hunted within its abysmal passageways—the Underpaths—since the beginning. Their Undercity is a sight to behold. Though this opening may have been sealed ere now, this marking would only be found on a path of significance. It is a likely route to their subterranean domain."

As the two waited, weapons drawn, Ken's pulse hammered, whether in anticipation of a battle or in contemplation of the unknown, he wasn't sure. If the wolves were proportionate to the rest of Weir, they would be an awesome predator.

Motioning with his sword, Aldren said, "I will need room to wield Caldorsbane. Stay to my back if possible. Your knife may be of little aid."

Although resenting Aldren's tone, Ken nevertheless complied. Each listened intently for the sound of their pursuers. Then Ken tried another tactic, letting his mind quest for that same undercurrent of sensory data that he had felt at the ruins. *Wow, it's there again. It's like a super-connected web of local energies…a rippling wave of life. I wonder if it has to do with particle vibrations at the atomic level? Wait. There's a change in the pattern, a disturbance. They're here.*

Discordant emanations washed over and around Ken's psyche. He stifled the upwelling of disgust building in his throat and pulled his attention back to the cave. With deadly calm, he ordered, "Light the fire."

Aldren didn't question the command; he set the torch to the tinder-dry brush. Within seconds, a crackling blaze erupted. Four hulking shapes materialized on the narrow Byway.

Ken could hardly believe his eyes. The wolves were massive, standing head-high. Their black claws looked like iron talons. Taut muscle and sinew bulged from everywhere under wiry coats matted with filth, and a terrible sickness flared from their eyes—a penetrating, phosphorescent evil.

A memory came back to Ken of when he was eight and visiting Uncle Dale. He had been playing in the glades above the north pasture when Rocky, one of Dale's aussie sheepdogs, had limped into view. Rocky, along with Milo and Scout, had been working the farmstead for years. They loved their occasional romps with Ken. It was unusual to encounter only one of the trio, as Dale used them as a team. Ken had shouted for Milo and Scout, waited a moment, and then, hoping the injury wasn't serious, run forward to Rocky. However, he had stopped short. Rocky was panting heavily, and foamy red bubbles oozed from his gums, and rather than tail wagging, a hoarse growl was building. Although Ken had been only eight years old, he had known a bad situation when he saw one. Ken tried reassuring words, but as he uttered them, the dog's feverish eyes had turned on him with deadly intent.... The dog would do anything to stop the pain. Before Ken had even turned to run, Rocky was thrown headfirst to the ground. A split second later, he heard the merciful gunshot from Dale's rifle. After the fear had subsided, Dale had explained to Ken that Rocky had been missing for a week, that they had found a torn-up raccoon near the mulch pile, and that a disease called rabies could change beloved housepets into crazed killers.

Returning to the present, Ken thought that whatever had afflicted these wolves made rabies look like the common cold.

The largest wolf inched into the fire's radius, raising a misshapen head. It sniffed in great lungfuls of air and then fixed its burning pupils on Ken. Aldren might as well have not existed.

Ken recognized the challenge as surely if a gauntlet had been thrown at his feet, and though there would be no acquitting bullet from Uncle Dale, Ken was also no longer eight years old. He had faced spots arguably tougher than this and lived. In this situation, there would be no bluffing and no clemency. He would respond to any attack with deadly force.

Raising his knife, he walked to the cave entrance.

Aldren issued no complaint. Honor demanded that he respect this human's sacrifice. As Ken passed him, Aldren nodded and thought, *No one, not even a human, should be denied the choosing of one's final fate.*

Ken reached the fire's corona. *So it's me you're after...compliments of Shadowalker, no doubt. Have to hand it to him, you are one hell of a hit squad. It's safe to say that there will be no peace for me until I deal with him and whoever is pulling his strings. The day of retribution is coming, but first things first... what am I going to do with you?*

Bathed in the flame's heat, Ken's adrenaline surged. He returned the wolf's gaze measure for measure and was shocked to feel its hungering presence touching the edges of his consciousness.

Ken's visceral reaction was to rebuff the encroachment. It was a Souldrinker, and of a creed far more alien than Shadowalker. Its crude animal intelligence had been cruelly mutated into something else, a perverse spawn that had been cast down from its rightful place on the land.

As much as Ken detested the barest melding with this creature, however, he realized there might be valuable information to gain. *The First Mother has changed me, my abilities. I am only beginning to understand the extent of the transformation. There is a link to the covert patterns of life. Welcome to a psychic hotline. I can feel this thing's presence as part of the resident energies, but we are distinct. I remain here, and it's there. How do I cross the divide? Out-of-body experience, astral travel, lucid dreaming—the goals are similar, but hardly achievable on command unless you happen to be the Dalai Lama, which I'm not. Running out of time, just do it. Look it in the eye and imagine yourself flying out of your body toward that....*

Ken was encased within a living darkness. Deafening bestial roars sounded and then faded. The Souldrinker was on the attack. A pressure wave surged before him. He thought *light.* A gargantuan head with sword-like teeth was briefly illuminated and then flickered back into the churning black miasma. Again and again, it tried to take him, without success. The roars dimmed. Ken attempted to probe further, seeking confrontation with the beast, but the darkness held. He sought to withdraw his presence and failed. It hadn't occurred to him that he might become trapped. *Great, lost forever in an astral plane or the consciousness of a Souldrinker or a dimension of dream, whatever you call this. No way.* He visualized the world as a seed in the fertile ground, life captured within a shell, waiting to erupt into the light. He was the impetus, clumsy and unpracticed, but there was power behind the intent. The blackness was swept aside. He stood amidst the landscape of Weir. Though his stroke had fallen short, his effort did not come up empty. Here were the vestiges of the once-wolf. These latent memories were of no use to the Souldrinker, and they were unprotected. A pack of wolves bounded among the tall grass. Then snow covered the land. In a warm den, a mother wolf nursed her young cubs. The scene shifted to a summer romp and fresh rabbit. As life before the Nosferu desecration unfolded before his eyes, pity filled Ken's heart, and perhaps the beast's as well, for it retreated. Ken did likewise, and his awareness was drawn back to the physical.

Ken blinked. He had returned. *Smoke from the burning wood, body odor absorbed in cotton, wind caressing my face, and the old heart is pounding reassuringly.*

Having been abruptly disconnected from such sensations, he now delighted in their input. The subjective experience had left him disjoined from objective events. His muscles were prepared to fight, while his mind integrated the merger effects.

The fire had intensified, but Ken no longer noticed. He would offer a last chance reprieve for both himself and the wolf. "You think to kill me, but I am not easy prey. I have walked other forests and survived greater dangers. If you cross these flames, you will die. Turn away and live. There may be a way to reverse the damage that has been done to you. I offer you hope."

Neither Ken nor the Souldrinker had moved during this contest of wills, but now, whether Ken had rekindled that forgotten fragment that might yet be wolf or conveyed in his words a more credible threat, the Souldrinker ebbed backward. Was it reconsidering?

Aldren saw the beast's hesitation and was awestruck. Such courage from a human was unprecedented. As he stared, he perceived a faint glow blurring the human's image, brightness beyond the dancing firelight. Shocked, Aldren felt his world and everything he knew teeter on the edge.

No! This cannot be! Never in the history of the Elder Race has a human wielded any such power. Yet the First Mother's Fire shows strongly, even if he doesn't realize the potential. A human possessing the Fire—what bodes this for our future?

At that pivotal intersection, Aldren's attitude underwent a dramatic reversal. Though he bore ill-will against humanity, he was loyal to the First Mother in all respects. This human's conjuring of the Fire demanded a startling conclusion. *There is only one source for magic as ours of old.*

Aldren silently chanted Aarondale's Oath. Finishing, he focused on the continuing standoff. *Mayhap these curs will heed the Fire.*

The wolf creature paced. The others kicked up dirt and snorted. Suddenly, as if responding to an unseen whip, the creature dove over the blazing barrier. Its stained teeth were bared to shred Ken's throat, and it was followed by its packmates.

Hefting Caldorsbane to strike, Aldren whispered with resolve, "So be it."

Ken reacted instantly to the Souldrinker's attack; he stepped forward, crouched, and braced himself for the impact on the Ka-Bar. Had he looked down, he would have seen the impossible, for he stood amidst the flames without injury. Instead, his attention was fixed on the descending

Souldrinker. The creature tried to shift in midair, but landed squarely on the knife's blade. The wolf's rib cage splintered and cracked as the blade pierced its heart. Sheer weight and speed carried the beast over Ken's head. The knife was ripped from his grasp.

Ken rolled to the side. He glimpsed Aldren, who was fully engaged, his long sword slicing through the air. After stopping his roll, Ken reoriented himself to retrieve his weapon. As he moved to the Souldrinker's bloody carcass, he was attacked from behind by one of it pack-mates. Pain exploded in his left shoulder as fangs rasped on bone. Hot saliva and blood sluiced across his shirt. Defying the pain, Ken tore free by spinning onto his back, only to find the creature's jaws descending once again. With both hands, Ken seized the mucus-coated fur under its muzzle and pushed back for his life; this close, the animal's fetid stench was overwhelming. Ken held on with a death grip.

"Every," he panted. "Every action has an equal and opposite reaction. Must hold the line."

His strength was disappearing with alarming speed. The once-wolf grew more frenzied, straining harder and harder to rend Ken's throat. His shoulder hurt like hell, and his arm trembled under the load.

As the animal lunged forward yet again, the flames at the cave entrance were reflected within its eyes.

Fire... Ken's memory hurtled to another blaze, not long ago, in Yellowstone National Park; there, as here, he had faced the possibility of death.

Just then, the creature twisted its grotesque head and embedded long canines into Ken's forearm. Ken's arm collapsed, and he screamed in desperation. Death was imminent. White light blasted from his hands. The burst was so intense that he was flash blind for several seconds.

The Souldrinker stiffened in his grip and jerked once as the light disappeared. Its odor was lost amid the scent of ozone and burning flesh. When Ken released his grasp, the creature slumped, stone-dead, atop him.

Aldren pulled Caldorsbane from the lifeless hulk of the last beast. He glanced to where its pack-mate lay upon the human.

"Human named Kenneth McNary, you fought more valiantly than any of the Elder Race would expect, and your death shall…"

"Hold the graveside service," Ken said weakly. "I'm not dead yet."

The heavy carcass fell aside, and Ken arose, wounded but very much alive.

Aldren limped over, eyeing the dead wolf. *Here is mystery worthy of the Eclesium. The Dwindling preys upon the Elder Race, consuming our ancient heritage as one empties a drinking vessel, while a human has conjured the Fire. Many would kill him outright if they knew. What counsel does this man keep, and what is my task? It is beyond me. Her will shall be my guide.* Aloud, he said, "It is good you survived. First Mother's blessing is upon us both."

Ken was slightly surprised. It wasn't like Aldren to express such concern for his well-being.

Walking to retrieve the Ka-Bar, Ken nearly tripped over his feet; they could have been made of stone. Had he just run a marathon? Trodding a straight line was also challenging; waves of dizziness struck him. He grabbed his knife and pulled it loose from the first beast's carcass. After cleaning the blade on his ruined vest, he returned it to the awaiting sheath. He sighed heavily. The danger was past; now for the aftermath.

Ken began, "I'm pretty sure that I don't have to tell you that these weren't normal wolves, even allowing for the divergence between Earth and Weir."

Aldren nodded. "They were Souldrinkers, twisted corruptions of true wolves, warped outwardly to match their inner evil. No doubt, they were sent by our enemies, by Him. These are not the first of such creatures that I have beheld, nor will they be the last. Many abominations have arisen as the Dwindling has progressed over the Cyclings. Our world has become that much darker with the advent of the Nosferu."

"Do I take it then," asked Ken, wiping his brow, "that you concede the Nosferu's guilt rather than that of humanity?"

Aldren hedged. "Do not force the issue. Let us agree that your people's role has been overstated. Now, if that is sufficient, we must turn to these injuries, lest they fester."

"Thank you," acknowledged Ken with a slight grimace as he removed his tattered vest and the rope. Both were shredded and probably the only reason his innards weren't scattered over the cave floor.

As Aldren carefully probed Ken's shoulder and forearm, Ken's gaze fell on his friend's slashed buckskins; the tanned hide was stained red from mid-thigh to calf-bottom.

"Can you manage that?" asked Ken. "I could rig a pressure bandage and slip tourniquet until the blood clots."

"I will stop the blood flow shortly. It is best that it bleed somewhat anyway, for our risk lies more in the tainted bites, yet, unlike you, I may have a semblance of immunity. I could have healed such a wound within a day during the Kevla Cycling, but now, I do not know."

Aldren's voice betrayed an uncharacteristic sadness.

Ken changed the subject. "What, or perhaps a more accurate question is, when was the Kevla Cycling?"

Feeling for fractures, Aldren pressed Ken's shoulder bones as he replied. "I forget that you are newly come to Weir. The Cyclings are how the Elder Race mark the passage of time, among other things. Near the Oakenhold, the Father of the Ancients flourishes, a mighty oak born of the seed of Arboron, Darath Oen a'Bith.

"Darth een a Bees?" repeated Ken, underplaying the accents.

"The One Tree of the World from which all other saplings sprang. Surely even one such as you must know this lore?"

Ken coughed. "There are many metaphors across human culture that include the concept of a world tree: the Tree of Knowledge in the Garden of Eden, the Hebrew Tree of Life, the Bo Tree under which Buddha gained enlightenment, and even Ygdrasil, the Norse Tree of Existence. It is an archetype among humanity, not an actual tree."

"Hmmf," snorted Aldren. "You have much to learn. Though the path is beyond your touch, Arboron is as real as I am standing before you."

"Don't take this the wrong way, but I've questioned that supposition once or twice."

Aldren promised, "At the least, you shall see with your own eyes the Father of the Ancients by whose sacred seed we measure the Cyclings. It takes nearly five thousand or so of your years to bear a single such seed. The intervening period between each seed is remembered as a Cycling. The Dwindling began in the latter part of the Morova Cycling. We are now in the Elsrad Cycling."

Realization dawned on Ken. "Wait a minute…you said you could have cured this bite during the Kevla Cycling… when did that end?"

The bombshell was delivered in a monotone: "The Kevla Cycling was three seed-births ago."

Ken sat in shock, absorbing the information. Then he asked, "How old are you?"

"Seven Cyclings have passed since I was birthed by Kiriana of Hemdall's Line. I am the newest scion of Hemdall's Line."

The implications were staggering. Ken could only imagine the span of Aldren's life. *To live that long…what would a person do with so much time, and how far could mankind develop if everyone lived for tens of thousands of years? We would experience the effects our present actions bestowed upon the future, upon our children. Society would assess the impact of actions on a time frame of centuries. Short-term solutions to the world's dilemmas would become obsolete, as everyone would be alive to suffer the consequences. Space exploration, education, science...*

Ken's reverie was broken as his shoulder erupted in pain. "Damn, be careful."

"You were elsewhere. As for your injuries, although I can not predict the extent of your danger, I do have a plant that may help."

Aldren rummaged through his satchel and produced two leaves. "These are the Crisenholly. The First Mother's influence runs strong within their fibers. They will halt the bleeding and give succor against such evil wounds."

Heart-shaped and lime-green, the leaves were thick with internal fluid. As Aldren ripped them apart, clear liquid oozed outward. He generously covered each of his and Ken's wounds and produced strips of cloth from his satchel.

Ken appreciated Aldren's effort but was kicking himself for forgetting the emergency kit in the backpack. He never traveled far without one... too much experience with unforeseen mishaps. Starting antibiotics onsite could be the determining factor between continuing on the trail and praying for a chopper evac to the nearest hospital. There was no telling what virulent germs might be lurking in the saliva of these creatures. He had tasted their horrible unnaturalness, warped constructs of an invading race. Even though common sense told him that Aldren's herb-lore might provide the more legitimate treatment for such wounds, a round of modern-day antibiotics would be reassuring.

More importantly, his meeting with the First Mother had taken on new meaning. As Ken adjusted the bandage on his forearm, he glared at the Souldrinker's smoking remains. *I just fried a living creature with my mind. Nobody should have this ability, this magic. Not just pulling a rabbit from a hat, but real and deadly power. For now, it was self-defense, it or me. What about the next encounter? Like any tool, it's a weapon for good or evil, depending on the knowledge and will of the user. I've got to crack the mechanism behind the magic. Until then, I'm like a kid playing with a loaded gun.... I wonder how much Aldren witnessed. He hasn't said anything yet. He might be a good source for understanding this gift. It sounds like before the Nosferu threw a wrench in the gears, the Elder Race had been wielding magic for thousands of years. Whatever you call it—gift, power, magic, sorcery—it must obey a law of science, even if humanity hasn't yet discovered which one. Einstein theorized that matter and energy are two ends of the same spectrum, that they can never be destroyed, but only change form. Can I suddenly convert matter into energy? Or is there existing energy within the environment or myself that I am now channeling to specific needs? The human body has electrical and chemical energy. Heck, each thought involves the firing of a multitude of electric impulses and nerve cells. Then there's nuclear technology... nuclear fusion with the hydrogen bomb, and fission with the atomic bomb. They amply demonstrate that a microscopic collision or fracture of matter can release fantastic amounts of energy. I can't have that type of technical discussion with Aldren, but his insight might help guide my analysis. Well, there will be ample opportunity to ask questions. We have a ways to travel.*

The fire at the entrance had dissipated.

"So, which way do we go from here?" asked Ken. "Is it to be the Byway, or are we heading underground?"

Wrapping his leg, Aldren said, "The Tuonim regularly patrol the Underpaths. We may soon require their aid should these wounds degenerate. Unless you have any premonitions to the contrary, it is best we continue into the mountain to rendezvous with such a party. I do not think it wise to push my leg on the Byway ascent."

"No premonitions, but I did have a thought. I have medicine in my backpack that might be as helpful as your Crisenholly. It's a good walk down the Byway, assuming I can locate it in the dark."

"I do not wish to give insult," said Aldren, "but I will place my trust in the Crisenholly. Even should your human medicine prove efficacious, in our present condition, any meeting with further abominations might be unfortunate."

"You think there are more Souldrinkers waiting for us?"

Aldren nodded.

"That changes things. If we're forced to fight, then we'll rise to the occasion. Otherwise, I'm in agreement to live to fight another day. Let's go with your suggestion. Give me a minute to secure our light."

Ken walked over to his vest and pulled stuffing aside as he dug for his flashlight. He found what was left of its metal casing. "Those claws tore deeper than I thought. All right, we'll Plan B it."

Ken withdrew several thick branches from the fire and gathered varying lengths of the damaged climbing line. Then he snuffed the burning ends of the wood in the dirt. The flames died, but the wood was hot. He began tightly wrapping the climbing line around each brand. It was a composite fiber…. The nylon core would melt to the wood and act like a wick, regulating the wood to a slow burn. The fumes would be strong initially as each torch was lit, but that wouldn't be a problem with the cavern's airflow.

"A clever adaptation of your rope," said Aldren. "The torches will only be necessary for a short distance. The Underpaths are magically illuminated by crystals embedded in the walls."

"I thought you said your race no longer has magic."

Aldren explained, "We have magic of relative insignificance, but no matter, for these spells were wrought long ago to provide permanent lighting."

Ken ignited the first torch from the embers of their erstwhile barrier and then handed it to Aldren. Ken carried the spares. They began their descent, Aldren limping slowly ahead.

Pausing, Ken drank in a last view of the cavern entrance. He had never been too enthusiastic when it came to cave exploration. Crawling in dark places beneath the earth was not his idea of fun. However, under current circumstances, he regretted his inexposure to spelunking. Maybe his climbing techniques would help.

Well, as the saying goes, no time like the present to learn. I never really understood the irony of that statement until now.

With that, he turned to follow Aldren.

CHAPTER 5
THE JOURNEY BELOW

As soon as the Souldrinker carcasses had melted into the gloom beyond Ken and Aldren's torchlight, the mountain, unrelenting and unyielding permanence, subdued all external sound. As for those sounds which Ken and Aldren might have generated to counter the sheer presence of so much rock, the two of them instead had kept silent counsel during the underground trudge. The silence was preferable to the hollow tones of their voices, grossly magnified and crushingly muted by the encroaching wall. With each hour, the light cast by the torch became more and more the confine of their world. Were they clinging to a tenuous umbilical cord that channeled safely through a mountain of stone or plunging into the abyss, never to be heard from again?

Aldren and Ken sat dejectedly on the craggy cave floor. Their thoughts were interrupted by a sputter from the torch. It was burning low, too low.

"Hand me that last torch," said Ken. "This one is just about licking my fingers."

Aldren complied, and Ken ignited the top knot of composite fiber. The torch flared and then steadied to a more balanced burn.

Ken checked his watch by the flickering light. *We've been walking for over sixteen hours, and no sign of glowing crystals or anything other than rock.*

He swept his hand along the cold stone and was rewarded with a fluffy coating of gray dust. *This can't be the right way. Aldren said that there is a network of passages under the Morningstars that intersects the Tuonim Undercity. We haven't even seen an adjoining tunnel, and this one's been tightening.*

Ken finished chewing the last mouthful of food that had been salvaged from the attack and reached for his canteen. He permitted himself two healthy swallows before returning the canteen to his belt. His water consumption would remain cautiously adequate until he could find a source to replenish the dwindling supply. Most people can tolerate hunger for several days without suffering dramatic physical problems, but dehydration is insidious. Water-induced fatigue and dementia could be just as crippling as any injury. He couldn't afford those extra liabilities; there was no way to estimate how much longer it would take to find the Tuonim. His gaze turned to Aldren.

Pale and sweaty, and he's lost a lot of blood. Leg looks like crud, too... probably infected. So much for his Crisenholly. "Now that I think about it," said Ken, extending his canteen to Aldren, "I haven't seen you drink since we met. Unless you've got an everlasting bottle of spring water in that satchel or the Elder Race is related to camels, you are welcome to what I can spare."

"Your sarcasm is not wasted. There is yet much that you do not know about my race and the inner Kingdom. As our aging differs from humans, so too does our need to eat, drink, and sleep. However, though you did not perceive it, there were opportunities while we rested when I received water gifts from the Frithlen Domloch."

"In English, if you please."

"The Spirits of Deepening Forest." Aldren flashed a wry smile. "Did you not sense that our trees are more lively than those of Earth?"

"Well, yeah, but I never anticipated that you could negotiate 'water gifts' from living wood. If you are in the right climate back home, you can extract water by opening tree seeds, notching a vine or fleshy stalk, slicing green bamboo, or shearing the entire base of some tropical trees. I have also jury-rigged a solar still with a clear plastic bag stuffed with leaves, though if you go with that construction, you have to make damn sure that the distilling leaves are from a nonpoisonous plant. I don't think I would have missed you relying on a derivation of those water procurement methods…. They all take a while to yield results."

"Indeed, my friend," said Aldren, "and such action here, in those sanctuaries where the effects of the Dwindling have yet to fully manifest, might provoke injury."

"So how do you convince the spirits to give you water? I can see where that might be a handy trick to know."

"I shall demonstrate after we leave the mountain, but that event will hold small significance to you. No human would fare successfully. The Frithlen Domloch do not respond to your race."

Ken laughed and shook his head grudgingly. "Yeah, why am I not surprised? The odds in your world do seem a bit tilted against us humans. Regardless, I'd be honored to see you do your water thing."

"Then when the time is right, I promise it shall be so. However, as to present circumstances, your water sharing is accepted."

Aldren reached for the canteen. "Not too much. We aren't going to find any tree spirits down here."

Aldren nodded. "You should be able to fill your drinking bottle anon, for there are many rivers within the heart of the Morningstars. However, it is sensible to conserve water for now."

As Aldren angled the canteen over his lips, Ken unbandaged his wounded shoulder. The bite punctures had sealed,

forming crusty scabs. Testing his range of motion, he was surprised to find that he had good movement and only mild pain.
After a cursory examination, he found that his other cuts and
bruises were in relatively similar shape.

Returning the canteen, Aldren rasped through labored
breathing, "Thank you for the water. I do not wish to inconvenience you further, but I require your help to continue our
journey. My leg wound is tainted. Its poison is rapidly affecting my body. You are fortunate to have been spared, for if this
affects me so, it would have killed you ere now. Only the Master of Dawn's Aerie may yet cure this injury."

Ken mused, "A lot of things have tried to kill me since I
arrived. I'm still here. I don't know if it's luck or the hand of
fate, but I do like to think that where there's a will, there's a
way, so cheer up. We'll get out of this."

Aldren scoffed. "You may, indeed. My prospects are
more guarded. If we do not find the Tuonim soon, I shall have
this dreary rock and a poor tale as my companions to the Nine
Circles." He would have smiled at the last had a muscle spasm
not left him panting for breath. Aldren grimaced before continuing, "I would not begrudge you for abandoning me. Your
chances of survival would improve greatly without my burden." His eyes narrowed on this human and all that his impo-
tent race had represented in the past.

Ken shook his head in disbelief and stood.

"I thought so," trailed Aldren smugly.

Ken left unsaid the questions troubling him; throwing
around accusations and arguing about what should have been
wouldn't do either of them any good. Instead, he replied, "You
idiot," with a wry smile. Then he slipped his arm around
Aldren's waist and helped him stand. With his other arm, Ken
held the torch aloft. They resumed their downward trek.

After more hours of seemingly endless lumbering along
the bumpy gradient, Ken was convinced that Aldren hadn't

the slightest notion of where they were heading. The weight pulling on Ken's arm had also grown heavy. His large companion was suffering.

His eyes are closed, and his respiration's been shallow. I'm the only thing that's keeping him from falling on his face. It won't be long before he's unconscious. What then? How far can I carry him?

Adding insult to injury, their last torch burned mere inches above Ken's hand. A wet strip of cloth cut from his shirt kept the heat at bay.

Aldren's life, and possibly my own, is hanging in the balance. We must find his Tuonim before our light fails.

The dark didn't hold any special fear for Ken. In fact, it had been more friend than foe on many occasions. The distinction was that here, deep underground, there would be no night vision, only uninterrupted blackness. Ken wasn't sure how he'd take that mentally. He had no caving experience. There was a walk through the Big Room at Carlsbad Caverns National Park, but that was so sanitized with lights and people that he might as well have been riding on the subway. His current position was far more tenuous. The ponderous mass around him and the absence of sound had combined to create an eerie, sepulchral feel for the journey.

He recalled a news story that had made headlines years ago in Florida. A group of four cave divers had been stranded and had drawn the ill luck of timing their trip during what had become the rainiest April on record. They had been dedicated cavers, loaded with equipment, and had left instructions with the local outfitter as to their whereabouts. When they turned up missing, the proper rescue authorities had been notified. There was concern, but not panic. Much of the cavern system had air pockets. A few days had passed before the flood waters receded. Though the water was murky with silt and other debris, the rescue team had entered the caves. After stringing lifelines and navigating the dive portion with rebreathers, the rescue team had finally emerged into the pitch-blackness of the first aerated chamber. The chamber had stunk of burned plastic and flesh. The air was toxic. The cavers were dead. By all accounts, the group should have survived, but the flashlights and chemical light sticks had failed early into the cavers' plight. The writer of the article had speculated that in the interval between the failure of the light and the arrival of the rescuers, the stress and darkness had pushed someone over the edge. Everything flammable, including the bodies, had been set on fire. Autopsies would later show that three of the cavers had died of stab wounds and the last had perished from smoke inhalation.

What was I thinking, coming down here with nothing to guide my way except a few wooden torches as a light source? Dumb move... meanwhile, we have maybe another hour before this fizzles out. When that happens, we've got two choices... retrace the path to daylight, a haul which Aldren won't survive, or continue to blindly crawl at a snail's pace for as long as the water and our strength hold. Either way, we're literally between a rock and a hard place.

Distracted by his thoughts, Ken overlooked a depression in the knobby cave floor. He and Aldren tumbled forward and separated. The torch flew into the air.

On his stomach, Ken watched the torch land in the dust. It sputtered, and, in a blink, the world became darkness.

All right, don't lose your cool. Keep it together and use your best asset... intelligence. I have to get that torch relit. Matches...matches... damn, they're in my pack on the Byway. There's no material in this tunnel to make a fire. I need Aldren. He can do his Elder Race bit and set flame to the wood. He called, "Aldren, are you okay? Aldren? If you can hear me, now would be a good time for you to say so." When he received no reply, Ken shouted, "Aldren!"

The continued lack of response caused Ken to adopt a different tack "Okay, I know you are close, so if you are too weak to talk, just hold on; I'll find you in a second."

Ken crawled sideways and edged forward, feeling his way along the cold rock. Suddenly, a startling realization hit him…. The cavern walls were materializing from the blackness. As his eyes adjusted further to the dim conditions, he could see that they had reached a sharp bend. The light source was brighter beyond it.

Ken spotted Aldren, who lay face down.

"Not good."

Rolling Aldren over, Ken attempted to wake him, shaking him gently. "Come on, big guy, give me a sign."

He slapped Aldren's face hard. "No reaction. Damn."

Moving his hand to Aldren's neck, Ken sighed. He couldn't feel a pulse. Of course, he wasn't a trained medic, nor could he say with certainty that the Elder Race's anatomy was identical to that of humanity. Aldren might be alive.

"Well, until I know you're dead, we're partners, so I can't leave you here."

He pulled Aldren to a seated position and, digging his good shoulder in at Aldren's waist, heaved. "Hrumphf… just my luck you had to be eight-plus feet tall. Why couldn't this fairytale be populated by dwarves?"

Balancing the hefty load, Ken rounded the bend. There, like an art-deco masterpiece, lay one of the Elder Race's light crystals.

"Finally," remarked Ken, "signs of life down under."

The crystal was mounted about five feet above the ground and was several inches in diameter. Ken couldn't resist the temptation to touch its lustrous surface. As he brushed it with his index finger, the light winked out. He tapped it again, hastily, and the pale white gemstone shone brightly. He repeated the process, with the same reassuring result.

"Makes sense to have an on/off switch even if I can't comprehend the energy powering the light. Behold, magic. There it is, bottled conveniently for sale like running to the hardware store for a sixty-watt bulb. Could it really be permanent? I suppose that when you live for thousands of years, you don't want to be saddled with changing a bulb every few weeks. What an amazing world."

Ken let his fingertips rest on the crystal. It went out again. Then he pushed his palm firmly against its smooth angular face, maintaining continuous contact. "It's cold to the touch. Our household lightbulbs are conduits for energy; they channel power from an external source. If I understand Aldren, these crystals should function more like batteries, storing the potential energy charge and activating on command. In a battery, that means the negatively charged electrons flow to the protons in the positive terminal, and that movement creates kinetic energy, which produces the light. I doubt magic works on the same rules, but it might be interesting to see what happens when a crystal with potential energy sufficient to provide light forever suddenly blows a fuse, fries a filament, or suffers the appropriate equivalent."

Withdrawing his hand from the light, Ken surveyed the chamber. The rock had lost its unfinished cave quality and had instead adopted a decidedly square construction. Looking down the corridor about thirty feet, Ken could see another crystal. Beyond it, a double door blocked the entire tunnel. Ken hurriedly crossed the distance with Aldren on his back and stood before the granite barrier.

"Fantastic."

The portal doors inspired awe. Carved into their stone were intricate and ornate designs: battles and fires, dragons and castles, mountains and forests. Mystical runes traced the borders nearest the passage walls, and in the center of the doors, a circular bas-relief depicted what looked like one of the Elder Race, victorious in battle. The man bore a silver circlet with a gleaming black stone upon his forehead and was dressed in armor of a similar ebony hue. In his right hand, he held a sword that transfixed a cloaked swordsman. Ken could only wonder at the opponent's identity and the history surrounding the memorialized combat scene.

Ken gently set Aldren on the ground and once again felt in a vain for a pulse. "Aldren, you might be past the point of hearing me or worrying about anything in this life, but if you're not, hang in there; your Tuonim can't be far."

Ken rose with determination. He would not let Aldren die without giving his best. Now he set about tackling the immediate obstacle to that goal. There were no obvious handles or mechanisms for opening the doors, so he did what came natural. He pushed with all his might. After nearly a minute without success, he stopped.

"I may as well heave until doomsday. If these doors are secured from the inside, there's not much to do. Then again, you'd think there would be a way to release them from either side. Even the inner sanctums of the Egyptian pharaohs had secret levers designed for ingress and egress. One could never tell when Osiris might resurrect a favored pharaoh from the dead and a quick exit be needed from a former eternal resting spot in the Valley of Kings."

Ken inspected the area where the doors abutted the walls. The joint was seamless. The stonemasons who had set these doors possessed unrivaled skills. Defeated temporarily, Ken sat beside Aldren to consider his next steps. Then he had a brainstorm. How about an introduction? It seemed silly, as had many of his recent actions, but he trusted his instincts more than ever since having found his way to this world, and maybe, just maybe, someone was listening.

Ken puffed his chest and announced, "I have here Aldren, son of Eril Dragonsbane, of Hemdall's Line, and my name is Kenneth Lugh McNary," then adding for good measure, "son of Ryan Edward McNary. Aldren's wounded, and we could use your assistance, and besides..." Ken was prepared to rant at the wall for another few minutes. Apparently, that was unnecessary. The center partition where the doors adjoined began to spread apart. Stone slid smoothly upon stone: The doors were swinging outward.

"Son of a gun." Ken was surprised. "It looks like an invitation's been extended. Wish I knew what to wear for the party."

Ken slid the Ka-Bar from its leather sheath and flattened himself against the wall. His intuition wasn't screaming any warning yet, but that didn't mean he should get reckless.

A moist, woody aroma, not at all what he had expecting this far below the surface, escaped from the air beyond the entryway. Glancing through the fully spread doors, Ken saw that the chamber within was illuminated by more crystals. Directly ahead, a rectangular, white stone altar was erected upon a dais.

A diminutive grin slipped across Ken's mouth. He was going to eat his earlier words to Aldren. Two colossal oak trees, living and healthy, flanked either side of the altar. There was no sign of who had operated the doors.

Ever so cautiously, he entered the chamber. The cavern arched upward as far as Ken could see; light thinned the higher he gazed until, finally, all was blackness. The oaks towered into the gloom, vanishing in the subterranean twilight. How they could exist without sunlight was a mystery to Ken, though it was an easy stretch to imagine that the undying energy within the crystals might be a factor. As for water, for he supposed that even magical trees might yet require such nourishment, a clear reservoir lapped weakly against the lower wall to his right.

"Hello," said Ken, "is anyone here?"

Receiving no answer, he explored further. As he approached the altar, he quickly discerned that his initial assessment had been erroneous. "That's not an altar; it's a sarcophagus."

The stone plate resting on top of the sarcophagus had the graven image of the warrior from the doors carved into its planar surface. There was also a flowing runic inscription, but Ken had no way of translating the text.

Allowing his view to swing full circle around the room, Ken found no connecting tunnels. "I'm not buying that we've blundered into a dead end. Someone or something moved those doors. Damn spooky even for this place."

Then, the silence was broken. Phantom whispers reverberated on the brooding stone.

Ken spun, not knowing from which direction contact would come. "I can hear you. Show yourself," he commanded.

Nobody appeared. The muttering persisted, low and steady and strangely unintelligible.

"We've been walking a long time to get here, and I don't have the patience for games." Ken returned the Ka-Bar to his waist and earnestly pleaded, "We mean you no harm. In fact, my friend is injured and needs help."

The whispering intensified for a moment and then ebbed to steady mumbling.

The cavern acoustics made pinpointing the source of the sound quite difficult. As Ken proceeded from one end of the cavern to the other, however, he reluctantly concluded that the strongest emanations were clearly being felt in one spot—the median point between the trees.

"With all I've experienced in this world, it's definitely possible. These two trees are the only living things I've encountered since we began our descent. Could these be the Spirits of Deepening Forest, or does each plant harbor a consciousness? And how do I tap into that presence, especially when Aldren assured me that no human has ever done so?"

Ken closed his eyes. For the first time since arriving in this mystical realm, he concentrated his resources on the trees. The First Mother's gift had made him more than human. He had perceived the environment in ways that no human could. Everything was possible.

First, Ken adjusted his inner path, pushing away all thoughts other than the sounds and the trees. Then he turned outward. He extended his senses, honing in on that biodynamic web of energy as he had done with the Souldrinker before the attack; it was there, and so were the trees. This was a friendlier contact than the Souldrinker. Ken followed the vibrations, letting his consciousness slide further from its physical anchor and closer to the trees. As Ken grasped for meaning where none seemed possible, he suddenly heard rhythm and cadence. Clearly, there was a language to decipher; he just lacked the matching key. He had not gone far enough. Fear kept his energy from them. Ken's experience with the Souldrinker had left him tentative and very much aware of his limitations. Maybe he could bridge the gap without losing himself. The Spirits were transmitting to him; could he do the same? Ken held firm to his position in the web and attempted to manipulate his own field of energy. He oriented his presence into a narrow wavelength and thrust it forward. A tendril of energy, far fainter than that which the trees put forth, reached its goal. As Ken listened, he felt the wind stirring, and then, all at once it clicked. The whispering became words.

"Has it happened so soon, such a fleeting creature to put such demands upon. It has no roots to withstand the storm. It is unbound in the firmament."

The other voice responded, "And yet, it has enabled the connection, transcending its kind. It is not as far from ours as once we had deemed."

"It listens… and the emanation is so incohesive, so chaotic. It is strange to be touched by this fledgling when other voices have been absent."

"Her influence lies upon this one like no other of its species. As She decreed it would be, so it has become. Our task is before us. We must forge the link between the strata."

There was a break in the conversation.

Have I lost the contact? Wait. Their energy is building. They are intensifying and warping the patterns into… what? The field is thickening but not expanding. It's like having a pair of binoculars that can focus at ten feet away or ten thousand feet, except you're using the same magnification to see everything during the same moment.

The voices synchronized, and continued.

"Awake, fell sword to Aarondale.
Arise, twilight sleeper from beyond.
The watchers of old summon thee,
Tharin Eberstone, Dreadlord's Bane;
First Kargon of the Morningstars.
Now is the day of Oath-keeping.

Awake, fell sword to Aarondale.
Arise…"

The charm was repeated over and over, louder and louder each time.

Branches of the great trees began whipping together. The disturbance forced Ken to disengage from the connection. The voices dimmed.

He opened his eyes.

A dust devil whirled among the boughs like a miniature tornado. As it moved downward, its revolutions became tighter and faster until it hovered directly over the stone sarcophagus. Without warning, the cyclone solidified into a man. It was the warrior depicted on the chamber doors and the sarcophagus lid, in battle array, but without his black body armor. He glared at Ken from atop his erstwhile resting place.

Why am I not surprised?

Standing there in person, he was obviously of the Elder Race and of a much fairer hue than Aldren.

"Sylvan-dre, Gaeath!" he shouted.

Ken's brow wrinkled with bewilderment.

The warrior tried again, "Ah yes, I forgot the language. The Base Speech, while practiced by my kindred, is relatively new to my tongue, so forgive me if I stumble. First Mother's blessing guide your way, my friend. It is good to see you once again, for it seems ages since our time of parting."

Ken was astounded by the man before him.

"Do not stand agape. Have you nothing to say to Tharin Eberstone?"

Ken thought, *Tharin Eberstone, I know we've never met until this day. How is it that his name rings familiar? I also sense that no matter what else Tharin might be, he is loyal to the First Mother. But how is that possible? Is there no end to Weir's magic?*

Tharin waited for acknowledgment.

Ken sputtered, "Greetings, Tharin, ah, I… who…"

"No," said Tharin, anticipating the confusion, "in your conscious awareness, our life paths have not crossed until this instance. And as you have discovered, there are other levels of perception and energies flowing through the tides of creation. Within the Nine Circles, time, space, and reality are more fluid than you can possibly imagine. I say to you, Kenneth McNary, that in the ashes of Cyclings long past by any reckoning, our deeds have been sung by the Tribes of the Elder Race."

Drawing his huge sword and thrusting it upward, Tharin cried, "Cor-Dreaden, Gaeath-Le!"

The words provoked a chain reaction of exhilaration within Ken. Adrenaline spiked, and his blood coursed strong. Though he couldn't remember hearing any such phrase before this day, his psyche apparently did, or perhaps it was more of the First Mother's doing. The sensations were not unlike those he had experienced at Windowmere Deep.

Tharin lowered his weapon. "No less than a hundred thousand Cyclings has the Father of Ancients seen since my last uttering upon Weir of the battle cry of Acadia, fortress-keep of the Elder Race." Tharin gave a huge bellowing laugh that resounded wildly in the cavern. Then he jumped down from the sarcophagus.

"By now, you must be aware of the power awakened unto you by the First Mother. The magic is woven into your being and will accomplish all that you truly desire, for the strength of the magic is the strength of the wielder. And then there is the seduction. Magic is a powerful calling that tempts the soul to achieve inspired deeds. The onus of such choices will rest with you alone. Yea, verily I give you this warning my friend: In its current incarnation, humanity was never intended to command the First Mother's Fire, for although the flame of your life burns hotly, it does not endure as ours does. Each time you summon the magic, you will expend energy, thereby decreasing your allotted span in this plane of existence. If you manage this gift wisely, the process will be slow, but you will eventually notice a lessening. You may repair wounds such as that of your companion and challenge those who seek the undoing of Weir. Whatever the need that you judge worthy, do not break Aarondale's Oath, for that is the path of disaster."

Seeing that Tharin waited, Ken searched his memory. He locked on to a mental picture of Aldren reciting Aarondale's Oath, and as the entire scene played in his mind, Ken spoke.

"Wisdom: to know root and tree, river and mountain.
Power: to defend the realms and preserve the dream.
Love: to temper power and forestall the doom.
All will matter lest Darkness reign supreme."

Tharin nodded approvingly. "That is indeed the Oath. Do not allow hatred to take hold of your heart, nor take energy for your own ends. Follow well its meaning, for you will lose yourself should you violate it. The newcomers, these Murschlok..."

"You mean the Nosferu," Ken guessed.

"Yes. If unstopped, they and their master will leave the First Mother's Kingdoms as no more than wastelands, barren and lifeless." Tharin strode to the sarcophagus and placed his hands on the capstone's intricate tracing. The stone lid pivoted sideways to reveal the morbid contents.

A withered skeleton was arrayed in fine clothes and black armor. It lay upon powdered white stone and was surrounded by green, interwoven braids of leafy plants. Ken could only identify one species of the assorted Weir flora, and that was because he had recently seen it. The Crisenholly, like the other plants, looked as if it had been harvested only moments ago.

Tharin laughed and said, "Did you not wonder at the meaning of the capstone inscription?"

Ken looked at the flowing runic language.

(runic inscription)

Tharin read, "Tirna'la Kargassa Eberstone primna Mehathmuir Minach e domeleth cor Brana Caer Accenach. Branachma'la Hadeth la're dreadnach Primaleth ceman Bramachlen."

"And that says…" prompted Ken with a blank expression.

"Ah, yes," mused Tharin, "you could not know of this yet. I forget my place. Eternity and memory do not fare well in the same bed. The language is the Old Tongue of the Elder Race. It proclaims, 'Buried here is Tharin Eberstone, First Kargon of the Morningstars and fallen hero of Acadia. Warriors of the Nine Circles, rejoice, for one of the mighty Firstborn joins your ranks.'"

Ken raised his eyes to Tharin and calmly said, "I take it that... well, you're dead?"

"In this reality, indeed," Tharin agreed, "my spirit has journeyed from the Nine Circles, for there were promises to honor. It is not by happenstance that we speak."

Reaching into the sarcophagus, Tharin removed the armor from his skeleton. Holding it before Ken, Tharin said, "I deliver to thee Soulstealer's Doom."

Ken stared at the black-within-black metal armor. There were no reflections or imperfections in the forged metal, only unyielding darkness.

"It is an ancient and magical heirloom from fallen Acadia," said Tharin.

"I don't like it," said Ken with obvious hesitation.

Tharin explained, "That is only natural, for its magic contradicts the patterns of life. Sorrow and violence are the legacy left by this heirloom. I cannot share the details, for the proper telling of such is not fated for our brief meeting this day. Suffice to say, it is a Souldrinker of sorts and will absorb the life energy of any creature challenging its wearer. Be forewarned! Over the Cyclings, Soulstealer's Doom has taken on the semblance of awareness. It is neither alive nor dead; in essence, it retains faint echoes of the thousands it has consumed—the Dreamers of Soulstealer's Doom. Do not fall prey to their influence."

"Well, if it's dangerous, why give it to me in the first place?"

In a serious tone, Tharin said, "The protection and power of Soulstealer's Doom is necessary for a time to fulfill your destiny. Mayhap there is risk, but one of great inner strength can silence its whispers. What say you?"

I like Tharin, he's a decent sort for an old ghost. There's another first for my life... talking with the dead, and it's not even my own race. Clearly, the First Mother had a direct hand in this appointed hour. However, was I predestined for this rendezvous, or did the First Mother choose me because I won the lottery? Again, I'm left with doubts on free will and fate. Grandma Gwen would say that we are all linked to the universe. Each of us has a place under God's creation. That doesn't really answer the question, though. The choices have always felt like they are mine. I can still decline this armor. However, speaking of higher powers, when a near god-like consciousness arranges a meet-and-greet with the dead after intervening eons, maybe there's a very good reason. Take it on faith.

Ken lifted the armor from Tharin's hands and buckled it on. Surprisingly, it weighed hardly anything, and though Ken had expected the armor to be too large for his upper body, it fit remarkably well. It was snug around his torso, and because it stopped just past his shoulders, it allowed free arm movement.

"Not a bad fit," said Ken admiringly.

Tharin chimed in, "It has certain magical features that you will more fully appreciate, and others yet to be discovered."

Pivoting toward the right, Tharin pointed to the pool.

"Travel under that wall a short span. You will intersect another cavern that my Tuonim descendants even now approach."

Pausing as if measuring his next words, Tharin continued, "Know this: Much has changed since the days of glory. The Tuonim have been corrupted by the influence of a Murschlok who, like a spider weaving its trap, has artfully sown the seeds of evil around Garondel Rohr-Kargon, Master of Dawn's Aerie. Yet all is not lost, for though deep rivers may run slow, strong is their course. I say to you, as a favor for the golden days of old, rekindle that which lies dormant. I cannot, for my time in this realm has passed."

These words touched Ken, and though it was another burden to an already long list, he promised, "Tharin, I will do what I can to improve the situation. Besides, I have a score to settle on account of the Nosferu." Ken rubbed his shoulder as he spoke. "We'll add your claim to their marker."

Tharin met Ken's eyes and said, "As always, you do not disappoint." Then, gripping Ken's shoulders in his massive hands, Tharin said, "I have fulfilled my appointed task. I may now continue the journey, for the Eternal War rages, and the Armies of the Nine Circles await my return. As to you, Kenneth McNary, though I cannot reveal more, know that there are higher forces pushing on the confluence of realities. What was so may not be, and what will be is in flux; thus, admitting that the path of your life's journey is uncertain, should you survive the perils ahead, our lines of destiny may once more touch. My friend and battle companion of old," said Tharin with a hint of parting sadness in his baritone voice, "keep thee well until next we fight side by side. It shall be your advantage then."

Tharin stepped back and faded beyond this existence.

Ken bid him farewell. "I will look forward to that day. Until then, take care, you old ghost."

Faint laughter sounded, followed by, "See to the Cairns of Arudhawn."

As Tharin disappeared, the sarcophagus capstone slid back into place. The chamber was left exactly as it had been when Ken had first entered.

Ken returned to Aldren, who was as yet unconscious outside the massive stone doors. He couldn't carry Aldren much further, and it was touch and go whether Aldren would survive to meet the Tuonim. There could be no better opportunity to put Tharin's words to the test.

Ken laid hold of Aldren's wounded leg and simply wished it to heal. The magic stirred but failed to manifest.

Damn it, what's the trigger for this power?

Ken reached back to the few instances when he had felt the magic.

Logic. Look for the common denominator and formulate a corresponding theory. With Shadowalker, I concentrated on the ocean, and that was the turning point for breaking his grip. With the wolf, I reached back to the Hayden Valley fire in Yellowstone. I was nearly burned alive in that blaze. That memory, the pain and Aldren's fire increased the adrenaline rush. Each episode involved potent images from nature and their effects. The strength of the ocean was the shield that I needed to block Shadowalker's assault, and the intense heat of the Yellowstone fire inspired the energy discharge that killed the wolf. It's clumsy, but nevertheless a workable theory. Now, let's see to the proof.

Ken grasped Aldren's leg and coupled his healing desire with specific images of spring in the forest. No memory dominated, but lumped together, they did the trick. His overarching vision of that season of rebirth, when new life bursts into the sun's nurturing warmth and all creatures lick the wounds of winter's bite, brought forth the magic. A soothing bright yellow light from Ken's hands bathed Aldren's injury. When he felt his mission was accomplished, Ken willed the energy to cease. As he did so, an acute weariness descended upon him.

Whew! It's good to know that power is not without its price. Tharin was right. This must be saved for emergencies only. That's my energy being expended, irrespective of the conversion mechanism. I doubt Einstein had this application in mind when he theorized matter and energy as opposites on the same continuum. Anyway, I'll have to see how long it takes for the aftereffects to dissipate.

Ken rested. As he recovered, he imagined that he was reclining on the porch at Uncle Dale's, sipping a tall glass of Aunt Louise's famous summer lemonade. Aunt Louise always said there was no better remedy on God's green Earth for complaints of the body. Up until now, Ken would not have disagreed.

Feeling better much sooner than he had expected, as only a few minutes had passed, Ken reached to remove Aldren's bandage. Shiny pink skin covered healing scars. *It puts a whole new spin on medical care,* Ken thought. *If only Dad could have seen this miracle. He has scant faith in the New-Age generation of alternative healers back home. Holistic medicine, Reiki practitioners, shamans, homeopathy providers—maybe those folks are on the true path. As Tharin said, humanity was never supposed to wield this level of magic. Notwithstanding that shortfall, advancement of those disciplines might be the highest medical achievement for which mankind can hope. It stands to reason that all humans must have the capability to influence energy and matter, but it's only the rare few who actually break through the barriers to unlock mere fragments of that potential. I wonder whether the First Mother chose to aid their vision quests or if they discovered the key on their own? Either way, it may be that thousands of years from today, all of humanity will wield aspects of the First Mother's Fire. Is such a destiny to be fulfilled through science or religion? Our scientific learning curve is rapidly progressing on the micro and macro functioning of the universe. Who knows what giant leaps might have been possible had Einstein completed his unified field theory linking nature's fundamental forces? Our physicists now have heavy ion and hadron colliders that are smashing particles together at near light speed to produce quarks and beyond.*

On the other front, I have now encountered a god-like sentience and stood face-to-face with a ghost who talks of an Eternal War continuing in the Nine Circles. The Eternal War must be the same battle that most of us unknowingly fight each day, the choice of good versus evil. But as I'm fond of arguing, those are relative terms depending on which position you straddle...good versus evil, order versus chaos, positive versus negative, known versus unknown. Maybe we're better off describing our conflict in terms of energy. Many physicists shun an allegorical view of the world. They see reality, includ-ing humanity, as consisting of energy: active in the case of pure energy and static in the guise of matter. Accelerate mat-ter to the speed-of-light squared, and bingo, you're back to pure energy. Plus, every system of energy can be character-ized as taking energy, giving energy, or lying in equilibrium for practical purposes.

Heck, one of the great questions of modern cosmology and Big Bang theory relates to the legendary missing repel-lent force, the cosmological constant that will determine the final result for omega—the mass density equation for the expansion of the universe. Simply put, will the ambient energy in the universe sustain the expansion of all cosmic matter, or is our ultimate fate going to be the second biggest collision in history as the universe rushes inward to collapse on itself? Some physicists have suggested that the answer lies in quan-tifying the amount of dark matter in the universe or unlocking the secrets of the super black holes.

Those mysteries are pretty much out of my hands, but recent events are more telling. The Nosferu and their follow-ers like Shadowalker drain and presumably store the energy of living beings, while I now have the ability to freely release my energy. Granted, these changes at first blush appear insignificant in the scheme of creation. What if they were mul-tiplied at fantastic rates, say every iota of energy, whether contained within living matter or more advanced forms of energy such as spiritual beings roaming the Nine Circles? And what if we applied the principle to higher energy systems, say, for example, the First Mother or the Enemy? Can it be that the expansion or contraction, the life or death, of the uni-verse will be determined by the conscious choice of the energy systems inhabiting its sphere? Is existence all about the strug-gle for dominance between the givers and takers of energy? And if victory in this universal tug-of-war is ever achieved by one side or the other, what's the end result?

Aldren stirred.

Figures you would wake up just as I'm piecing together slices of the big picture. Of course, you could also be sparing my beleaguered brain. I'm no quantum theorist, so my version of events could be nothing more than personal fantasy. And as much as I might yearn right now to be in the thick of a late-night meaning-of-life jam session with the law school crew, it'll have to wait. There are more pressing concerns for us lowly mortal forms of energy.

Ken gave Aldren a light shake.

Aldren groggily opened his eyes before lapsing back into unconsciousness.

"I know you could use the rest to help heal. I'm also dragging from the magic, but we've got a date with the Tuonim.

Ken brought Aldren to the pool's edge. The water was crystal clear and had amply nourished the two trees. The pragmatist in Ken took over. "We may as well take advantage of the water." He thought of his early days with Uncle Dale. *Moving water's best. If it needs filtering and you don't have the tool off the shelf, there's always ways. That'll just clear the grit. Doesn't mean it won't eventually knock you down… diarrhea or worse viral bugs. You can sample the goods for obvious taint, but the human tongue is hardly a foolproof indicator of purity. Plenty of folks happily eat poison without a notion of the trouble they're swallowing. Sometimes you don't have a choice, though. You got to take what Mother Nature provides.*

Ken removed his canteen and dunked a cupped hand into the pool.

"Whew. That's cold like the morning frost. Good sign. At this temperature, it's less likely to harbor unfriendly bacteria."

He brought a palmful to his mouth.

"No unusual odor."

He took a cautious taste, barely dipping his tongue.

The water was wonderful, earthy and refreshing. He gulped as much as he needed and then filled the canteen.

"Now for the big plunge. No unnecessary efforts; five minutes in this icebox, and I won't feel my arms, let alone be able to carry Aldren."

He strode into the pool and waded to the wall. The cold water sent his heart racing; it would be hard to hold his breath.

"Tharin, I hope you meant a short distance."

After hyperventilating three times, Ken submerged and swam. Half a minute later, he resurfaced in the pool and made his way to Aldren.

As Ken grabbed Aldren, the granite doors at the cavern's entrance slid shut, sealing the chamber with a "whoom!"

"Goodbye to you, too, Tharin."

Ken pulled Aldren into the chilly pool. As soon as Aldren touched water, his eyes flew open. This time, the spark of awareness shone from their depths.

"Where are we?" came Aldren's faint whisper.

"Welcome back from the near dead," responded Ken. "I can't explain now. You've got to trust me. I'll do the work. All you have to do is hold your breath for about ten seconds; we're gonna be traveling underwater."

Aldren locked his arm around Ken's shoulder and said with more confidence, "I am ready."

"Good," replied Ken. "We're going on the count of three: one, two, three!"

Ken propelled them through the narrow channel in the rock. They popped up on the other side a few seconds later. They stood chest deep in a side eddy of a large underground waterway. A dazzling show greeted their arrival. There was only a smattering of crystals in the cavern, but the effect was spectacular as the light was amplified and reflected by the river and exposed minerals.

Ken mumbled, "Better than the special effects at a Las Vegas Fourth of July concert."

"What?" Aldren asked, puzzled.

"Nothing. Let's go. I'm freezing."

The two made their way to the river's bank. Ken boosted Aldren onto dry stone and then followed.

Aldren stood firmly and was carefully probing his former leg injury. "Perhaps you should tell me more of this tale. And of the armor coat that now wards you."

"I was wondering how long it would take you to notice. Let's skip the expanded version for a second. The *Reader's Digest* summary is that a Tuonim ghost gave me the armor and I managed to heal your leg."

There was much unsaid, but Aldren's eyes widened. "The First Mother's Fire?"

"I'm a wizard in training." Ken hoped the levity would ease the tension.

Aldren bowed gracefully.

"It is hard for one of the Elder Race..." Aldren paused reflectively and then went to the heart of the matter as he said, "I did not fully trust you before, as you are human, and much evil has been done in the name of humanity. You, Kenneth McNary, have now twice saved my life, acting without hesitation and with risk to your own life. I never dreamed that I might encounter one such as you. That is, the only humans I have known are servants in Remeth's Court. You are very unusual—I should say unique—for your race. Your selfless actions have placed an honor debt upon my Line that must be repaid. I would name you Oath-Companion and ask you to accept my bond of friendship."

Slightly embarrassed and needing a chance to gather his thoughts, Ken cleared his throat. "Aldren, I consider us friends, but yours is the last word. This view of humans as servants won't do. My friendship is reserved for equals, people whom I respect and who return that in kind. I am nobody's servant but my own. On Earth, the human race has fought wars against those among us who would endanger freedom.

Though we died by the hundreds of thousands, even millions, we persevered in the cause of freedom. I'm too young to have participated in those conflicts, but I will never forsake that birthright, even if it means my death in this world."

Aldren replied, "Human or not, your words and deeds are worthy. And though you may perish in this realm, it will not be by my hands, nor would I desire it so. If need be, I will stand by your side though it mean my passage to the Nine Circles."

From the discussion with Tharin, Ken understood Aldren's reference to the Elder Race's afterlife. He could not ask for a stronger promise. Ken extended his hand. "You've got yourself an Oath-Companion."

Aldren received Ken's hand.

Releasing Aldren's grip, Ken said, "We'll have company soon. In the interim, if we can find something to burn, a fire wouldn't hurt. These clothes…" He stopped speaking. The faint sounds of tinkling metal and footsteps were barely audible over the river's gurgling. "That will be the Tuonim," he said.

Both looked to the far side of the cavern. There, five individuals emerged from a rocky portal, one of several connecting tunnels. The newcomers had Aldren's height and corresponding bone structure overlaid with fair skin and white hair. All wore vests forged of metal, with varying symbols engraved in the breastplates. They circled the two strangers and drew their swords.

Ken instinctively set his back against Aldren's, but before he could reach for his knife, Aldren whispered, "Do not provoke them into improvident action. Confrontation should be unnecessary."

Aloud, Aldren announced, "I am Aldren, son of Eril Dragonsbane, of Hemdall's Line. I share the path with my Oath-Companion."

Several eyes swiveled dubiously to Ken and his smooth black armor. Nevertheless, one warrior, with a falcon symbol on his breastplate, stepped forward and said, "I am Swayne, of Gunderhad's Line. It has been many Cyclings since one of Hemdall's scions walked among our presence. That does not mean we turn a blind eye to the deeds of our fellow Tribesman. Do you not serve Stellrod, High Cleric to King Remeth?"

"Indeed, and as such, I am familiar with the Falcon Clan. I am honored to meet you."

Swayne's response was less friendly. "You are far from Remeth's Court." He surveyed their dripping-wet attire. "And I am curious as to how you and this Oath-Companion come to be wandering within the Morningstars."

"That is…" Aldren began.

"Hold," enjoined Swayne. "The story is not mine to hear first. I shall escort you to Garondel Rohr-Kargon, Master of Dawn's Aerie, for it is he who shall hear your tale and determine your fate."

Swayne called another Tuonim to his side and whispered a command. The soldier nodded and ran from the chamber.

No doubt a messenger, Ken thought.

Swayne motioned for Aldren and Ken to walk with him. The rest of the Tuonim sheathed their weapons and proceeded single-file behind the trio.

As Swayne piloted them through the subterranean warren, Ken reflected on the Tuonim. *Everything that I've seen indicates that the Tuonim, as well as Aldren, probably the Elder Race as a whole, place emphasis on social formalities. Aldren mentioned a King, which usually means a royal court, and then there's the ritual greeting and heraldic symbols on the Tuonim's armor. It fits together, I suppose, but it's going to work against my purpose. In Weir, I'm the bottom of the social ladder. Heck, I might not even rate that low if you count the iron collars worn by Shadowalker's thugs. It's no wonder the Tuonim were staring. While tall for a human, I'd probably be considered a runt for one of the Elder Race. And my plain black armor lacks any heraldic symbol.... Even in this getup, they probably don't ascribe much status to me: I'm like a lordless knight from the Middle Ages who tinted his armor black because he couldn't afford to keep it polished. Aldren introduced me as his Oath-Companion. That wasn't a bad move. He avoided revealing that I'm human. However, I cannot, and I will not, let this masquerade continue for long. It would be nice to be accepted by these people, but not at the price of my humanity.*

After a short time, the passages they traversed spoke of civilization. Raw tunnel walls gave way to precision-jointed, smooth-crafted blocks. The flooring resembled inlaid cobblestone. Moreover, the entrances to new chambers and branching paths became more ornate; there were vaulted stone archways, carved pillars, marble accents, and decorative inscriptions in the same runic language as that displayed on Tharin's sarcophagus. A more ominous sign, however, was the armed sentries posted at the key junctions—typically the intersection of three or more passages. Swayne offered quick acknowledgment to each Tuonim but never missed a step. The raised eyebrows and inquisitive glances could wait. Word of Swayne's find would travel of its own volition.

The procession had been winding uphill for about an hour when Swayne bade them halt before a passageway that was secured by a ponderous metal portcullis. A gate such as this would have been right at home in front of any medieval castle. Within this underground mountain domain, however, it was truly awe-inspiring. Four burly Tuonim stood guard on either side of the gate, wielding swords and long polearms.

Ken didn't like the look of this. *Can't be sure of the gate's metal; it might be cast iron. Like everything else in this world of extremes, it's probably of surprisingly strong construction. Either way, whether it's plain iron or magically enhanced, that's one heck of a formidable gate. That checkerboard design of foot-thick beams does justice to every latenight Robin Hood movie I've seen. It must weigh several tons.*

One of the guards pulled a lever, and the gate slowly rose into the ceiling, accompanied by the sound of clinking chain and gears. As Ken passed underneath the curved entryway, his mouth dropped at the sheer vision before him. The light of thousands of wall crystals revealed an underground kingdom of fantastic beauty. No description by Aldren could have possibly captured the reality of the Tuonim's Undercity. The elegant buildings seemed of white alabaster and meandered across rising levels in an expanse that could have swallowed Mount Everest. The Undercity's towers, spires, and pinnacles rose gracefully into the heights. Their swirled columns and stone artistry were mirrored in architectural forms crafted into the ceiling far overhead. And from the cavern's opposite cliff face, in the distance, a waterfall plummeted thousands of feet, continuing its subterranean voyage as a river through the mountain. Eerie patches of white mist hovered among the city's lower environs, coalescing with the white stone. It seemed more like a sky city floating among the clouds than an earthbound metropolis. But looks can be deceiving. The Undercity had its ugly side.

Swayne guided the procession into the cavern. A narrow stone lane was laid from the gate to the beginning of the city's structures. Droplets of cool mist gathered on every surface. Ken would have noticed his clothes leeching the moisture had they not been damp from the soaking in Tharin's pool. The upper city was hidden from sight. As Ken passed the white stone walls of the first buildings on either side, he could see no seams or joints in the stone. He appreciated the decorative etchings, though their grandeur had lost its sheen. A greenish-black carpet of living material thrived on the foundations, creeping higher where deeper shadows permitted growth. Decaying refuse littered the white stone cobbles. As Ken's boots sloshed through a rivulet of brown, murky liquid destined for the nethermost sewer of this subterranean kingdom, fumes of ammonia and excrement stung his nose. He exchanged a dubious glance with Aldren.

"Oath-Companion," Swayne said, surprising Ken, "I take it you have never visited the Undercity."

"This is my first time," replied Ken, hoping that Swayne would not press the discussion.

"Then judge not precipitously. We, too, suffer from the Dwindling. Aspects of the Undercity that were once dispelled at will, must now be left to other means. Our people adjust reluctantly. Bide a moment; the view improves."

Ken nodded politely and continued his observations. There were few windows in these lower walls. Those that he did see were shaped in wavy patterns and whimsical curves. There was no glass to ward the mist or the putrid odors, only dingy wood shuttering the openings from the interior. The air was heavy. Every breath felt like a skirmish to wrest oxygen from the stale, mist-laden soup. An asthmatic would have perished in minutes, but there was life within the viscous fog. One could hear scrapings, shufflings, and muffled voices, though the exact origin of such was impossible to tell. Figures formed, and just as quickly faded, in the gloom. Most had hooded cloaks offering protection from the dreary conditions. None got very close. Swayne alone held the path.

The road began to wind uphill, and as it did so, the fog gave up its secrets. The party approached a gate to an arched passageway. Three Tuonim sat by the opening, eating. Upon seeing Swayne, two of them rose reluctantly. Their armor was unkempt and strained against loose paunches. The image of an open hand above a balance scale was etched on the chest of each set of armor.

"Lord Gunderhad," said the bolder, "what brings these travelers to our realm?"

Swayne warned, "Braxius, the Merchant's Guild has no business this day. Move aside; the Rohr-Kargon awaits."

"Of course." The jovial reply rang hollow. "It is our pleasure to serve the needs of the Falcon Clan." It was a not-so-subtle reminder that all the Tuonim Clans now depended on the Merchant's Guild for basic necessities. It was also the only reason why Swayne had not killed Braxius on the spot.

On this upper level, the fog was more attenuated, a smoky white veil gently blurring the strange architecture of this underground world. There were no separate buildings; the structure in this area was one gigantic creature, linked vertically and horizontally, for other than the dreamy window openings, no seam, break, or gap was visible on the etched white stone. Catwalk-like avenues defied gravity as they looped among the city at all heights, occasionally branching off to dimly lit doors. Ken looked over the edge of the lane on which he stood. Dense fog eclipsed any view of the ground. His gaze returned above. The steep construction made the walls appear to hunch outward, his neck hurt from the awkward view. There were no buttresses, columns, or other supports to be seen. The stone spans should have collapsed under their own weight, never mind that of the ample pedestrian traffic. Cloaked citizens, many much smaller than he had expected for the Elder Race, though he supposed they might be children, walked purposefully along the gridwork, going about their daily tasks. Day had little relevance here, however. The perpetual gleam of the crystals had supplanted nature's clock, casting an adequate but diffuse light across the Undercity.

As Ken strode with the procession, his eye caught the sign of a hammer and anvil directly above one of the doors. With all the other artistic carvings in the white stone, it was tricky to spy these advertisements unless one knew exactly where to look. The ringing clang of metal on metal was heard. *It's a smithy, and over there, above that door, a cape. That's most likely a tailor. And there's a...*

"Oomphf!" Ken knocked into a passerby. Baskets spilled onto the walkway, and one was lost to the foggy abyss as a petite Tuonim fell backward.

"Narsa, stupid clumsy girl. Have I not told you to mind your place? You're lucky not to have fallen to your death. My

Lord," a Tuonim woman pleaded with Ken, "my deepest apologies. These young humans are difficult to train. I assure you, she will be punished."

The flustered girl scrambled to reload the bundled wares into the baskets.

Ken stared at the girl's gaunt arms and ghostly white skin. *So that's it... all the smaller figures... they're humans, not Tuonim.*

He bent down and handed Narsa a package by his feet. Her eyes remained downcast as a delicate hand grasped the bundle from him. Peering into her hood, Ken was able to see blonde hair, shoulder length and flaccid, framing pale, clammy skin.

Swayne waited in slight annoyance but said nothing.

Ken retrieved the final package and then offered his hand to help the girl up.

The Tuonim woman blundered, "My Lord, do not spoil the girl. Narsa, thank your benefactor and let us proceed."

Narsa nodded silently and scurried forward, with the Tuonim woman a whipping-step behind.

"Oath-Companion," Swayne finally prompted, "we are expected above."

Ken nodded and followed. He had no idea of what "above" meant in the present context. There were numerous slender stone spires and broader towers dancing and curling upward in ways that no stone should. Swayne shunned all these ways, however. He appeared to be closing upon the waterfall, and its raw power now vibrated underfoot.

As they progressed, Ken's disgust threatened to dispel the illusion that he maintained for his Tuonim escorts. Humanity was under dire siege in this deep domain. Everywhere Swayne led, similar vignettes played, whether it be plying a craft, trading wares, or simply traversing the catwalks—Tuonim were always attended by humans. Indeed, humanity far outnumbered the Tuonim, and they performed all manner of duties for their overseers.

Slavery, servitude, whatever the exact relationship between human and Tuonim, it's damn clear that my fellow humans are severely in need of an upgrade in their personal freedom. I would have expected that living for tens of thousands of years would have engendered a modicum of wisdom, morality, and compassion commensurate with that enhanced existence. Apparently not... I can't believe the First Mother would ever support such a societal practice. I wonder why she hasn't intervened more directly before my arrival? Then again, don't question a near-deity.

That's funny; the Bible has Moses asking God "Who am I, oh Lord, that I should go unto Pharaoh, and that I should bring forth the children of Israel out of Egypt?" While I certainly am not a Moses, I don't remember him getting a good reply, either. So be it. Until the First Mother tells me otherwise, I intend to be Mr. Fix-It. Before my time in Weir is over, I'm going to empower my people. Wish I had a clue how, though. I'm no guru on political science. These are real lives. I know the foundation underlying constitutional government, but such a government presumes individual rights, for the people and by the people. By definition, "people" has to include humans. That minor fact might have escaped the Tuonim, especially when the absence of magic has forced them to put so much reliance on their human servants. Slavery in any form is pernicious. Abraham Lincoln had the rule of law and the might of half the nation, and he managed to produce one of the bloodiest wars in human history. Even after the victory over the South, the remnants of slavery lingered for generations. And apart from the United States, many third-world countries and some not-so–third-world players still haven't as yet stamped it out. There isn't going to be a silver bullet for this situation. Freedom will take time, but I've got to put the wheels in motion...somehow....

Ken momentarily curled his hands and then released the tension.

Swayne was an astute observer. "Something troubles you, Oath-Companion?"

Ken forced a grin and answered nonchalantly, "No, just stiff from the dampness." His demeanor told a much different story, one that Swayne was not insensitive to perceiving.

This Oath-Companion is a strange one, Swayne thought, *and his countenance is unsuited to any of the Tribal lines; he bears close watching.*

The waterfall, which initially had seemed so far away, now loomed before them. For the first time, Ken noticed fractured catwalks, bridges to nowhere, over his head. Jagged cracks raced along the length of the nearest walls, and creeping fungus once again darkened the white stone.

Swayne explained, "The vibrations take their toll; new cracks develop even as the Stonemasons struggle to repair the damage. They cannot weave the Song of Shaping as before. The Dwindling has seen to that, as well."

Eventually, the group stopped. They stood single-file on a ledge overlooking the bottom of the waterfall. The sound of the cascading water pounding the riverbed not more than twenty-five feet away was thunderous. Conversation was impossible. Moist wind from the falling water drenched Ken's face. Human women worked below, standing downstream in the calmer river shallows. Some were laundering clothes, while others were carting buckets of water back to the elevated bank, where Tuonim gave further orders. The women in the water had next to nothing covering their wet bodies. The sight was pathetic. There was neither color nor life to their exposed skin. Dull white leather stretched over scraggly arms, and spindly legs supported cadaverous torsos.

Ken shook his head in denial of the misery. *Humans weren't meant to live underground for extended periods. No sunlight, no Vitamin D production. Without that vitamin, as a species, we're wide open to disease and deformities. Needless pain and suffering, but why care if you have a steady supply of breeding humans? God, who's the true enemy in this world— the Nosferu, the Tuonim, or both?*

Aldren put his hand on Ken's shoulder.

Ken had almost forgotten his large friend, but as he looked in Aldren's eyes, he saw something that gave him hope for humanity. It was sympathy... as much as he would find in any of the Elder Race. He also saw a message: *not now*.

Aldren motioned upward.

A hexagonal platform was rapidly descending. In no time, it touched ground in front of the party. The platform had slender stone railings that arched to form a dome-like roof. It could have been a summer gazebo but for a thin chain secured to the central dome that originated from a thousand feet above. Swayne opened a small swinging gate in the railing and ushered the others inside.

The ascent began. The air warmed as they rose. Although the river dispersed its share of the thermal energy, the Undercity nevertheless generated substantial heat. The fog, which was the byproduct of the water vapor condensing in the cool lower-level conditions, had completely dissipated a few hundred feet above the cavern floor.

Ken was an accomplished climber, so the dizzying height held no fear for him. He wasn't nearly as comfortable with the tensile strength of the chain that supported the primitive elevator, however, especially given the intervening distance. To keep from dwelling on the risk, he stared at the spectacular waterfall. It was poetry in motion.

At the halfway point, the water's diminishing crash permitted loud conversation.

Aldren leaned to Ken and, for his ears only, said, "Here within the mountain, the river is called Nithel're, which translates as the Mist That Roars. It has a gentler voice where it flows topside along the southern spur of the Morningstars."

"Definitely appropriate," remarked Ken. His view traced the riverbed to the far wall of the enormous cavern. "Aldren," he asked in a whisper, "if we had the opportunity, could we safely ride the river to its surface channel?"

"The opening is left unattended, for it means death to all."

The ascent continued.

Soon, they passed the blowhole from which Nithel're spouted. It was a mouth-like trough glazed with crystalline deposits and green, mossy plants.

They finally neared the cavern ceiling. Its gothic stonework conjured the impression of a colossal cathedral. The Tuonim Stonemasons must have had skill beyond belief to have accomplished such a Herculean labor, Ken thought. It was the culmination of lifetimes.

Quite suddenly, the domed elevator halted. Ken turned away from the stone artistry. They had reached the end of the ride—a natural clifftop in this underground world. The party debarked. Massive stalactites hung ominously above their heads, but these, too, displayed the decorative imprints of the Stonemasons. The inlaid path on which they trod led only a short way, for the cavern's roof curved sharply down to meet the cliff. There, a rising stairway was cut into the mountain. Huge metallic doors, obsidian black and rune-covered, were hinged into the stone on each side. These doors made those of Tharin's tomb resemble a child's creation; they were more than three stories high and were at least two feet thick. Greased locking bolts as thick as a man were fashioned along their length.

A hot wind, heat from the Undercity venting to the out-side, blew lightly at the party's backs. As they crossed the threshold of the doors, Aldren whispered, "Impressive, are they not? Their forging was said to be fifty years' labor by Havkir Surefist, Master Smith of the Tuonim. Should the need arise, these doors will seal the Undercity from all who seek entry from above."

Ken cocked his head to indicate that he was impressed, and then, peering ahead, he commented, "There's natural light above. Could it be we've reached Dawn's Aerie?"

"Indeed. Yet to leave is another matter. Ware thyself." Aldren's hand brushed Caldorsbane gingerly, a portent of things to come.

Compared to the quiet of the stairway tunnel, Aldren's grim warning seemed loud.

CHAPTER 6

THE MASTER OF DAWN'S AERIE

Ken inhaled briskly as they climbed into daylight. The cold mountain air bit his lungs, but after being underground for so long, he gratefully bore the discomfort.

They had emerged from the Undercity onto the only high bluff within the main bailey of Dawn's Aerie. As Swayne shepherded them down the sloping rock to the busy courtyard, Ken used the vantage to observe the keep's strategic design. Two massive walls were structured as one circle within another. The outer ring was only slightly lower than the inner. Ken guessed that both were nearly two hundred feet thick and maybe half that high. This construction would make them incredibly resistant to traditional siege techniques. Sentries walked along the outer parapets, armed with long bows and displaying sheathed swords. The battlements had the classic merlon-and-crenel pattern, allowing for defensive cover or offensive attack from a clear field of fire. Reinforced circular tower units were uniformly spaced opposite each other on both rings. There was only one primary gate leading to the outer bailey, and it was fortified with an interior barbican and second portcullis. No doubt, various machicolations would be embedded in its roof to mercilessly slaughter attacking forces from above. Peering through the gate's tunnel-like passage provided a view of only the exterior ring rather than of another gate; it was a further defensive ingenuity to make life harder for enemy soldiers. The opening in the outer ring was most likely positioned far from the inner loop entrance, probably one hundred and eighty degrees away along the exterior ring. Though Ken couldn't be sure about the outer loop, he saw that the interior face of the inner ring had T-shaped window cuts—airflow, sunlight, and shielded attack positions all in one package. The stonework of Dawn's Aerie was the converse to that of the Undercity: Its smooth walls and towers were as free from blemish, crack, seam, and imperfection as were the Undercity's adorned with extravagantly carved artistry. Functionality screamed from every component of this mountain keep.

As they reached ground level, Swayne angled the group to one of three nondescript iron doors that provided access to the living space within the main ring. Unlike the castles of medieval Earth, the courtyard of Dawn's Aerie had no visible merchant stands, smithies, stables, kennels, mews, or outbuildings of any kind. Instead, Tuonim warriors avidly trained in all manner of weaponry and unarmed combat, while human attendants stood on the ready to provide new arms, clothes, refreshments, or whatever else their lords might demand.

The door chosen by Swayne to pierce the heart of Dawn's Aerie was identical to the remaining pair and offered no clue as to what lay beyond. It was also part of the grand design that no Keep element should signal the location of the Aerie's vitals. Though Ken was unaware of it, the three-person–wide hallway he now traveled was the single primary thoroughfare within the inner loop. It ran centrally like an artery but permitted traffic in both directions, with numerous quarters branching out on either side. Infrequently, the corridor widened sufficiently to accommodate several Tuonim standing shoulder-to-shoulder if the need arose. The magic crystals that he had observed while underground were also prevalent in the Keep. By their light, he was able to descry snippets of Tuonim and humans actively at work in the various connecting chambers. Surprisingly, many rooms were lifeless and dark; Ken felt as if they had been forgotten.

In short order, the company stood on the threshold of the great hall of Dawn's Aerie. It had served as throne room, audience chamber, and festival hall of every Kargon of the Morningstars. The great hall's vaulted ceilings extended to formidable trusses just underlying the uppermost parapets. Its horizontal space stretched as far as the structural integrity would permit while maintaining ample rock between the hall and the outside courtyard.

Swayne ushered them toward his liege as the gathered entourage of Tuonim lords and ladies melted into the foreground. Select human servants stood at the heels of their respective Tuonim superiors.

These humans look healthier than the ones below...greater muscle density, and there's a range of skin tones other than white. Big question is how screwed up they are on the inside...have they accepted an existence of servitude, are they indoctrinated to the culture? How long has this society of near-immortals endured with humans as fodder? People don't forget freedom once tasted... once tasted. What if they've never known it? The Roman Empire lasted five hundred years with its system of citizenship and slavery before it rotted from within... it was never overthrown.

Few of the humans met Ken's gaze, preferring the safety of anonymity. In their eyes, he was an Elder Lord. His business was none of their affair, a survival mechanism for any human among the Tuonim Nobility.

At the end of the great hall, a pensive Garondel Rohr-Kargon sat on his throne. No mere chair was this throne: It was birthed from the Aerie's granite. Like the wedding bed of Greek legend crafted by Ulysses for faithful Penelope, the Rohr-Kargon's seat of power was yet rooted to the Aerie's bedrock. There was no pillow, cushion, or other adornment separating the Rohr-Kargon from his Keep. Gemstones artfully grafted into the throne's chiseled stone reflected laser points of light into the great hall's farthest corners.

Swayne bade Ken and Aldren stop a spear's length from the throne. At this distance, the Rohr-Kargon cut an impressive figure; he was Ken's vision of Odin-King, the Norse god, poised upon his throne in Hlidskjalf, Asgard's highest watchtower. The Rohr-Kargon was arrayed in snow-white armor, and a silver scabbard hung from the throne, the bejeweled hilt of an immense broadsword visible. A dazzling ivory pearl rested in the pommel, but its brilliance paled before the Rohr-Kargon's long white hair and winter-blue eyes. Ken would have guessed that Garondel was around fifty-five years old, save for those eyes; in their cool reflection, a hint of his true age could be found for those willing to plumb such depths. Two neatly braided locks framed Garondel's square jaw before plummeting like daggers to the breastplate of his barrel chest. Engraved on the chest armor was a familiar image: two trees flanking a sarcophagus, the burial site of Tharin Eberstone, First Kargon of the Morningstars.

Aldren genuflected with his head slightly bowed.

Ken ignored the deferential posturing. He met the Rohr-Kargon's regal presence head on. Subtlety had never been his strong suit.

Abruptly breaking the silence, the Rohr-Kargon said, "Step closer." The deep bass of his voice easily carried to the farthest member of his Court.

The Rohr-Kargon focused his attention on Aldren. "Swayne's messenger spoke truth when he named you son of Eril Dragonsbane; Hemdall's Bloodline did ever stand out. I knew your father of old, and if memory serves, it was you who visited our court in the Loranna Cycling, accompanied by the High Cleric?"

"I am honored that you remember so trifling an event."

Shifting his gaze to Ken and staring at the black armor, the Rohr-Kargon wrinkled his brow in puzzlement, "You, brazen youth, who I am told is honored as Oath-Companion to a line of the Firstborn, of what kinship are you?"

As Ken stumbled for a response, Aldren quickly offered, "My Lord, the Oath-Companion hails from the Hinterlands, and his Line is of less consequence."

Eyes narrowing in suspicion, the Rohr-Kargon pressed onward, "Nevertheless, I will have an answer, and not from you, son of Eril Dragonsbane."

Ken gambled as he boldly said, "My Lord, I have sworn to forsake my family name until I perform a deed that would bring further honor to my Line."

Whispers erupted among the Nobles. The soldiers under Swayne's command crowded nearer.

"Thou has much pride for one so small. For now, I shall accept that response," said Garondel. Pausing the conversation, the Rohr-Kargon reached for a stone goblet that resembled a trophy cup; a human servant rapidly filled the receptacle with a foamy beverage. After taking a great draught, Garondel asked, "How does a scion of Hemdall's Line come to be wandering unannounced among my Underpaths?"

Aldren responded guardedly, "My Lord, Stellrod bade us journey to the Deep to seek the First Mother's guidance. Upon our return, She, in Her infinite wisdom, delivered us to your dominion."

"Hmmph," snorted the Rohr-Kargon. "And no doubt, little assistance was found from Her at Windowmere Deep. You would do better to consult the Nosferu. At least they provide advice in place of silence. For that matter, where is Mendac? Send at once for him, and we shall see what tidings the omens bear."

One of Swayne's men darted from the great hall.

The Rohr-Kargon's irreverence to the First Mother was intolerable. Though normally respectful, Aldren spoke impertinently, "King Remeth would not speak so of the First Mother."

Garondel laughed cynically. "King Remeth... King indeed. What has he done for the Elder Race? While the Realms continue to diminish and the Elder Race falls from its glory, he merely prattles to the High Cleric."

"Rohr-Kargon or not," there was an edge to Aldren's words that Ken had not heard before, "be advised that I serve as Chosen Apprentice to the High Cleric."

"Indeed. Then you tread a path that has lost its purpose. You will find no Clerics within my Kingdom. I need warriors. I would rise to action," Garondel slapped his broadsword, "and lead our people in battle did I know the true cause of our decay. I have my suspicions." The Rohr-Kargon turned his angry glance on the now-cowering humans present in the hall. As each struggled to hide behind his or her master or mistress, the Rohr-Kargon spat and took another draught of his beverage.

Ken sighed at the pooling spit. *Tharin asked me to help the Rohr-Kargon, but it's going to be challenging to overcome such hatred. Reason won't be convincing. The message needs to be delivered in undeniable terms that Garondel can understand, but how?*

Ken's thoughts were interrupted by a disturbance at the entrance to the great hall. The court Nobles who had clustered together for a better view of the spectacle hastily fled to the hall's borders. No one dared tempt fate. A wedge of flaming magma might have caused less concern. Everyone's world seemed to revolve around a man-sized hooded figure in black robes approaching the throne; a preternatural darkness lingered on its steps. With each footfall, the stones of the great hall groaned in defiance of this loathsome burden. Sadly, such was the decline of the Tuonim Bloodline that these warnings passed unheeded.

The monkish figure fused into coiling shadows now dimming Garondel's throne. Though the robes concealed much, they couldn't camouflage the stench of evil. Even without a face, the Enemy's taint on this figure was easily recognized. Shadowalker had exuded corruption, but this creature embodied the contagion.

Before Ken could say anything, he was thrown awry by a wave of dizziness. He shut his eyes. When he opened them a moment later, he was dealt another blow. Silence had descended on the gathering. He might have been admiring a still-life tableau hanging in New York's Metropolitan Museum of Art; the great hall's entire assembly lay utterly motionless. Physical reality as Ken knew it had come to a grinding halt, as time and space temporarily resided in unaccustomed orbits. He could not say whether it was his perception of time alone that was altered, or whether all of Weir had been cast into limbo. The effect was astounding.

Like everyone else, Ken felt his muscles suspended in etheric cement. Had they not been, he certainly would have jumped as disembodied voices shattered the vacuum. They emanated from everywhere and nowhere; they sounded within his consciousness. Random conversations overlapped—threatening screams, taunting whispers, veiled promises, maniacal babble—it was rapidly becoming unbearable. Had he lost his sanity? Not without a fight, he hoped.

Ken's thought screamed into the chaos: *Who are you?*

The schizophrenic chorus surprised him by responding as one: *We are those who remain, and we are your salvation.*

Where are you, and why have you chosen to plague me?

We are with only you. There is no other.

And then he knew. *You are the Dreamers of Soulstealer's Doom. I have been told of your presence. What do you want?*

We have much to offer should you choose to embrace us.

A mental image flashed of Ken commanding legions of humanity.

This one before you is the first obstacle; do not stay your hand, strike now....

Ken recalled Tharin's warning, but the movie playing in his mind's eye was not unpleasant. Indeed, part of him yearned to explore this new possibility. He would free humanity from their Tuonim bondage.

The voices cried in excitement. *Yes! Join us!*

And then more images came. Soulstealer's Doom had the power to defeat Mendac and Garondel Rohr-Kargon. Ken stood triumphantly amidst a throne room teeming with humanity. A royal crown descended to his brow. Women worshipped at his feet. The Realms were his for the taking.

What of the First Mother's purpose? Surely this is not in the plan... nor do I wish the mantel of kingship. Beneficent ruler is a far cry from government for the people by the people.

They had gone too far. Ken understood the siren's lure for what it was. These were not his dreams, but the ambitions of the once-living. *Every person harbors tremendous potential for deeds of awe-inspiring good or terrifying evil, yet whichever the path, the key is choice. Who would have thought that I'd be debating metaphysics, but my world has been turned upside down. The First Mother, the Enemy, Souldrinkers, and power on a scale that I never dreamed possible—despite all these curveballs, the hallmark of my humanity is self-determination. To lose that freedom would be to lose myself. The First Mother has claimed a piece of me; I can't deny it. I'm hoping that it was Hers already and I just needed a reminder. I'll be damned if I let any more go out the door. But She gave me Soulstealer's Doom. What if it's a way to preserve my humanity? Let the armor do the heavy lifting.*

No more magic, and no more sacrificing Ken McNary. I don't know how it works. What if every time I use the Fire, I'm renouncing more than my old age? Am I leaking my essence to the universe in dribs and drabs that can never again be me? Could be that's our fate upon death anyway. Does a soul have mass... or, as proffered by St. Thomas Aquinas in his Summa Theologica, how many angels can dance on the point of a pin? It's the question that the First Mother asked me before all this began—the illusion of physicality... the paradox of flesh. What am I? Why is our human mythos replete with tales of the Devil purchasing souls in exchange for granting magical powers? Are these vestigial metaphors, latent warnings for a secret that ancient humans once suspected? There is a path to greatness, but the price is too high. There's no Devil waiting to take your soul; the Devil is you. If I embrace the worldly power promised to me by the armor and Dreamers, as distasteful as that sounds, it might save me from a destiny with infinite consequences. The Elder Race is practically immortal, and as Tharin said, the rules are fundamentally different for them. They can wield the First Mother's Fire with relative impunity. Do they really care if I'm erased from the scheme of existence? Am I simply a tool, designed for use until worn out or broken?

The Dreamers encouraged him. *You have foresight beyond your breeding to consider such matters. Let us be your guides and protectors.*

This was more of a debate than Ken had thought possible. Doubts had shaken but not displaced his faith in himself and the First Mother. *If I let you in, I'll never know who's running the show. I'm not amenable to that risk just yet. Dreamers, or whoever you are, listen up: Return things to normal. I have promises to keep.*

The voices screamed in protest. *Do not dismiss us! Awaken! You, Kenneth McNary, have the power! Fulfill your true destiny....*

Ken hardened his will to such possibilities.

The voices persisted but became fainter. *No! Do not be so proud as to ignore us. No!*

He shut them out. Whatever door they had opened was rapidly closing. A last whisper beckoned. *We shall await....*

The Dreamers of Soulstealer's Doom faded into the void from whence they had come. As if waking from a daydream, Ken experienced sound and movement once again gracing the great hall of Dawn's Aerie. Physical reality resumed its natural course.

Ken wondered at the forces wielded by Soulstealer's Doom; had he been drawn away for minutes or milliseconds? Either way; it seemed that no one else had shared the episode.

Whoops, maybe someone did, Garondel is paying entirely too much attention to me.

Garondel Rohr-Kargon continued his scrutiny. The battle-earned wisdom of millennia had taught him to study his opponents lest he underestimate one, and though his powers were a mere shade of that before the Dwindling, he sensed secrets withheld in the Oath-Companion.

Perhaps it is nothing dire, yet this Oath-Companion bespeaks another tale. Verily, there are other methods to unveil that which lies buried.

Pointing to Ken, Garondel leaned toward his Nosferu advisor. "Mendac, what say the omens for this traveler from Remeth's Court?"

Mendac produced a plum-sized crystal from a fold in his robe and placed it into his jaundiced palm; long yellow fingernails locked around its crystalline edge. His other hand, fingers outspread, slowly revolved clockwise around the gem. The crystal produced a reddish gleam as Mendac's hoarse pronouncement crept throughout the assembly, "Thou art neither of Remeth's Court nor sprung from the loins of the Elder Race."

Ken's hand slid to his knife in anticipation. Likewise, Aldren reached for Caldorsbane as Mendac delivered the coup de grace: "Thou art a human pretender."

Pandemonium erupted. The lords and ladies fell back, shouting, "Human! Deceiver!" Swayne's men charged, swords drawn.

Ken deflected a soldier's sword with the Ka-Bar's steel guard and then ducked underneath another's attacking swipe. His canteen was torn from his belt as he dodged another blade thrust. Outnumbered and comparatively unarmed, Ken knew it was only a matter of time before a sword would reach him. He glimpsed Aldren dueling three Tuonim. Caldorsbane performed like a buzzsaw, letting sparks fly each time metal clashed with metal. Ken and Aldren wouldn't escape alive without using the First Mother's magic. Ken struggled to gather his willpower amidst the frenzied assault.

Think fast; it's now or never....

Before the thought was completed, Ken's concentration was shattered by a bone-jarring impact to his back. Simultaneously, he heard screeching metal snap. Bracing his bruised back with one hand, he pivoted with the Ka-Bar in the other to confront his nemesis. His efforts were unnecessary, however. Motion had again ceased within the great hall, but only as a consequence of a much more mundane event from his perspective.

Swayne stood a yard away, astonishment and horror evident on his face. His long Tuonim blade, Yoshirim, the Clan Sword of his father, his father's father, and all ancestral leaders of the Falcon Clan, lay torn asunder. The piece held aloft in Swayne's grip was no bigger than the Ka-Bar; the other, upon the floor, was five-plus feet of broken metal.

From the throne, Garondel Rohr-Kargon also stared at this wonder. In all his Cyclings, he had never witnessed such an occurrence. Gazing at the black-within-black armor that the human wore, Garondel felt a fleeting recollection surface but then flee before taking substance. An explanation had to be found. *Perhaps the records in the Chronicles of Stone... yes. Aristorn will search through the night; such toil would appeal to his bookish curiosity.*

Asserting control, Garondel broke the unnatural quiet, his level tone revealing little of his unease. "Surrender. You wage a losing battle."

A constant influx of Tuonim soldiers flooded the hall; perhaps thirty or more now surrounded them.

Garondel is holding the winning hand for now, Ken observed. *Besides, there's still the matter of that favor owed to Tharin. Ouch. Make that a debt of gratitude. That old ghost was right about the armor. I would have been dead before I hit the ground.*

Ken rubbed his aching back. *Okay, prisoners for the short term, I hope.*

He dropped the Ka-Bar and nodded for Aldren to do likewise with Caldorsbane.

Garondel suspected that Aldren had intentionally protected this human. That thought gave seed to anger. A human such as this posed an invasive threat to the Elder Race. Fear already raced among the Nobles.

"Son of Eril Dragonsbane, scion of Hemdall's Line, you would knowingly dishonor your name over one such as this?" Garondel asked, a dangerous edge riding his voice.

Aldren spoke loudly for all to hear, "My Lord, for reasons of my own choosing, I have named this human Oath-Companion to Hemdall's Line, and having done so, I stand with him to the last."

Several Tuonim gasped; disbelief and disgust registered throughout the Nobility.

The Rohr-Kargon found himself grudgingly admiring such loyalty but unable to pardon the crime. "And you, human, before I pass judgment, have you anything to say?"

"You can start by calling me Ken. I will not be referred to as 'human.'"

Garondel's reddened face nearly exploded at this audacious correction.

"When you thought I was one of the Elder Race, you were willing to let us explain. Now, because I am human, we stand condemned. What justice is this, and where lies your precious honor? While I may be different than you, I think, I breathe, and I hurt, just as you do. What could possibly give you the right to dominate my kind and decide our fate?"

Garondel rose from the throne. "The Despoiler is a curse upon this land. You are nothing remotely like the Elder Race. Your kind has decimated the outer Realm, and now the very substance of your transgressions has fouled the patterns of Weir. Because of humanity, the Elder Race has lost its way. We, who have endured since the beginning, watching your pathetic development from four-legged beasts to two-legged predators; we, who are Her Firstborn and most favored; we, who live for a thousand of your lifetimes, are now witnessing the theft of our future. You are our undoing. Is that not sufficient cause, man-child?"

"I might respect your position if your conclusion was correct," responded Ken, "but your aim shoots wide of the mark. Earlier you said that if you knew the cause of the Elder Race's demise, you would act. Hear me now, Garondel Rohr-Kargon, for I bear a simple message: Look to the shadows." Ken pointed to Mendac. "The Nosferu are preying on you, me, and this entire world. Your hatred, which burns so fiercely against humanity, blinds you to your true enemies."

Mendac inched toward Ken. The deformed hand bearing the crystal was open and upturned. As the bony fingers formed a skull-like fist, grasping pressure slammed down on Ken. Mendac did not bother to invade the human's consciousness; in times of haste, Souldrinking could be wielded to cause an expedient death without absorbing the victim's energy.

Ken winced at the increasing pain shooting through his mind but continued, "I'm willing to bet that the Nosferu have encouraged your grudge against humanity. It serves their purpose to have your suspicion directed upon the First Mother's other children. Have you ever heard the saying, divide and conquer? I ask you, Garondel Rohr-Kargon, Master of Dawn's Aerie, who rules the Morningstars—you or the creature at your side?"

Garondel roared, "Silence your insolence! Mendac, desist with your sorcery."

Mendac spun as if to challenge the Rohr-Kargon.

Before Mendac's turn was finished, Garondel's hand rested on the pommel of his broadsword; battle scars rippling upon his forearm conveyed a far better warning than words.

Reconsidering, Mendac whispered curtly, "As thou wish, my Lord."

The force assailing Ken abruptly stopped. Ken was relieved but showed no reaction. The confrontation between Garondel and Mendac was far more interesting than the throbbing in his head. *So, the leash is beginning to burn around Mendac's neck. Good. It may provide the opening I need to change Garondel's opinion of humanity and the true enemy.*

The Rohr-Kargon redirected his ire. "I would not offend Mendac further lest you fall prey to an untimely death. As for your accusation, listen well. The Nosferu have provided guidance and healing in a time of desperation. They alone resist the Dwindling that devours us from within and heralds the doom of Weir. The Nosferu would locate that which curses my people and destroy it. Remeth and the High Cleric place their fate in the First Mother, yet I feel She has abandoned the First-born. I can foresee only ruin. If there be salvation, it lies in the skills of the Nosferu, not the unsupported denunciations of a human renegade."

Mendac bowed before the Rohr-Kargon; such wonderfully naïve praise was unexpected. Perhaps his indiscretion would be forgotten.

Garondel nodded.

Aldren opened his mouth, preparing to loose a volley of support for Ken, but the Rohr-Kargon was faster.

"Scion of Hemdall's Line, I am in no mood to hear further protest. Guards, place these prisoners in suitable quarters below while I decide the measure of my justice."

Under the shadows of his hood, Mendac broke into a sinister grin at the sight of the pair being escorted to the dungeons. *Whoever thou art, human, thou wilt not survive a fortnight. I shall see to thee and thy companion personally, for thy knowledge of the Nosferu is most disturbing. Indeed, the Master must be told of thee.*

Mendac excused himself from the Rohr-Kargon's presence and glided undisturbed through the agitated Nobles.

Garondel Rohr-Kargon had many questions this day. As he was apt to do, he rose from the throne and strode from the great hall to embrace the solitude of the Aerie's less-traveled paths. As his personal guard took position on his flank, the Rohr-Kargon waved them off. "I would walk alone."

Garondel chose a meandering route to Aristorn's library as he reflected on previous events. Mendac's reaction to the human had been troubling, as was his own. *Could there be truth behind the human's outburst?*

Though circumstances had forced him to confine the human to the dungeon, this strange human was both fascinating and compelling. *In all my days, I have never met a human such as this. He bears little semblance to the meek servants within the Aerie. He is Oath-Companion to one of Hemdall's Line, no small feat. And to challenge Mendac took either great courage or great foolishness. Only time will reveal which.*

Most disturbing of all was the recurring image of Swayne's broken Clan Sword.

No fool's trick there; perhaps, it will be great courage.

As the Rohr-Kargon turned into the next passageway, he saw the arras hanging undisturbed. For a moment, he admired the grandeur of the mountain vista depicted on the material. Then, remembering his purpose, he pulled it aside. A dim stairway ascended into shadows. He was fond of this concealed path to the library; the stonemasons had cast a wondrous spell of remembrance in its masonry, a magic craft lost for generations. If one had the strength and desire, he could hear the stones sing the early ballads, tales beyond recollection of the oldest Clan. Of late, he had been unable to awaken their melody. He dwelled not upon this feebleness. Climbing these stairs transported his thoughts, instead, to that fateful meeting with Aristorn.

Aristorn had possessed the gift of Stoneshaping, and so great was his skill that the Stonewright's Guild had deemed him worthy of Master Mason status before the end of his fourth Cycling. In so doing, they had given him access to the combined storehouse of knowledge of the entire Guild—the oral tradition handed down from generation to generation. This was a great boon to Aristorn, for he was overly scholarly for one of the Stonewright's Guild. Aristorn absorbed the Keep's tales of old, wherever they might be found, among the Guild or otherwise. As he put it, to understand the stone, one must understand the Tuonim. Thus it came to pass that of all else living, none other, save perhaps Isrenel Rohr-Kargon, sire of Garondel, held so much of the Keep's secrets. Yet always, Aristorn hungered for more knowledge, for the Aerie had endured since the time of the Oath. Its foundation was hewn from the mountain's bones, and deep excavation had continued during much of the rise of the Elder Race. Indeed, many are the forgotten shafts delved into places better left unfound.

In the fullness of his fifth Cycling, Aristorn had vowed to rediscover Kalan-Bath, the Lost Tunnel. Legend held that Kalan-Bath led to the tomb of the First Kargon of the Morningstars. Through his research, which consisted of prying ballads from the elder Stonemasons, Aristorn reasoned that Kalan-Bath's entrance lay below the outer bastion of the East Wall. It had been one stanza from the memory of Aristorn's father's father, Arodnee, a Master Mason in his own right, that told of the First Mother sealing the tomb after the morning light cast its blessing upon the site. Only the hardiest climbers could undertake such an exploration. Where the Aerie's East Wall rose from the mountain, a sheer cliff descended for a thousand feet, but for a youthful Master Mason of the Stonewright's Guild, the taste of raw stone on one's fingers at such heights was to be envied. And so, the dangerous quest had been undertaken. The hand of fate, however, had held other plans. Misfortune struck in the guise of a fierce ice storm. All rescue efforts were in vain as white death had locked its teeth on the Morningstars. Days after the storm had eased, Aristorn's broken body had been found in a chasm abutting the Byway. Yet, hardy was the Bloodline of Amontyr, Firstborn of the Elder Race, for Aristorn had survived.

Isrenel Rohr-Kargon had possessed the puissance to heal Aristorn, but straightening the Master Mason's twisted spine had been beyond his reach. Thus, burdened with a permanent hunch and other debilitating effects from such damage, Aristorn was unable to muster the magic for true Stoneshaping. For a Master Mason of his caliber, death might have been kinder. Cursed with this dishonorable existence, Aristorn had withdrawn from the Guild. He shunned his fellow Tuonim and had begun a self-imposed exile into the mountain's underbelly.

Fate had once again intervened, however, for, many Cyclings later, a newly crowned Garondel Rohr-Kargon, strolling the Keep, had happened upon a curious figure scuttling among the corridors. It was Aristorn. Though marked with a crippling bent, he had strong arms, which clutched tome after tome, a rare sight. Garondel had followed but had found, upon rounding a corner, that Aristorn had vanished without a trace. Seconds later, muffled whispers had arisen from the colored fabric of an arras. As he lifted it, Garondel discovered that the walls sang and that Aristorn lay upon a stairway, delicately inscribing the Old Tongue on page after page of tomes.

After brief explanation, Garondel had understood that this was Aristorn's place of dreams. Since finding these bygone stairs to the neglected library, for the Tuonim were a people much enamored of the oral tradition, Aristorn had chronicled all that he heard. Thus, a friendship had been born, and with it, the restoration of Aristorn's honor, for shortly thereafter, Dawn's Aerie, ancient Fortress-Keep of the Tuonim, for the first time in its long history, had boasted a Royal Librarian.

Reaching the thick wooden door, Garondel withdrew a silver key from his waist, turned the key in the iron lock, and quietly opened the portal. Aristorn sat reading at his desk and looked up as he registered the intrusion.

"My friend," the Rohr-Kargon warmly greeted, "I have a request that suits your unique talents...."

Thereafter, idle conversation among the sentries stalking the Keep's windswept parapets turned to Aristorn's latest fancy, for the light from his library window burned brightly through the night and well into the next evening.

CHAPTER 7

In the Dungeons of Dawn's Aerie

Mendac had related all that had occurred in the great hall, including the human's strange ability to resist the spell of Souldrinking. Though there was not ample time to bring the Souldrinking's full potency to bear, the human should have succumbed to the initial probe. His tolerance was remarkable. Mendac wondered if there could be more to this human than the other specimens of his weakling race. Given the choice, he would have preferred to study and drain this human at his leisure. The table within his chambers had been idle of late. Its leather harnesses and straps were stiffening from lack of attention. However, the Master had been firm in his instructions. Mendac sighed. It was not to be. He was to discover the human's secrets with all alacrity and then kill both the human and his companion. The Master insisted that the deaths appear natural. There must be no verifiable suspicion from the Rohr-Kargon. It would seem peculiar for both to die but could be blamed on unknown contamination from the human filth.

Mendac turned to his apothecary shelves and gathered the necessary supplies... mortar, pestle, candles... and removed a wax-sealed jar from a shelf.

As he began concocting the delicate poison, a light knock sounded on the door.

That would be Junagra with the information, ever eager to please. Perhaps I shall let him endure long enough to meet the Master.

Mendac hissed, "Enter."

As Swordmaster of the Tiger Clan, Junagra was unaccustomed to being commanded like a servant, for he was mighty even for one of the Elder Race. Nevertheless, he permitted this with Mendac. With the advent of the Dwindling, it would be foolish to test metal against magic.

"The human scum and the High Cleric's messenger have been imprisoned in the third tier of cells, nearest the South Wall of the outer rampart."

"Gather thy best," ordered Mendac. "Thou shalt have work to do tomorrow's eve. The human and Elder Lord must die. And Junagra, fetch thee a human female from the under-brothels, unbruised if possible. I would have entertainment after this night's labor is accomplished."

Junagra glanced distastefully at Mendac's torture table, nodded quickly, and then left.

Mendac resumed the grinding and mixing with renewed fervor. "Human, thou wilt trouble the Coven no more."

Much later, as the muffled screams of Mendac's latest victim became hopeless whimpers and the morning light chased the night demons off the Keep's battlements, Ken suddenly jerked upright from his stone bed. Rubbing his forehead, he felt the fog of sleepiness fade. After the skirmish, he and Aldren had been taken several levels under the great hall and then escorted down a winding passage through guarded iron gates before being deposited in their cell. As he had done when they were first imprisoned, Ken set his thoughts on Mendac and escape.

Whoever said stone walls and iron bars do not a prison make definitely wasn't locked up. Even with the First Mother's magic and Aldren's help, it's not going to be a walk in the park. How do I get to Mendac? And assuming I can, do I have the power to stop him? And if I'm lucky enough to survive, where does that leave me with the Rohr-Kargon? Defeating his pet magician won't improve my ratings....

Ken gazed across to where Aldren lay sleeping; the Elder Race might need less rest than humans, but the Souldrinker had claimed its pound of flesh, despite Ken's healing of Aldren's leg injury.

Ken rose and once again examined their prison. Without resorting to magic, it seemed impregnable—solid granite, no exterior windows, and an iron door. Well, there were a few other features. A privy hole lurked in the far corner of the floor. Next to it was a wooden bucket filled with water. Two ragged cloths lay beside it.

"Not exactly modern sanitation, but it might be more unpleasant if I weren't locked up with one of the Elder Race."

Ken walked over and peered in vain down the dark sewer opening. There was only so much rock between them and the roof of the Undercity's cavern; this hole had to link up with a larger system fairly soon. He relieved himself, making his contribution to the pollution now befouling the Nithel're. The torchlight filtering in through the cell door's rectangular grate did little to brighten their quarters, but it did provide a small measure of privacy.

Old-fashioned torchlight... there were light crystals mounted in the corridor as we made our way down here. Many were dim; others were dark. I'm guessing that they weren't just turned off. I've learned enough to know that the First Mother's magic is complicated in its manifestations, but Aldren has been clear in saying that the Elder Race performed magic by giving their energy. Tharin suggested the same. So if I'm right that these crystals function like batteries

storing a charge of sufficient duration to be called permanent,
then the fact that they might be dead or dying suggests that,
whatever the mechanism, the Nosferu are stealing all forms of
soul energy in Weir.

Aldren stirred and sat upright. "I had hoped for a better greeting from the Tuonim. The dungeons of Dawn's Aerie are no place for Hemdall's Line. My father would never tolerate such insult."

"What would he do that you haven't already done?" asked Ken.

"My father is one of King Remeth's finest warriors. When all others failed, he alone was victorious over Taleeth, the plundering dragon of the White Mountains. All respect the name of Eril Dragonsbane. The Rohr-Kargon would never dare to imprison him, whereas I—"

"Whereas you had the courage to look beyond your race and call a human friend. Would your father have done that?"

"No. Indeed, he would have never set forth for Windowmere Deep. Like much of my people, he has lost faith in the First Mother."

Ken reassured him. "Exactly. This might sound familiar, but I don't think that chance had anything to do with our meeting. Consider that while you—"

A gate slammed, followed by footsteps.

A burly guard appeared at their door. He thrust a plate and water bowl through the grate and said, "A morning feast for those who treat with humans."

Aldren grabbed the offering.

The guard's mocking laughter stung Aldren's ears but faded as he continued his duties of spreading good cheer among the rest of the dungeon's pathetic occupants. The few prisoners that Ken and Aldren had passed on their arrival had been humans.

Aldren handed the plate to Ken and said, "Poor fare for one of the Elder Race."

Their breakfast consisted of bread and cheese, and although sparing in quantity, the food showed no sign of mold or other unsavory tampering.

Ken smelled the cheese and said, "Might not be up to your standards, but, Elder Race or not, you look like you could use a meal."

Ken broke off a half share and began to eat.

After suitable brooding, Aldren resigned himself to the banquet.

Between bites, Ken asked, "Don't mean to bring the subject back to your father… about this Taleeth… on Earth the only real dragons we had were the dinosaurs. They became extinct ages ago. When you say dragon, are we talking about an overblown flying reptile or a magical creature of the fire-breathing type?"

"I am unaware of your dinosaur and reptile," Aldren mused. "However, the dragons of Weir, few as they may be, can be fearsome enemies or stalwart friends, though the latter is spoken of only in the tales of the Lore Masters. Unfortunately, the battle with Taleeth was the Elder Race's last encounter with dragonkind, and that occurred well before my time. For the most part, dragons attend to all things dragon, avoiding contact with my people and the other creatures. Their dens are secreted within the shrouded wilds of Weir. The Lore Masters hold that dragons age as do we of the Elder Race and that some dragons fly, while others inhabit water; all resemble four-legged lizards. Do you remember the Old One under which you camped the night that we first met?"

"Old One," said Ken, thinking back. "Do you mean that huge redwood tree on the hill?"

"Yes, that tree, as you say. Taleeth would be of equal length and was of the winged variety."

Ken whistled and said, "What about magic and breathing fire?"

"I know of no fire, but dragons can spit venom. If you are the unfortunate recipient of such an outburst, I have no doubt that, in your remaining seconds of life, you would feel as if you were burning alive. As to magic, it is a question of some intrigue among the Lore Masters. Though no counter-spell was ever detected, all attempts to direct the First Mother's Fire to advantage against Taleeth proved ineffectual."

Ken shook his head, "Living dragons… the journey gets ever stranger."

Aldren added, "If such is your desire, when we reach the Oakenhold, you may inquire to my father for the particulars of his namesake." Reminded of his task, Aldren stood and tested his leg.

"Eril Dragonsbane," said Ken.

"Indeed," replied Aldren as he reexamined the scar beneath his ripped buckskins, "However, we have more vital matters to discuss than your fancy with dragons."

Ken refocused, as well, "How's it doing?"

"It is fully healed. I would never have conceived a human capable of wielding the First Mother's Fire, much less with the power to cure the corruption in my leg. It is one item among several for which I have been waiting for explanation."

"You're right," agreed Ken. "I owe you that much. But a word of warning… you're getting the whole truth and nothing but the truth. You might not like the implications for humanity and the Elder Race."

Aldren said tersely, "Let me judge the merit of your account."

At that, Ken started his tale at the best place—the beginning. He related everything in detail. He spoke of his dream, the First Mother, the Nosferu, and his black armor. Aldren showed fascination throughout the recitation, and at various points interjected questions for clarification. As the story unfolded, Aldren's demeanor brightened. Apparently, it was one thing to align his fate with a human of questionable origin and another spin altogether to become embroiled in a mission blessed by the First Mother.

After an hour, Ken wrapped up his tale and said, "So you see, although I have the power to release us from this prison, I won't do so without honoring my promise to Tharin Eberstone. Dawn's Aerie must awake to the Nosferu threat."

Aldren, who had walked the Path of Honor for three hundred times the lifespan of the human before him, only too well understood the obligations placed on Ken.

"My friend," consoled a thoughtful Aldren, "we shall find a way to do that which must be done. Trust in the First Mother, and the fullness of time shall reveal all."

"That's one interpretation. But I've never been the patient sort. There's a saying back on Earth: 'God helps those who help themselves.' I admit that recent events have lessened its impact, but you get my drift. I intend to confront Mendac. The rub is that he must release his hold on this Keep in a manner that vindicates humanity. I don't know any other way to reach the Rohr-Kargon."

Aldren nodded. "I shall follow your choice. It will not be easy to find him among the Aerie's labyrinth of rooms, nor can we underestimate his power. Unlike Shadowalker, whom you have challenged, Mendac is one of the Nosferu. His capabilities may be far greater. Even with the First Mother's Fire and your bravery, I do not know if we can prevail. The spell of Souldrinking is formidable magic."

"I'll take that chance."

"And what of your life? "First Mother's Fire or not," cautioned Aldren, "you are yet human. Are you willing to have the sands of your hourglass ebb before their allotted time?"

"Tharin said it would take a while to feel the effects of the magic. I'm prepared to go the distance, though I admit to hoping that less will be more."

"Then it is settled. Rest for now and gather strength. Tonight, when the guard is stretched thin and the shadows take hold, we shall move against this Nosferu."

CHAPTER 8

TROUBLE AHEAD

C orin Shadowalker let his mount pick the trail. His hands were better suited to the warmth of his travel furs than to the clasp of reins. It was an ill-tempered beast and he rarely gave it such latitude, but though recalcitrant, his steed was not dumb. Surprising intelligence resided within its tiny equine brain. It had caught wind of their goal, and that scent held the promise of soft hay and fine provisions. Even without these lures, it would have been hard to miss their destination. All paths west of the Morningstars had but one conclusion—the glistening waters of the Gylderhorn, the mighty tributary bisecting the Eastern Rim of Weir.

In the distance, dim lights reflected off the Gylderhorn's unceasing tide, a sure sign that within the hour, he would reach Delvin's Landing. The night air had blown cold in the Valley of Twins, and though he would now be named among the mightiest if he let it be so, there was that remnant yet within him that could relish a tasty meal by a hot fire. For the first time in days, he had forgotten the human. Delvin's Landing offered other pleasures of a more personal nature. He was recalling one Tuonim wench who had enjoyed his special attentions, when the Nosferu's beckoning interrupted his thoughts. A flicker of concern wiped away his lurid smile. This Nosferu did not seek him without serious provocation. Checking his horse, Shadowalker dismounted and withdrew the crystal from his saddlebag. Focusing his mind, Shadowalker saw a pale face floating in the crystal's center facet.

"The Soul-Chase has failed thee. Thine human yet walks the land of Weir."

Shadowalker tensed. "How can a mere human have escaped the Soul-Chase?"

"I cannot tell thee. However, be thou assured, thine human must be dealt with, for he threatens much that we have gained."

"What do you mean, the human threatens? What of the High Cleric's protégé?" Shadowalker's voice deepened.

"Hemdall's Line is insignificant. Thine human has precedent knowledge of our intent and has demonstrated, shall we say, an uncanny talent for survival. Perhaps, even more. That possibility is of far greater concern to the Coven, for it heralds a presence that was believed silent. We shall see. For now, thine human is waylaid within the dungeons of Garondel Rohr-Kargon. Events have been orchestrated to enable his termination. Should our agent fail in this duty for any reason, a new task falls to thee anon. See to it that thine human is captured and brought alive before the Coven."

"Alive will be more difficult," said Shadowalker. "If he is to be killed anyway, why the concern?"

"My brethren now deem him of special interest. His mind must be probed with more finesse than thee may yet possess. Once we have learned our fill, only then shall we feast upon his soul."

Shadowalker had wanted that pleasure to be his alone. He hedged, "And if this human should suffer an unfortunate accident?"

"The Coven is dismayed at thy performance already. Wouldst thou continue to test our patience?"

Shadowalker retreated, "One human arrayed against the Coven will hardly tip the balance of power. Why not bring the northern forces into play? Conquer Dawn's Aerie before the human or Stellrod's chosen can pose any interference."

"Do not presume to question us," the Nosferu testily rebuked. "The forces of which thou speakest have another mission. All resistance in thine Hinterlands must be vanquished ere we move upon the Rohr-Kargon. And we must stock ample feed for our hungry allies."

Shadowalker understood the subtlety immediately but was beyond caring. The humans eking an existence in the Hinterlands were pests to be eradicated, whatever the method of their death.

"As you wish," said Shadowalker. "I will delay my return to the Oakenhold until after the human is delivered to the Coven, but no longer. I have a preordained audience with His Majesty, King Remeth."

The image in the crystal faded.

Shadowalker was left to his thoughts as heavy snow fell on the land. A white blanket soon smothered the valley floor. Such cover storms were common during the movements of the Nosferu and their allies. He normally found the inclement weather inconvenient. In this instance, he would use it to his ends. He would need such help as he lay concealed nearby, waiting for his command.

"To catch a hare," mused Shadowalker, "one must first lay the snare. Should this human evade the Nosferu within the Aerie, he will no doubt venture to the Oakenhold. The High Cleric's pup will insist on returning. There is only one likely place where they will cross the Gylderhorn with ease. That will be their undoing. Its destruction is regrettable, but one must suffer such sacrifices on the path to power."

Shadowalker repacked the crystal, mounted, and nudged the chilly mount toward what would in all likelihood be his final stay at Delvin's Landing.

CHAPTER 9

A Reckoning

In the dungeons of Dawn's Aerie, Ken anxiously scanned his watch. There was a little more than an hour until midnight. Soon, they would put their plan into effect. At midday, when the guard had returned to feed his pets, Ken had attempted to knock him unconscious using his magic. Within seconds after handing them food, the guard had fallen to the ground, senseless. He had awoken unharmed shortly thereafter. Ken and Aldren had acted as if nothing had occurred. However, the event had been a milestone for the wizard in training—the First Mother's Fire could now be wielded to their advantage without killing anyone. In another hour, they would be on the move, an all or nothing gambit.

Elsewhere within the Keep, Garondel Rohr-Kargon tossed uncomfortably within a feverish dream. The lush furs in his chamber held no comfort this night and seemed to choke the Rohr-Kargon.

An insistent but gentle tapping on the door released the Rohr-Kargon from the ghosts haunting his royal slumber.

"Who," grumbled a thick-throated Garondel, "interrupts my rest?"

"My Lord, it is only Aristorn," replied his private guard.

Weary, but awake, Garondel sat upright. "Allow him to enter."

The Rohr-Kargon relaxed at seeing his old friend. Aristorn was among the few whom Garondel trusted absolutely. His wisdom had oft proved helpful, and this night was no different.

"I have just had a most disturbing dream. Would you humor me by listening?" requested Garondel.

Aristorn hobbled to the nearest chair. "If I can be of service, the news I bear can abide."

"I found myself alone in the outer bailey near the Eastern Gate. The freezing air was slowly stealing the vigor from my flesh. The guards were gone. I had no way to enter. I drew my arm back and hammered the rampart. As I struck, my blow pierced the barrier with ease. The magnificent stonework of Dawn's Aerie crumbled to dust. I struck again and again, and when I finally delved to the other side, the cold sharpened its claws a thousand fold. There, in the Keep's inner courtyard, lay my warriors. The pride of Dawn's Aerie was brought to its knees, covered in ice and unmoving. The sleep of the Nine Circles held firm. I opened my mouth to give alarm, but no sound issued. I sought to wake the nearest warrior, but my limbs failed; I stood stiff and unyielding. I stared unwillingly at this horror until my sight faded into darkness. 'Twas your presence that released me from that unwelcome abyss. Aristorn, my friend and counselor, what say you to this tale?"

Aristorn nodded sympathetically. "I am not surprised, for though our magic has lessened and the seeds of despair find fertile soil, I believe that the First Mother has broken Her silence in more ways than one. I have an answer to your query, though you knew the result all along."

Aristorn held out a dusty book and said, "One of the earliest fragments, my Lord."

The tome smelled of rotten parchment and was nigh to crumbling, yet the Old Tongue flowed powerfully along the page marked by Aristorn. As he read, the Rohr-Kargon's eyes widened.

"Do you believe this to be true?" asked Garondel.

Aristorn nodded.

"Then it may be that I have erred. And yet, I cannot say which way the scales may tip, for in its presence, evil deeds are just as likely as good."

Garondel Rohr-Kargon rose and began to dress.

Aristorn queried, "My Lord?"

"Omens of such portent are not to be ignored, lest dire consequences fall. I will attend this matter now."

Aristorn bowed, and as he departed, he heard the Rohr-Kargon calling for his personal guard.

In the dungeon below, Ken nodded to Aldren and said, "I'm still getting the hang of the magic, so stand back. I'll focus on the lock, but the door might not cooperate."

Aldren stood. "I am ready. Alas, for such a task, would that Caldorsbane rested at my side."

Ken agreed with such sentiment. He would have liked the Ka-Bar on his hip. "We'll scrounge what we find along the way."

Suddenly, the steel door whined in the outer corridor.

"Quick," whispered Ken, "back to sleep!"

Footsteps approached. Mendac gazed through the port in the cell door.

"Human, awake thyself. Awake, I say!" commanded an impatient Mendac.

Ken and Aldren stirred as if waking from a deep sleep.

"Human, I shall introduce myself more formally than the last time thee and I met. I am Mendac of the Nosferu, Follower of Borgath and Servant to the Coven, and I am thy death."

A key turned in the lock.

Ken and Aldren jumped up and retreated to back of the cell.

Mendac and six armed Tuonim entered. Four Tuonim had swords drawn; another held a glass decanter containing a black liquid; the sixth was large even by Elder Race standards.

Ken stalled while figuring his next move. "I'm surprised you couldn't do your dirty work alone."

"These are the fortunate," was the agitated reply. "They will be overlords when the Coven takes control."

"And when will that be?" said Ken.

"Soon, but not before thy life is stolen. Our forces are nearing completion. Even now, they approach numbers sufficient to destroy Garondel Rohr-Kargon and Remeth."

Aldren countered, "King Remeth has legions at his command. Surely, the Nosferu, who are few, cannot hope to defeat his power. Though you have the spell of Souldrinking, we will sacrifice as many warriors to the Nine Circles as are needed to rid us of your presence."

Mendac's hoarse laughter echoed against the surrounding rock. "Foolish youth, we will not strike alone."

Ken thought, *how right you are.*

Salvation stood behind them in the form of Garondel Rohr-Kargon and two of his personal guard. The Rohr-Kargon had not yet spoken, but the righteous look of indignation and anger told volumes.

No telling how much Garondel's overheard. But Mendac hasn't seen them yet. Let's press home the point.

Ken baited the hook. "From what I've seen of this fortress, it's gonna take one hell of an army to conquer Dawn's Aerie. Last time I checked, I seem to remember a certain Nosferu whelp—that would be you—tucking his cowardly tail between his legs when confronted by the Rohr-Kargon."

Mendac positively fumed. "Dawn's Aerie is mine. The Coven shall feed upon Garondel Rohr-Kargon like the other cattle."

Garondel Rohr-Kargon's voice thundered in the dungeon's confines, "Deceiving wretch! Traitors, all! The only thing you'll taste is the steel of my sword!"

Mendac turned and cursed silently. He had gone too far to back down. Pointing at three of his henchmen, he ordered, "Thou art with me. Junagra, thee and the others see to these meddlers."

The three charged the Rohr-Kargon, forcing him into the dungeon corridor, with Mendac close behind.

Junagra eyed Aldren. "I have no need of weapons to release you to the Nine Circles. As for the human..." He turned to his two comrades. "He's yours."

The heck with that, Ken thought.

Ken made the first move. Targeting the weakest link, he flew forward and slammed the base of his palm into the chin of the Tuonim holding the glass jar. The force of the strike hurled the Tuonim, glass jar and all, into the cell wall. Ken didn't wait to see the results but distinctly heard smashing glass as he ducked low to his right in anticipation of the other Tuonim's attack. Ken wasn't disappointed; the sword impact on his shoulder drove his knee to the ground.

Pain ignited in Ken's arm. Soulstealer's Doom had protected him from the initial stroke but had deflected the blade onto his exposed arm. A gash across his bicep began spilling what seemed like gallons of blood. His opponent moved in to finish the job.

Ken glanced over to see Aldren and Junagra locked in combat. *No help from that quarter.*

Still on the ground, Ken refocused on the threat.

The Tuonim lifted his sword to deliver the death strike.

Ken pivoted on his knee and lashed out with a roundhouse sweep, catching his foe's legs at mid-calf. As the stunned Tuonim fell onto his back, Ken pounced. He kicked twice in the face, knowing the heavy damage that his boots would wreak. Ken fought down a wave of nausea and was preparing another kick when the injured Tuonim mercifully passed out.

Looking to the far wall, Ken saw that the first Tuonim he had hit lay motionless. Fear gripped Ken's heart. He had never killed anyone in his life. However, seeing that Aldren and Junagra were fighting, Ken moved to aid his friend, further thoughts of murder leaving his mind. The moral consequences of his actions could be dealt with later.

Holding his injured bicep, Ken retrieved a sword from the ground. He edged near the titanic pair, waiting for the right opening. Junagra's style was easy to read, pure power. Aldren was the more skilled, avoiding Junagra's wild swings and deflecting those that came near. Junagra was expending tremendous energy, while Aldren nimbly evaded his grasp. Ken had several opportunities to run the blade through Junagra's exposed body, but each time, he hesitated to deliver metal to flesh.

The sound of fighting from the corridor caught Ken's attention. Although he wished to help the Rohr-Kargon, he would not leave Aldren.

As if reading his mind, Aldren yelled, "See to the Rohr-Kargon! I can hold Junagra here."

Sensing that the tide had changed, Junagra backed away from Aldren and drew his sword. He was breathing heavily and said, "A Swordmaster of the Tiger Clan has no fear of a Cleric's blade. Human, after I slaughter this one, I shall enjoy tearing you apart limb by limb."

Ken responded evenly, "I think not. You're panting. He's fresh. I've also seen his swordsmanship. The smart money's on him, given a level playing field, and I can help with that."

Ken tossed his sword to Aldren, who deftly caught the blade. Aldren smiled briefly and pivoted to face Junagra.

Ken turned and stepped cautiously into the corridor. A moment later, he heard steel clanging on steel behind him. He hoped his assessment of Aldren's and Junagra's fight would prove true as he walked down the hallway. He found the first of Mendac's traitors sprawled awkwardly against the wall and paused only long enough to rip a piece of cloth from the dead Tuonim to secure a bandage over his own throbbing arm. He moved along the dungeon alleyway. Another of Mendac's conspirators had been sent to the Nine Circles. He stepped over the body. Nearing a bend, Ken felt a brief chill at hearing agonizing screams. As he peered around the wall, he was sickened by the vision before him.

All the Tuonim, including the last of Mendac's henchman, writhed violently on the ground. Mendac's arm was outstretched, and within his hand, he bore a glowing red crystal. As the crystal pulsed brighter, Mendac laughed wildly.

Ken strode into view.

Tharin, I hope you knew what you were talking about.

Mendac ceased laughing.

"I will not permit this to happen," threatened Ken.

"Thou art incapable of preventing my victory. These belong to the Nosferu, as do all creatures within our domain. The Master knows of thee and has sentenced thee to death. That is unusual, if not unique, to one of thy base stature, yet the Elder Race is long-lived and sweet to our taste. Bide a while, human, and thou shalt have the privilege of dying last."

The disdain in Mendac's voice increased Ken's determination. He stepped closer.

"Thou wouldst choose the instant of thy death. I would not expect this from the likes of thee. Thy race is ever full of cowardice. Feel the death that thou so avidly seekest to embrace."

Cruel talons of power scraped against Ken's mind, but as Mendac sought to rend his way deeper, Ken erected a mental barrier.

The human's resistance was again surprising to the Nosferu. Mendac had swallowed the souls of entire civilizations during his artificially extended life, and very few individuals had shown such ability. In a long-forgotten corner of his twisted spirit, a silent alarm sounded, *beware thine human...* But he was a Follower of Borgath, Destroyer of Worlds. There would be a costly tithe for fleeing this moment of triumph. He pressed on, assailing the human's consciousness, heedless of that which argued for caution. Mendac bled more and more life from the Tuonim, pouring every effort into breaching this human's defense.

Ken imagined a bunker of concrete and steel. As one rift opened, he would repair it, but no matter how hard he tried, he could not keep pace. As the seconds ticked by, Ken grew dizzy.

Must focus on the wall. Concentrate. Nevertheless, his defenses began to crumble. Mendac would prevail after all.

Mendac, too, sensed impending success. Yet, just as the human's will was about to collapse, the attack was abruptly thrust aside. Fear shook Mendac's being as a ponderous force assaulted him.

Soulstealer's Doom, with the unquenchable desire of thousands upon thousands of souls, greedily devoured Mendac's power. An energy beam streamed from Mendac's crystal to the breastplate of Soulstealer's Doom.

As Ken looked on, Mendac shrunk in stature; his bright red crystal flickered and dimmed.

Mendac screamed, and fell to his knees. The crystal exploded into dust.

As Mendac cowered, Ken fought with the Dreamers of Soulstealer's Doom for the sanctity of his soul. "I will not be ruled by Mendac or by the likes of you."

A definitive line would be drawn. In a last tremendous effort, he regained control, or at least Soulstealer's Doom let it appear as such. The Dreamers receded into their twilight slumber; the energy beam disappeared. Mendac lay unconscious.

Ken held his pounding head, inhaled deeply, and grabbed the Rohr-Kargon's warblade. He approached Mendac and held the warblade above the creature's motionless body. But even now, Ken could not slay in cold blood. Mendac hardly posed a threat in his weakened state.

Ken turned. Garondel Rohr-Kargon alone had survived Mendac's draining. The other Tuonim were dead, their flesh withered from the bone. It seemed that the Dwindling had not left the Rohr-Kargon entirely bereft of magic.

Ken knelt and helped Garondel sit up. "Rest easy, Rohr-Kargon. The effects will pass. Don't ask me how I know, I just do."

Garondel nodded but was too weak for speech. Suddenly, he gripped Ken's arm.

Ken saw the raised knife reflected in the Rohr-Kargon's eyes. He leapt sideways and, without thinking, thrust the war-blade through Mendac's exposed flank. The knife tumbled from Mendac's hand, clattering harmlessly against stone. Mendac screamed once, grasped the sword feebly, and then fell, destined never again to rise.

Ken looked at the warblade in his hands and then to the fallen Nosferu. His mind replayed over and over the bone-splitting crunch, the flowing dark blood, the permeating odor of stomach acid. He had killed a sentient being. And while the ignorant might have experienced pleasure and the sage might have cried for innocence lost, Ken pondered the cards fate had dealt and the meaning of his actions.

Uncle Dale once said that even in death, lessons are learned; he was right. Hard times call for hard measures.

Death was the natural result of life. He had taken another's life when necessary for survival. Although Ken would never be the same, there was a substantial part of him that would never be different.

Ken turned to the Rohr-Kargon and, remembering Aldren, said, "I'll be back."

Garondel simply said, "Go."

Ken hurried as best he could to their former prison. Fatigue and blood loss slowed him considerably, but the noise-less corridor hastened his steps. Clearly, the battle between Junagra and Aldren had ended.

I know Aldren had the upper hand....

Doubts began to surface.

Why hasn't he joined us already? Could Junagra have won? Fearing the worst, Ken reached the cell and entered, warblade extended. His precaution was unnecessary. Aldren was propped against the wall just inside the door, eyes open, and breathing.

Aldren coughed and spat red. "Not a bad piece of sword-play, eh?"

To his left, Junagra's massive form lay on the floor, sur-rounded by blood. As Ken proceeded to Aldren's side, he saw that Junagra's head was nearly severed from the body. It was obvious to Ken, looking at Aldren, that the victory had not been gained without cost. Aldren was a mess. He had blood oozing and dripping from several minor gashes, but of para-mount concern was a chest wound that continued to bleed through the fingers of Aldren's clenched palm.

Kneeling, Ken lifted Aldren's hand; air bubbles and blood frothed outward. Granted, Ken knew only basic emer-gency first aid, however, it didn't take a medical degree to fig-ure out the damage. The blade had split ribs on its way through the lungs and beyond. Ken applied pressure with his hand.

Aldren asked, "What... of the Rohr-Kargon and Men-dac?"

"Mendac is history. The Rohr-Kargon lives and, given time to rest, should recover. You, on the other hand, look lousy."

Aldren coughed and spat blood again. "It was an honor-able fight. I shall be welcomed in the Nine Circles."

Ken shook his head. "You aren't going anywhere just yet." Closing his eyes, Ken summoned the First Mother's Fire. It didn't take long for the magic to gather. Each time, he became more adept. The power came from within, but in his weakened state, he toppled forward. His hands found the stone of Dawn's Aerie, which responded to the contact. Crafted by the Firstborn and imbued with the mighty power of old, the living stone of Dawn's Aerie answered Ken's need. Energy surged into him. He would not falter. As before, he seized upon nature's imagery and envisioned the wound healing. Opening his eyes, he guided the First Mother's Fire in repairing, sealing, rebuilding. He was now beyond weary, but he refused to stop the healing process prematurely.

A commotion erupted in the outer dungeon. Tuonim guards were approaching.

He ignored them and continued his work. The room spun. His breath labored. After what seemed an eternity but was only another few seconds, Ken finally felt Aldren's skin knit beneath his hand.

That'll do it.

The First Mother's Fire ceased. Weak, sweaty, and worn to the bone, Ken wanted to sleep for a week, but Swayne and several guards had entered. He tried to muster the strength to stand. Instead, he found himself flat on his back, looking at the ceiling. The cool caress of the stone seemed a welcome relief. As he passed into unconsciousness, the last thing he heard was the Rohr-Kargon's unmistakable bark, "Leave the human be!"

CHAPTER 10

Awakenings

K en drifted in the no-man's-land between sleep and wake-
fulness, enjoying the soft flannel sheets of his bedroom
at Uncle Dale's. Wistful tunes played from Aunt Louise's
Steinway. Ken opened his eyes. As the castle stonework solidified into waking reality, he turned to see a beautiful Tuonim
woman sitting by the window with her fingers weaving across
a golden harp. He remembered.

Shielding his eyes from bright sunbeams, Ken rasped,
"How, uggh, how long have I been here?"

The Tuonim woman continued the gentle strumming,
ignoring the interruption.

Ken lifted his head from the warm folds of the pillows
but stopped short of getting out of bed. He was naked. A fresh
bandage was wrapped over his bicep. However, he hardly felt
the injury. Removing the dressing, he discovered a healing
scar. As he marveled at the magic, a sudden concern materialized. Soulstealer's Doom was nowhere in sight. Of course,
he was not exactly being tortured. Deciding to hold his
tongue, he listened to the music. It was strange to his ears but
not unpleasant.

The woman sang.

The days grow long; faith, mine armor,
Wanes with the coming twilight.
How shall I find the way home?
The Lady of the Wood answers not.

My Prince quests for thee,
His priceless treasure forgotten,
A fair flower challenging Winter's burn.
The Lady of the Wood answers not.

Duty, oh valiant foe to restless fate,
Gird my heart for that to come.
Hope, your blessing eternal,
The Lady of the Wood answers not.

Ancient beast, spoiler to some,
Endurance you shall see here;
Love is not undone;
Fertile yet is the seed of the Firstborn.
The Lady of the Wood answers not.

The Lady of the Wood answers not,
Then I shall speak for her.

As the woman ended her performance, she gracefully rose and moved to Ken's side. He could not help but appreciate the cut of her silk dress and the way it accentuated her sensuous curves. Here was a Tuonim woman in her prime—long, white shimmering hair, high-set cheekbones, and golden-hued eyes. The ravages of time had been cheated their due. Her looks would endure. He was not above fantasizing what it would be like to make love to a near-immortal and suddenly found the situation slightly embarrassing.

To cover his embarrassment, Ken said, "You play beautifully. Please don't be upset with me for saying it seemed a sad song."

"There is much to admire in sadness, for without it, who could know joy? Yet, be not overly concerned; the mood of the Ballad of Elodreth and Pelham changes in the later stanzas."

"You would find me an eager audience." Ken sought to prolong the company of this charming lady. He asked tentatively, "May I know your name?"

The words from her lips quenched any desire he had felt. "I am Mereth, and you lie within the home of Swayne, of Gunderhad's Line—my husband. This is the third day that the morning light has greeted your rest in our arms."

"Three days," he sputtered before saying, "Thank you for taking care of me. I trust I haven't been too much of a burden."

"We all have our obligations, and I must attend to mine now."

"You're right," he agreed. "Elodreth and Pelham will keep for another day. However, I could really use my clothes and armor now."

A rumbling sound from his stomach reminded Ken of a more pressing need. "Again, my thanks. Would it be possible for you to get me some food, as well?"

"Do not thank me. You are here at the behest of Garondel Rohr-Kargon. Your armor and weaponry are in my husband's safekeeping. As for your clothes, they were in need of cleaning and lie not far. I shall have them brought to you, along with stew."

"What about my armor?"

Mereth smiled, "Yes, I see that you are feeling better. You act far more like a Clansman than a human. How strange to find one such as you, a ruddy-skinned human, virile and gifted beyond any human heretofore known to the Elder Race. That is, if the rumors are true."

Ken felt like a lab specimen and said curtly, "My armor."

"Very well, I shall advise my husband of your request."

As Mereth departed, Ken eased back into a light slumber. He awoke later to find Aldren quietly entering his chamber. Ken's clothes had been draped over a nearby chair, and the table across the room had ample food. The pungent aroma of spicy broth and fresh bread had his mouth watering.

"I'm awake already. You don't have to sneak in like a thief, or are we still prisoners?"

Aldren laughed heartily. "We are honored guests of the Rohr-Kargon."

"Well, that certainly has a better ring to it."

Although unsteady, Ken wasted no time getting out of bed. Between putting on his clothes and swallowing mouthfuls of soup, he managed to continue the conversation. "I see that you're in one piece, and for that I am happy. Is Mendac dead, or did I dream that part?"

"Rest easy, my friend. Your sword stroke was true. Mendac's soul has returned from whence it came, perhaps even to the Nine Circles, where I should be thrice over, but for your intervention. Let none say I chose poorly when I named thee Oath-Companion."

"Indeed." Ken smiled. "What else has occurred while I slept?"

"Much has happened since your blow against Mendac. Word of your deed has spread throughout this Keep. I'm afraid that the tale grows with each telling and that few know what really happened. You will have to enlighten me, as well, about how you survived when circumstances permit. Some doubt that you are truly human, but all within the Keep acknowledge the honor-debt owed to you by Garondel Rohr-Kargon."

Ken scoffed, "Swayne's wife didn't exactly roll out the red carpet."

Aldren lifted an eyebrow. "What?"

"She wasn't very friendly."

"I am not surprised. Many of the Elder Race, and especially the Tuonim, have viewed humanity as the bane of Weir. Your deeds and Mendac's treachery raise the possibility that the case is otherwise, and this truth has caused great unrest. The Tuonim have turned to Garondel for guidance, yet he is secluded within the great hall, seeing none save the Clan Chiefs. Movement among the Keep's guardsmen has increased, and the Undercity whispers that Garondel is preparing for battle."

"Who is the Rohr-Kargon—" Two loud raps sounded on the chamber door, interrupting Ken's question.

Swayne entered, followed by one of his soldiers. The guard dropped Soulstealer's Doom, the Ka-Bar and its leather sheath, and the canteen at Ken's feet and then left.

A consummate warrior, Swayne understood the human's need for his weaponry. Swayne had spent centuries upon centuries perfecting his technique and achieving oneness of spirit with his Clan Sword. Beyond memory, Yoshirim had been entrusted to the Falcon Clan Chief. Though five Cyclings had passed, Swayne swelled with the pride upon recalling his ceremony of leadership, when his father, Dane, had placed Yoshirim in Swayne's scabbard and, with it, had awarded the honor of Clan Chief. The memory touched a chord of melancholy, as well. It had been a time of parting. The ceremony was as much a farewell as it had been confirmation of Swayne's promotion, for, that very day, Swayne resolutely watched his parents vanish into the Oaken Corridors. Dane had no longer been able to deny the Unum-par, the wanderlust that had called so many of the Elder Race to worlds beyond the Gateways. In choosing to transfer leadership and to journey without Yoshirim, Dane could not have conveyed a clearer message about the likelihood of his return. Swayne's mother, Sigurd, would not be parted with her love, and so had followed where Dane led.

And yet, as honored as Swayne had felt when he first gripped Yoshirim, he had only recently come to realize that an unforeseen weakness had lain dormant in the cradle of tradition, and now, great was his shame. The impossible had occurred with the arrival of this perplexing human and that smooth black armor. Yoshirim lay broken, and with it, Swayne's spirit. From the highest Noble to the lowliest servant, all knew of his embarrassment.

Gripping his empty scabbard, Swayne relived the moment of Yoshirim's shattering and found his thoughts hardening anew toward this human. A battle raged within him, for in his heart, he knew that, however unlikely, this human, Oath-Companion to Hemdall's Blood, walked with honor and had defended Garondel Rohr-Kargon though it meant possible death. And then there was the healing of Aldren, son of Eril Dragonsbane; Swayne had arrived in time to see the impossible: The human had used the First Mother's Fire to pour life into Aldren. The only one to behold the power, Swayne had not spoken of the incident for fear of further ridicule from the Nobles.

Swayne's thoughts stopped as the human bent to inspect his equipment.

"But for your metal water holder which was pierced by a sword in the great hall, you will find your things in good order. Your knife is strange to me, yet the blade has strength and balance. The armor, however, is most impressive, the more so because *you* wear it. Can you tell me of its forging?"

Ken noticed Swayne's empty scabbard and read the full depth of the question. He did not want to lie, but at the same time, he detected hostility and was not prepared to trust this Tuonim.

"It was a gift from a friend and traces its history to Acadia. More than that, I cannot say."

Swayne's surprise at the mention of Acadia was evident. He quickly regained his composure and stated, "The Rohr-Kargon wishes to hear both of your counsel."

"Now?" asked Ken, his exasperation showing. "Let me put a bit more in my stomach."

Swayne nodded. "A few moments, then. Make haste."

Ken put a hunk of bread in his mouth as he examined his canteen. It was a complete loss. On the bright side, a destroyed canteen was much preferable to feeling a sword in his gut. He took another bite of the bread and a last gulp of stew before securing the Ka-Bar against his leg. Finally, he stared at Soulstealer's Doom. They had unfinished business. Reluctantly, he again buckled on the enigmatic black armor.

Aldren smiled approvingly.

Swayne rapidly wove the trio through the Keep's hallways, slowing only when the doors of the great hall lay in sight. As the trio entered, they were greeted by a gathering much altered from before. Gone were the lords and ladies, the human servants, and the circus spectacle. Sweat filled the air. A handful of dour-faced Tuonim turned their attentions from various maps strewn across a stone table near the throne to the newcomers. Even the Rohr-Kargon's dominating presence, and that of his learned counsel, Aristorn, could not dissuade the Clan Chiefs from a firsthand view of Ken. This human had achieved a notoriety unheard of among the Tuonim, not only for his shocking status as Oath-Companion to Hemdall's Line, but more from his single-handed destruction of Mendac. In their weakened state from the Dwindling, many of the Clansmen had not believed such a feat was possible, let alone from a human. Ken was a loose cannon in their otherwise ordered world, and none could say what deeds might follow in his passing.

Garondel announced, "Let there be none who doubt. This day, I acknowledge the honor-debt owed to the human, Kenneth McNary. Further, I offer my domain as sanctuary until such time as he regains his strength and wishes to depart."

Garondel clapped his hands, and two servants entered bearing velvet-covered parcels.

"I ask you to accept these tokens of esteem."

Garondel reached under the first cloth and, from a small stone box, produced a ring.

"This has been crafted from the white bedrock of Dawn's Aerie. To the Tuonim, it identifies the bearer as one of the First Mark. As such, it signifies everlasting friendship with the Tuonim and the freedom to journey unchecked within our territories."

Aldren urged Ken to accept the ring. "It is a precious gift that few claim to hold."

Ken eyed the thin plain white ring. It was polished to perfection. He wondered at the stone's brittleness after such fine shaping, and whether it would survive the rigors ahead.

There's only one way to find out.

Ken held out his hand and permitted the Rohr-Kargon to place the ring on his index finger. It fit perfectly.

Moving to the second parcel, the Rohr-Kargon produced a sheath and sword. "You have not worn a sword since first I laid eyes upon your person. If you do not have one, I offer the training blade from my youth, Stonegrinder."

Ken looked at the sheath, a time-washed leather harness to be worn across the back; it was lackluster but serviceable. The sword mirrored the sheath's humble image: hardened rawhide provided ample grip on the two-handed hilt, and neither adornments nor etchings graced any part of the four-odd feet of stone-gray metal. In place of adornment, a vein-like network of shallow scratches and a sheared-off tip bore their own testimony to this sword's ancient history.

Ken smiled. He liked Stonegrinder immensely. If he had been offered a jeweled masterpiece, he would have accepted it begrudgingly because it would catch too many prying eyes; he would have had to forever watch his back for thieves and envious Nobles. This was an unremarkable sword, plain and sturdy.

Misreading Ken's hesitation, the Rohr-Kargon offered encouragement. "Do not be deceived by appearances; Stone-grinder has proven an experienced teacher and mighty ally."

As Ken removed Stonegrinder from the Rohr-Kargon's hands, he said, "I am honored. Thank you. Now all I need is someone to show me the best way to use it."

With a look from the Rohr-Kargon, Swayne reluctantly stepped forward. "I will impart what I can of my skill."

Aldren piped in, "I, too, would be glad to help."

As Ken finished donning the back harness, the Rohr-Kargon nodded his approval before saying, "Let us turn to more critical matters."

Garondel dismissed the servants and beckoned Aldren and Ken to the area where the Clan Chiefs waited with their maps.

The maps depicted the countryside surrounding Dawn's Aerie. As the Rohr-Kargon discussed scouting reports with his Clan Chiefs, Ken listened intently, welcoming the chance to learn more about Weir.

Garondel began, "Lord Keshire, what of your Clans-men?"

Lord Keshire of the Fox Clan responded, "My scouts tracking the eastern border of Dawn's Aerie report no unusual movement. As ever, the Spirits of Deepening Forest guard their own."

"Let us hope it stays so," interrupted Garondel. "And what of the southern front?"

"I have instructed my scouts in the east to turn their foray to the southern foot of the Morningstars. They will jour-ney to Fingol's Bay and send a runner if aught is amiss."

"Even so," muttered Garondel, "any such news will be long in arriving."

Lord Keshire continued, "As my Lord is aware, the mountains to our west are a formidable deterrent. However, I took the precaution of placing a watcher with a trade caravan from the Undercity that left to restock Delvin's Landing. My Clansman will monitor the shores of the Gylderhorn for any threat."

Garondel nodded approval and moved on. "And you, Lord MacTyre, what says the Wolf Clan?"

A lean, muscled Tuonim next to Ken responded, "It is a se'nnight's journey north through the Valley of Twins. My scouts will remain in Three Corners at the entrance to the Valley and send reports anon. However, one of our Clansmen has recently returned to the Aerie from an earlier expedition."

"How much earlier?" queried Garondel.

"A month," replied Lord MacTyre.

Garondel nodded.

"He was dispatched when the party reached the village of Karsey. There was no indication from our people of aught amiss, and yet…"

"This is no time to hold back. Out with it."

"The humans in Karsey talked of unrest in the Hinterlands. It is said that the Dark Riders skirmish with an unknown foe deep in the northern wastes."

All the Lords turned to the Rohr-Kargon.

Garondel, like most of his people, had heard tales of the Dark Riders—a mounted group of human warriors said to patrol the Hinterlands during the eve hours and protect renegade settlements. If, indeed, they existed, they were a relatively new development, for none of the Tuonim had yet encountered these humans. This oversight was partly his to blame, for as this supposed group confined its activities to the Hinterlands, he had seen no reason to intervene.

"In these times," Garondel said as he eyed Ken, "even rumor may prove useful. Lord MacTyre, what of your remaining scouts from the earlier expedition?

"They split at Karsey. Half continued northeast, seeking to journey through Bryn's Aisle, while the rest moved northwest toward the Reinhold Outpost. A messenger is likely from either party, but I cannot say when such will happen. For obvious reasons, they are ignorant of our current circumstances."

Garondel asked, "When was our last communication with the Rheinhold Outpost?"

None of the Clan Chiefs spoke.

Finally, Aristorn broke the silence. "Of late, there have been few available or desirous of walking the Outpost's cold stone. I believe a small group of our warriors remain, for I received a letter from one of my Clansmen. Arulan is the Outpost's Stonemason; he is sister-son to me. His letter did not reveal any news of interest. As I think on it, I realize that was more than a year back, perhaps two."

Garondel paced and then mused aloud, "I had hoped for more. Mendac's threat was sure, and as he was not one to idly boast, we must be prepared to strike."

The Rohr-Kargon turned his penetrating stare on Ken. "Oath-Companion, you were first to accuse the Nosferu of treachery when all else seemed blind. What counsel would you give?"

Ken had the floor. He took a moment to assess his audience. *You're an outsider, a threat to their way of life. No embellishment now; give them the nutshell version.*

"You can choose to believe as you will, but while camping at Windowmere Deep, I had a dream in which an elderly woman appeared to me. She stood on the water's surface and told me that she was the First Mother. She spoke of the Nosferu as the enemy of all life. Shortly thereafter, I helped Aldren escape from another of the Elder Race."

Many of the Clan Chiefs exchanged startled looks. While many knew the history of the First Mother's manifestations, few of the Great Scions who still strode the land could actually remember Her last appearance. Even more appalling was the suggestion that the First Mother had visited a human.

In response to the Clan Chiefs' reaction, Aldren spoke, "I believe his vision is true. As for the rest, you are aware that the High Cleric dispatched me to the Deep. I was taken prisoner in Deepening Forest just west of the Grove. I was tricked by one of Remeth's counselors. I will not mention his name openly lest I bring ill luck upon our purpose, but I will write it in the Base Speech so that you may forewarn all Tuonim of his deception."

Aldren paused briefly and inscribed Shadowalker's name using stylus and parchment handed to him by Aristorn. That done, Aldren resumed his testimony. "This counselor tried to force information from me using the Nosferu's evil, the spell of Souldrinking. He would have succeeded but for the Oath-Companion's rescue. I never suspected such betrayal from one of the Elder Race. After our escape, the Oath-Companion and I began the journey to the Oakenhold. As Chosen Apprentice to the High Cleric, my first duty then and now is to report these events to Stellrod. It was not my intention to pass through your domain, but Her will dictated otherwise, and well that it did, for there was wrong to be set right."

Ken finished their tale. "When we arrived, I was also, let us say obligated to help you discover the true enemy. I don't know what threat the Nosferu have placed along your borders, but I'll lend insight where I can. Let me get a closer look at these maps. You've got too much territory to deploy your forces blindly. Reconnaissance and communications are solid strategies for now. Besides these, I would think that it's critical to warn Stellrod and King Remeth of the Nosferu plan. If the Nosferu have assembled an army of sufficient power to challenge Dawn's Aerie, you need all the resources and allies that you can get. There's also a strong possibility that the Nosferu are moving against the Oakenhold. If we can beat them to the punch, they might be caught with their pants down, and a two-front attack is to our advantage."

As he paused, Ken stroked his chin in thought. "Aldren and I were already on our way to King Remeth, and, with your permission, I see no reason to delay the trip now. Once we inform him of the danger, we'll return with what support he can give."

Ken pivoted to face Aldren. "How long will it take us to reach the Oakenhold?"

Aldren's hand found the map. "Horses are unsuited to the heights of Lavlir's Pass, and that is our more expedient route from here. Once through…" His finger traced due west. "We can trade for horses and ferry across the Gylderhorn at Delvin's Landing. If we encounter no resistance and the horses are lightly rested, we should arrive within forty days."

The Rohr-Kargon uttered a concern foremost on Ken's thoughts, "Aldren, son of Eril Dragonsbane, and Oath-Companion, the warning that you seek to deliver to the Oakenhold may come too late. Both of you have demonstrated strength and bravery; will you not stay and help my warriors uproot the evil lurking within our borders?"

Aldren tensed and threw a pleading glance to Ken.

Reading the signs, Ken responded tactfully, "We appreciate the offer, but we may do you the greatest good through King Remeth. And who knows, we might find other help along the way. Every creature on Weir has a stake in the outcome of this conflict with the Nosferu."

Aldren exhaled in relief.

Not one to let an intelligence opportunity pass, Lord Keshire jumped in. "If you and the Oath-Companion could keep an open ear for tidings… Delvin's Landing attracts certain company that may have useful news. Should a message to the Aerie be necessary, many of my Clansmen can be found in unlooked-for places."

Ken assured him, "No problem. I appreciate the value of information in any campaign."

The Rohr-Kargon pushed away from the table. "It is settled, then. You shall leave in the morning. In the meantime, I commend you to Swayne."

Aldren and Ken nodded, while Swayne bowed. The trio then marched out of the great hall, followed by several members of the Falcon Clan as they burst into the afternoon sun in the main courtyard.

"Oath-Companion, we have several hours before the evening fare. I would begin your training now."

"Let's do it," said Ken, warming to the challenge.

Swayne stripped his armor and gave it to one of his Clansmen. Ken did likewise, leaving Soulstealer's Doom with Aldren. For the first hour, Swayne assessed Ken's skills and reaction time. Side by side, Swayne demonstrated fundamental defenses, attacks, and countermoves for Ken to repeat. Aldren offered encouragement and pointers during the process. Ken's greatest difficulty was in dealing with the weight and balance of the sword. He was proficient with the Ka-Bar, but adding several feet of metal required significant adjustment in both the strike and follow-through.

"Hold," said Swayne. "Let us see how you fence with a real opponent."

Swayne called to the two Clansmen who had been watching the lesson; they produced leather jerkins. As the Clansmen fitted the protective armor on Ken and Swayne, Ken posed a question. "We spar with our blades?"

"Oath-Companion, we do not play. Your life depends on obtaining oneness of spirit with Stonegrinder. As a human wielding a Tuonim blade, it is unlikely that you can awaken the Swordsong. But there are other approaches. The sword is an extension of your hand, the hand is connected to your arm, and the arm obeys the commands of the will. Mistakes have consequences, and you must embrace the risk to master the blade."

"Okay, I get the message."

Almost before Ken was ready, Swayne struck on the offensive.

Aldren shouted, "Focus on the sword. Understand the pattern of his attack."

Using basic defense, Ken deflected many blows. Those hits that did score resulted in throbbing bruises but, thankfully, no bloodshed.

Swayne is enjoying himself. Could it be he's dishing out payback for his broken sword? If so, the street runs in both directions.

Ken saw his opening and took a powerful swing.

Swayne effortlessly met the blade with his own. Ken, however, felt the impact down to his toes and nearly dropped his weapon. *Correction, make that a one-way street.*

Swayne paused. "I thought as much. An offensive strike with the sword magnifies the concussive force far in excess of that felt with your knife."

Ken flexed his hand and rubbed his arm. "Point taken."

Swayne grinned.

Thereafter, the pair traded blows for the next few hours until Swayne called a halt. Aldren, holding Soulstealer's Doom, greeted each with a pitcher of water.

Hot, exhausted and feeling the strain in his arms, Ken took a few gulps of the proffered water and poured the remainder over his head.

Aldren laughed. "I worked up an appetite just watching you two."

"That is good, for Mereth expects us. Come with me."

As Swayne led them onward through the Aerie to the Falcon Clan's holdings, Ken was impressed anew by the Keep's vastness but was again troubled as they passed one empty chamber after another. *Even allowing for the activities below, the Tuonim population is small. So far, I've seen maybe a thousand Tuonim. Add ten times that in humans. A decent number of folk, but even without the Undercity, the Aerie could comfortably support five times that number. Either they have intentionally overbuilt or their population has undergone a significant downsizing. The Tuonim are going to need a lot more warriors if there's a war coming.*

Swayne stopped before their rooms and said, "Mereth sets a timely table. See that you join us—through that hallway and then to your left—as the evening watch tolls."

"Can you be a bit more specific on the time?" asked Ken.

Swayne walked to nearest window and pointed at an immense bell mounted on the tower closest to gatehouse of the inner ring.

"Twice daily at the changing of the guard—" explained Swayne, "at the coming dawn and evening dusk, the Hammer of Destiny will sound. Have you not heard it?"

"Now that you mention it, yes, but sound doesn't travel well in the lower dungeons."

Aldren cracked a smile.

Swayne remained unmoved at Ken's humor and said, "You will each find a fresh scented washbasin, towel, and new clothing in your chambers. If there is aught else you desire, pull the knotted rope hanging near the bed. A house servant will fulfill your wishes. Otherwise, we shall expect your company at the appropriate hour."

Swayne departed.

Ken entered his room and hung his sweat-soaked shirt on the bed. Staring into the nearby mirror, he found there was one other luxury he could use. On a whim, he pulled the rope near the bed. A few minutes later, a knock sounded on the door.

Ken went to the door.

An attractive young woman tentatively asked, "What does my Lord desire?"

Ken smiled, touched his jaw, and said, "I've been on the trail a while. Can you find me a razor to trim this stubble?"

She nodded and left.

Though Ken knew his five o'clock shadow would return, he was having dinner with a lady. Even if Mereth were the only woman present, he wanted to make a better impression.

Shortly, another knock sounded.

Ken replied, "Come in."

A neatly dressed elderly manservant entered. He held a basin of soapy water and a straight razor.

Ken was mildly disappointed. The woman had been a whole lot nicer to look at.

"I am called Bushon. I would be happy to assist, my Lord."

"Thanks, I can handle it myself," replied Ken. He had learned to use a straight razor at Uncle Dale's. Disposable razors had never figured prominently in Dale's camping pack; their wastefulness insulted his country frugality.

Bushon nodded but hurriedly closed the door and stalked forward.

Ken backed toward Stonegrinder.

"Please, my Lord, I intend you no harm," reassured Bushon, who put the razor and basin down. "I am Senior House Chamberlain to the Falcon Clan. We haven't much time. I am at risk being here, but my presence is linked to you. First, are you truly human?"

Ken was intrigued. "Yes, I'm human. However, I'm not of this realm…. Ah, let me rephrase that…. Have you heard of Earth?"

Bushon nodded. "I am one who knows somewhat of the outer homeworld. My ancestor, more than twenty generations ago, was brought from there in his fourteenth year of life. They did so to save him from death, and our line has served the Falcon Clan ever since. His stories have been passed down within my family. Forgive me; I babble when time is precious. I am told that you spoke treason before the Rohr-Kargon, defending humans and assailing the Tuonim's right to control our destiny. Is this so?"

"That's correct. Humans are meant to be free."

"Then you may be interested to know that there are those among us who secretly resist the servitude. I am one such."

"Good to hear it. I was beginning to believe that the instinct had been removed from everyone. Are there many who feel this way?"

"A great many," whispered Bushon. "Some have fled to the freedom of the Hinterlands. Others have been taken away and never seen again. Within the mountain, there is a growing movement preparing for the day when humans shall walk unchallenged upon Weir. It is for this reason that I sought you. Your coming has sparked the movement. You wear the ring of the First Mark. If the rumors are true, you have rescued the Rohr-Kargon from death. None of us has ever dreamed of obtaining this status. You have power and influence to help our people, and I beg you to do so."

"Stop." Ken cut off Bushon more firmly than he had intended, and the older manservant backed away in fright. Ken said, "No, relax. You have nothing to be afraid of…. I was just going to say that you don't have to beg me for anything; you are preaching to the choir. I will do all I can to help you and our people."

Footsteps sounded in the corridor.

Bushon shot a fearful glance at the door and said, "Thank you, my Lord."

"Please call me Ken. I make no claim to nobility of any kind. In fact, I'm from a more humble lineage than you might imagine."

"My Lord Ken, I understand your wish," Bushon said in a conciliatory tone, "but I dare not do otherwise. I would be severely punished by the Tuonim for such disrespect. I must go now, but my message is this: You have friends. If you ask aught of us, we shall heed your call."

"Thanks for the vote of confidence and the good word. I'll see what I can do."

Bushon bowed gracefully and guardedly opened the door. Scanning the hallway, he waved and then left.

Ken walked to the washbasin and splashed soapy water on his face. He picked up the razor gingerly. It was foolish to have too much on your mind while swiping with a straight razor.

Just my luck, he thought.

A short while later, the Hammer of Destiny sounded. A sore but clean-shaven Ken met Aldren outside his door.

Aldren commented, "Your appearance has improved. However, would it not be prudent to wear your armor?"

Ken laughed, "We're going to dinner, not to a battle."

"You may change your opinion, depending on the company," said Aldren.

"That may be," said Ken, slapping Aldren on the back, "but I don't want to offend Swayne and Mereth. We are their guests, and I trust that they'll see to our welfare. Plus, it's hard to relax wearing that thing."

"I share your reticence. In the Oakenhold, such garb is reserved only for times of conflict. Even then, those under the Eclesium's jurisdiction will not don such protection. Their fortune lies in the arms of the First Mother."

"Eclesium?" said Ken.

"The Order of Clerics and Lore Masters," replied Aldren. "As Chosen Apprentice to Stellrod, I stand in good stead among its members."

Turning the corner, they saw two Clansmen flanking an archway that opened into the Falcon Clan's dining chamber. They paused at the entryway.

As their presence became known, conversation stopped among the seated Tuonim. There were six other dinner guests this night, all unfamiliar to Ken save for Lord Keshire, whom he recognized from the Clan Chiefs in the Rohr-Kargon's great hall.

Swayne and Mereth anchored either head of the elegant table. Four places were set on each side, though the fine-hewn granite slab could have accommodated thrice as many. A comfortable fire blazed in the hearth behind Swayne, while Mereth's end of the table backed into the kitchen area. Wonderful aromas teased Ken's nose.

Mereth directed, "Aldren, son of Eril Dragonsbane, of Hemdall's Line, this place is yours. Oath-Companion, if you will."

Ken walked to the only other empty chair at the table.

"Introductions are in order," said Swayne. Gesturing to his left, he said, "I present Lord and Lady Keshire of the Fox Clan, and to your left, son of Eril Dragonsbane, is Lady Orphiam, Mistress of the Weaver's Guild." Indicating those to the right of him, Swayne said, "Lord Barak, Master of the Armorer's Guild and his consort, Lady Emeryle of the Dragon Clan. And to your right, Oath-Companion, sits Aristorn, our Royal Librarian and Keeper of the Chronicles of Stone."

Mereth gently clapped her hands, and several humans hustled from the kitchen entry, toting trays and flagons. Fortunately for Ken, the only badge of servitude these humans displayed was a single iron bracelet on the left wrist. Neck collars might have prompted him to action that he might later regret. The trays were placed on the table, revealing warm breads; cheeses; and assorted fruits and vegetables, both raw and masterfully cooked. There was also an enormous roasted bird. Ken couldn't identify its breed, but it looked delicious.

As Ken's goblet was filled with what appeared to be red wine, he observed the fine tracing of a falcon on the human servant's bracelet.

"Please enjoy our bounty," said Mereth, encouraging everyone to begin the meal.

Ken loaded his plate with various offerings. He had worked up a ferocious appetite and was grateful for the feast.

From across the table, Aldren was getting an eyeful of Lady Emeryle.

Ken sympathized. Lady Emeryle was breathtaking, built to last, and her jade-colored armor seemed more apt for sex appeal than defense. She presented a dramatic contrast to the thin, aristocratic Lord and Lady Keshire and the grandmotherly Lady Orphiam. Mereth could hold her own against Lady Emeryle, though; Ken wagered she could hold her own against any woman, Tuonim or otherwise.

Lord Barak wore the only other armor at the table, and from his hip hung a decorative scabbard and sword. Despite the graying hair that complimented his silver chainmail, he looked more than adequate should a challenge occur.

Aristorn opened the conversation. "Aldren, upon your return to the Oakenhold, please convey my greetings to the High Cleric. The absence of Clerics in the Aerie has made for poor correspondence. It seems like ages since the last great gathering of the Eclesium. In truth, perhaps that is in part responsible for the current situation. Instead of turning to the Nosferu for aid with the Dwindling, we would have been better served to look within and renew our trust with the First Mother. The High Cleric's judgment in sending you to the Ancients must have been truly inspired by Her, for it has awakened the Elder Race to a danger like few others recorded in the Chronicles of Stone."

"The Rohr-Kargon's growing contempt for the Order of Clerics has greatly perplexed Stellrod," Aldren replied. "For this reason, it was not my intent to seek out Dawn's Aerie; however, the higher path oft involves putting one foot in front of the other. I am honored to carry your message to Stellrod. He will rejoice at the tidings, tempered as they may be with dark events, for although Stellrod has suspected the Nosferu role, he must be told the full extent of their treachery. Souldrinking is a depraved and deadly power. It will take all our remaining strength to combat this evil and whatever army lies in wait. I can only hope that we reach the High Cleric before the Nosferu act."

Mereth interjected, "My husband tells me that you and the Oath-Companion will be leaving tomorrow for that purpose. I have made extra provision for your journey through the mountains."

"Speaking of provision," offered Ken, "I would like to thank you for this gracious meal and the fresh clothes. They are very comfortable. I had a spare set in my pack, but circumstances forced me to stow it on our way to Dawn's Aerie."

"Well spoken," Lady Orphiam gracefully replied. "The clothes are yours to keep. They are a trifle for the Weaver's Guild to do for those who have forestalled Garondel Rohr-Kargon's departure to the Nine Circles. We have great need for his guidance in these *strange* times."

"Strange indeed," said Lady Emeryle, who then turned to Ken. "Is it truth that *you* slew Mendac, and without ever having handled a blade?"

Beautiful and blunt, thought Ken. *So much for the chitchat and light dinner conversation. You probably meant to ask how a mere human could kill Mendac.*

"Well, in part," Ken answered cautiously, "while I had no experience with a sword, I did have years of practice using my knife."

Lord Barak said, "I briefly inspected it under Lord Gunderhad's supervision while you rested in his care. It is an unremarkable tool of efficient design. I deem it from a skilled craftsman, as far as humans go. The armor is another matter, though. Though it lacks Clan markings, it is Tuonim in origin and not of recent forging. I am unaware of any Tuonim armor that will shatter a Clan Blade."

Lord Barak pointed to Yoshirim's remains on the fireplace mantle behind Swayne and asked, "Oath-Companion, how did you come by it?"

Swayne paused his meal to say, "I will hear no more on this subject, Lord Barak."

Mereth heard her husband's tone and thought, *careful my love, it will not do to insult one whom you will shortly ask the likelihood of reforging Yoshirim. It is no accident that he,*

nor any of our guests, sits within our demesne this night. She
interceded quickly on his behalf. "We have arranged a performance tonight," said Mereth, softening the brisk mood. "The
Oath-Companion wished to hear more of the Ballad of Elodreth and Pelham." She clapped her hands twice.

From the entranceway, a handsome Tuonim couple
approached the seated gathering, arm in arm. They were
dressed in elegant white, the woman in a flowing gown that
billowed ethereally with each movement, and the man in a
loose-fitting tunic and tights. A full-length, shimmering,
black-raven motif had been cleverly embroidered into their
garments so that with a bit of imagination, one could simply
see two ravens, wings extended, soaring in the heavens.

The couple bowed before their audience. The woman
strummed on a harp as the man plucked a four-stringed dul-
cimer-like instrument. Both instruments were finely sculpted
from the Aerie's white bedrock. While the melody was pleas-
ingly simple, the vibrating strings on the sacred stone generated musical tones the likes of which Ken had never heard
before.

Everyone ate heartily as the duet serenaded the repast.
Ken followed the example of the table guests and, like them,
kept his own counsel during the captivating rendition. The
artists simultaneously played, sang, and interpreted the composition with free-style body movements. And Mereth had
been right, Ken thought, the later stanzas *did* conclude on a
more cheerful note.

When they had finished their performance, the couple
bowed.

Mereth tilted her head regally in salute and said, "The
Falcon Clan accepts this unique gift in the spirit of which it is
offered; the Line of Gunderhad will remember."

With that, the duo departed and table talk resumed.

Ken listened to snippets of the conversation as he
chewed his last helping of meat. Lady Orphiam was asking

Aldren his impression of the Ballad, and Lord Keshire whispered covertly to Swayne while Lady Keshire flattered Lord Barak despite a predatory stare from Lady Emeryle.

Ken reached for his wine goblet but knocked it over as his forearm knotted. Everyone's attention swung to him.

"My apologies," said Ken meekly. "My muscles are feeling the sword training from this afternoon." He rubbed the kink out, flexing his hand.

Lady Emeryle pounced on his weakness. "The way of the sword requires inner steel to complement the outer, mastery is unachievable in a human lifetime."

"Scars there are," Swayne said defensively of his new pupil, "yet he did well for having never before hefted an Elder blade."

"High praise, indeed, for a human," jeered Lord Barak. "Still, these days, it takes more than sword skills to avoid the Nine Circles. There's magic afoot, dark and deadly, which the Dwindling has left us ill-prepared to counter."

Lady Emeryle redirected the conversation. "And what of the spell of Souldrinking, Oath-Companion? Surely Mendac did not fall without its protection?"

Ken hesitated. *You keep asking the hard questions.* "It wasn't as effective on me as he had hoped."

"You, a human, resisted his power while the Rohr-Kargon's personal guard was dispatched to the Nine Circles?" exclaimed Lady Emeryle.

"That's right."

"I don't believe you."

"And yet," said Aldren reprovingly, "Mendac is vanquished and the Oath-Companion remains. Is that not testament enough?"

Lady Emeryle rose to the occasion. "And what of you, son of Eril Dragonsbane? They say that the dungeon cell where you were found evidenced a great struggle and that yours was not the only sword dipped in blood. Are we to believe that Junagra, Swordmaster of the Tiger Clan, passed to the Nine Circles without leaving you so much as a scratch to remember him by?"

"No, Junagra scored heavily. My injuries were healed before Lord Gunderhad's arrival," replied Aldren.

Swayne stopped eating and riveted his attention to the conversation.

Lord Barak countered, "From what source did this supposed healing arise, when all know that the First Mother's Fire has left the Realm?"

Aldren simply pointed at Ken.

Silence filled the room.

And then rolling laughter bellowed from Lord Barak. "A good jest; well played, indeed. I had marked Clerics as a normally austere lot," he said.

Nobody else was smiling.

Ken changed the topic. "Aristorn, you mentioned the Chronicles of Stone. What are they?"

In attending tonight's fare, Aristorn had, in part, hoped for closer scrutiny of the Oath-Companion's armor and for explanation as to how a human had come to possess the lost might of Acadia. He kept such counsel to himself, however, as he answered. "The Chronicles are the last remaining written records of the history of our Tribe, but they are only remnants, fragments of our past that hardly weave a tale. You must understand that the passage of time is of less concern to us than to humans. Even happenings of great import may become as fleeting ripples on the Gylderhorn, leaving no trace, save in the memories of those witnessing their coming and going. I have set the task upon myself to preserve a fuller accounting of the Tuonim. It is a difficult labor, for as a race, we do not often look backward, but forward to the joy of discovering what each new moment shall bestow. Indeed, it is this very quality that may be our undoing."

"How is that possible?" asked Ken.

"My friends," interrupted Lord Keshire, "we should leave that discussion for another day. This topic can be of no interest to the Oath-Companion."

"It concerns humans and Tuonim alike," replied Aristorn. "Oath-Companion, I suspect by now that you have probably noticed several aspects of our life. It cannot have escaped your perception that we utilize humans as a servant class."

"Does that apply to all humans?" Ken asked defensively.

Aristorn considered his next words carefully. "There are those outside of the Aerie who do not fall within our dominion. These humans are tolerated, so long as they do not interfere. The worst of the lot, however—those who seek the path of destruction—are hunted, captured, and sentenced to the mines of Kalan Minach, the Forgotten Mountain. Their lives end as rock slaves, scraping metal ores from the mountain's core. This was not always the practice, however. In days long past by your reckoning, the small population of humans that had gained entrance to Weir were left to their own ends. We were amused by your primitive race, and so short-lived were its members that their deeds passed without memory, but as the Cyclings turn and our days continue, seemingly endless, with few children born, the Elder Race has been decimated.

"Not from strife, famine, disease, or the hand of any enemy has ever so mighty a blow been driven; we have only ourselves to blame. Our undoing may be named the Unumpar. In the Base Speech, a close translation would be 'the lust that comes from boredom.' Clansmen who have tired of our regimented life atop the Aerie's parapets are able, for a time, to fill their inner voids by striding forth into the far recesses of Weir. Alas, eventually, they and many others of the Elder Race have crossed beyond the Oaken Corridors to places hitherto unknown. None to our knowledge has ever returned."

"I am not totally surprised," Ken avowed. "Dawn's Aerie can support a huge population, yet I've observed room after empty room and a comparatively small number of Tuonim. I must confess that I never suspected the cause, however. Long life can have its disadvantages."

"Quite correct," agreed Aristorn.

Ken seized the opportunity to turn the conversation, though he risked further alienation. "Now I can understand why you chose humanity for labor, but the injustice of slavery in any form cannot be countenanced by any civilized society. Apart from the food of freedom, what about the health of the humans below? You must have noticed their poor conditions. We aren't a subterranean species. They need open air and sunlight."

Lady Keshire gasped in shock.

Aristorn wanted to reply but held his tongue. Aldren, too, kept his own thoughts. Mereth was uncomfortable and looked to Swayne for guidance. Other reactions were less guarded.

"Oath-Companion, you go too far," warned Lord Keshire, his eyes narrowing suspiciously. "We are Her Firstborn and the chosen stewards of the Realms. Our actions are not to be questioned."

Lord Barak added, "You speak of civilization, and yet humanity has barely advanced from its barbaric infancy. Those of your race finding their way into Weir have been ignorant, selfish, and destructive to all they touch. There is no balance as was intended by the First Mother."

"I can't deny the existence of those traits in humanity, but I share a belief with many humans that we are evolving beyond these limitations with each succeeding generation. Acknowledging that we have our flaws, however, the Elder Race could have elected to teach humanity to rise to greatness rather than imposing bondage."

Ken gestured to the nearest human, a young woman standing nearby with wine pitcher in hand. "Is this to be her drudgery until the day she dies? What a waste of potential for her and you. Our lives are comparatively short to yours. That's all the more reason why we must live life to its fullest and make a difference while we can. Given a chance, you'll find that we will accomplish much more than your minimal expectations."

Then the perfect example came to Ken. *Time to put your money where your mouth is...hope I haven't bitten off more than I can chew.*

"Some lives will be shorter than others," Lady Emeryle said ominously.

"Maybe so," snapped Ken, "but consider this. You say that the Elder Race is the First Mother's chosen and that gives you license to dominate humanity. How does that proposition stand in the face of the First Mother contacting humanity?"

"You raise an interesting discussion point," mused Aristorn. "We have heard of your visitation by the First Mother, but we have only your word on this. Good as that may be, there is no evidence to proffer."

"That's about to change. With patience, guidance, and self-determination, humanity can rise up from its barbaric infancy, Lord Barak, to stand together with the Elder Race as contributing members of this world, and beyond." Ken rose, proceeded to the mantle, and grabbed Yoshirim's two pieces.

"Oath-Companion," growled Swayne warningly, "what are your intentions? Broken it may be, but Yoshirim is the Clan Chief symbol of the Falcon Clan."

"Can it be repaired? And if so, how long will the process take?" asked Ken.

Swayne hesitated. "There are others present more qualified to judge than I."

"Bring it here," ordered Lord Barak.

Ken handed over the hilt and mangled blade.

After several minutes and a private conference with Lady Emeryle, Lord Barak placed the pieces on the table and pronounced, "Lord Gunderhad, the Armorer's Guild can forge you a sword worthy of any Clan Chief, but mending this now is a lost cause. Yoshirim's heart has been torn asunder from within, and the Swordsong is silent. Even were we not faced with the effects of the Dwindling, such a task would be nigh impossible. I am truly sorry."

Swayne sank into his chair. Mereth went to his side, for she knew the impact of such tidings.

Ken said, "Swayne, the damage to Yoshirim is my fault, and as such, I intend to be the remedy."

"You have done enough," Swayne muttered through gritted teeth. "Leave be while the Falcon Clan yet extends you hospitality."

Ken grabbed the two fragments and moved to the crackling hearth behind Swayne. "You have asked for proof of what I say. I pray this will provide the necessary foundation for treating humanity as something other than a footstool."

With his right hand, Ken held the severed blade together. He focused on summoning the magic; it was there, sooner than he had anticipated. As soon as he felt it, he plunged the blade and his hand and upper arm into the fire.

The servant with the wine pitcher screamed.

Aldren continued eating.

The Tuonim, as one, rose from the table and stared in disbelief. All save Swayne. For him, there was affirmation of Aldren's healing in the dungeon cell. And there was hope.

A white glow surrounded Ken's body, insulating him from the flame. Indeed, the First Mother's Fire burned hotter than any mere wood fire.

Feel the break, imagine the pieces fusing together on a molecular level. Ouch. What the heck is that?...A spark of life in metal, barely detectable. Could that be the Swordsong that Lord Barak referenced? It's almost a presence in the sword on the energetic level. What if I feed it some of mine? There, it's blossoming, surging in spirit and strength. But the energy path is blocked, running from the hilt through my arm instead of the sword. Must reconnect and reforge.

There's too much resistance. I need more heat, more power. How much am I giving of myself? Can't stop now... too much waste, and there's zero tolerance for failure with this crowd. More heat, more energy, the power of a white-hot molten volcano, where the elemental forces of nature clash and are born together.

Ken was immersed in his task, intent on healing Yoshirim. Otherwise, he would have heard Swayne command, "Back, stand away at your peril; the heat is amassing beyond his control."

Lord Barak mumbled, "A human, it cannot be possible." His face was drained of color.

"Yet it is happening," replied Aldren.

Lord Keshire glowered fanatically, perceiving disaster and opportunity. *The Rohr-Kargon has erred in his generosity. We must find a way to bend this human to our will or break him.*

Ken was oblivious to the world around him, riding the wave of power that he'd summoned. The Tuonim, the room, and the fireplace mantel had faded. He was in the heart of a mountain volcano, where magma boiled and churned in smoking eddies. The sword in his grasp had transmuted to a lance of living fire, yet he felt no pain.

That's it. There. The energy is free flowing, pulsing. It's...well, I'll be damned, it's singing. Now, reconstitute the metal. Pressure upon pressure, like carbon to diamond, searing flame to flawless blade, sharpen the edge, smooth and unblemished. Yes. Cool the blade.

Ken was now secreted within a glacial ice chamber. The venerable blue ice sublimated on contact. Steam filled the recess, and the cold caressed the magical blade into quiescence.

Finished.

He dispelled the First Mother's Fire and turned to face the awestruck Tuonim. Staggering slightly, he dropped the newly reborn Yoshirim into Swayne's outstretched arms.

"Water," said Ken. His voice croaked dryly.

Lady Emeryle thrust her goblet to him and glared hungrily as he quaffed the contents. She, too, recognized opportunity.

Ken then sought Mereth's attention. "Lady Gunderhad," he puffed, "thank you for an entertaining dinner. I'll be retiring for the evening. Aldren, you might accompany me. After all…" He gulped for air. "We need our rest for tomorrow's journey."

Tears in her eyes, Mereth bowed her head.

"Please excuse me, as well," said Aldren, taking a last draught of wine. "The Oath-Companion is correct."

Aldren walked beside Ken, matching his leisurely pace. Beyond the arched doorway to the dining chamber and safely out of view, Ken collapsed upon Aldren, who immediately offered a hand.

"Thanks," gasped Ken. "That took more than I had anticipated."

"It is no small accomplishment to weave the Swordsong," replied Aldren, "for our weapons are much more than the dead metal crafted by humanity. I understand your purpose, and the deed was well done. Your people will be proud of the seed you have planted this night, for I believe they shall reap the benefits." As the two stopped at Ken's door, Aldren commented, "Enjoy your sleep, for tomorrow's trail bed will be less comfortable."

"Thanks for the reminder, but tonight won't be a problem. I'm beat. Do me a favor and make sure I'm awake at a decent hour tomorrow."

"Am I to be mother to my Oath-Companion?"

"No," quipped Ken, "I just meant… well…"

Aldren laughed.

The mirth was contagious. Ken laughed, too. He then bid Aldren goodnight before closing his door.

Dawn came without incident.

The Hammer of Destiny was an ideal alarm clock. *Gong, gong, gong.* Its resounding peals penetrated Ken's dreamless purgatory.

A squinty eye cracked open. "God, my head feels like a truck ran over me." Ken rose, rubbing an aching neck, and then dragged himself to the wash basin for a morning splash. It felt like someone had tied a hundred-pound steel chain to him. He cupped the cold water and let it stream down his head; and again, and again.

"That's a step in the right direction. It would be naïve not to expect to feel something after last night's feat of wizardry."

A knock on his door drew his attention away from magic and his spiraling fate.

"Yes, come in," he groaned.

Aldren entered. "The Tuonim are assembling…. Do you require anything?"

"Thanks for the concern," said Ken, realizing that Aldren was testing him, checking to see how much the First Mother's Fire had sucked from him. "Can you scare up some food while I get my things together?"

Aldren handed him a cloth bundle with a falcon crest design stitched on the sturdy fabric. "Lady Gunderhad did not want you to depart without a full stomach, nor, apparently, a memento of her."

Ken unwrapped the corners of the cloth. Inside were two delicious-looking round muffins. Chunks of fruit and other tasty treats had been baked within the muffins. Alongside the muffins were several cornbread-like cakes in another silk-like handkerchief. Ken lifted the bundle for closer inspection. He sniffed.

"Are these cakes what I think they are? Hala?" he asked.

"Indeed, you have made an impression," said Aldren, "and such gifts are better appreciated on our journey."

Ken took the muffins, stuffed the outer material in a pocket, and gave the rest back to Aldren. "Can you hold this in your waist satchel until we need it?"

Aldren nodded.

"Good," said Ken, cramming pieces of muffin into his mouth, "now for the road ahead."

As Ken stood beside Aldren in the Aerie's outer bailey, he would have given any price for a mug of hot coffee. A biting wind whisked by, funneling through the barren trough between the inner and outer walls. Several hundred Tuonim warriors were assembled with them. Aristorn and Garondel were in front of the Clansmen.

Aldren had just finished renewing his promise to Aristorn that he would contact the High Cleric as soon as possible and was now thanking the Rohr-Kargon for fresh provisions that were laded in two carriers resembling saddle bags with long straps. Aldren put one over his head, strap crossing down his chest to the opposite side, and gave the other to Ken, who did likewise.

Garondel Rohr-Kargon then turned to Ken. "Human, Kenneth McNary, Oath-Companion to Hemdall's Line, I have not been surprised in countless Cyclings. Yea, verily, you have done that and more. All within my domain have heard of Mendac's death and of Yoshirim's reforging. Many of my people refuse to believe that any human could wield the First Mother's Fire while her Firstborn are bereft of this gift. I do not fault them in their perspective. Before yesterday, it was an unimaginable event in our world. But now, there is no denying the deed.

"You have questioned our oversight of your race, openly declaring what many of the Nobility consider treason, and for that, there are many in my realm who as yet advocate your death. On this have I brooded; no human has ever occupied my thoughts for as long. I have concluded that there is more to you, Kenneth McNary, than any of us might suspect; and perhaps that is the case, as well, with humanity. And so, let it be known that here and now, I acknowledge that we have erred in condemning your race. It may be that the answer for the Dwindling lies with the Nosferu, as do other evils afoot. Ere these events, I had lost faith in the First Mother, but there is no denying her hand in sending us a human who can wield the Fire. There is a message therein for her Firstborn. We can only pray that it has not arrived in vain."

"Does that mean that the humans in the Aerie are free?" quizzed Ken.

The Rohr-Kargon's response was guarded. "Although I cannot promise rapid change, for we Tuonim do not make hasty decisions, the matter will receive due consideration."

Apparently, Ken hadn't made as much progress as he had thought, but he didn't want to seem ungrateful either. "I'm glad that you're starting to see things our way," replied Ken diplomatically. "Often, the hardest step can simply be admitting that you may be wrong. I thank you for having the wisdom and courage to surmount that hurdle. Part of me desperately wants to stay to help nurture a transition between your people and mine, but I've got this nagging fear that there might not be anyone left alive if we don't mobilize all our forces against the Nosferu. If it works out, I'll return as soon as I can to see how everyone is faring."

"I will look forward to that day," said Garondel. "As for the Nosferu, until I know more about their plans, I cannot spare any warriors from the defense of Dawn's Aerie. Indeed, it is we who may ultimately need assistance. Be that as it may, however, a petition has been presented. Though I am reluctant to release my best, I shall not deny an honor-debt."

Lord Gunderhad stepped forward from the ranks, along with two members of the Falcon Clan. With hand resting on a newly polished Yoshirim, Swayne said, "Oath-Companion, I would continue your sword training. These two are Cable and Durn, my personal guard."

Ken detected the hint of a smile on the normally taciturn Tuonim's face. Chuckling aloud, he said, "We're glad for the company, but I think my sword arm is already beginning to ache."

After brief goodbyes, the company embarked from the outer ring. As they passed through the barbican of the Western Gate, the Rohr-Kargon issued a final farewell: "May the blessing of Dawn's Aerie give comfort in your hour of need."

Ken thought of his promise to Tharin Eberstone. *I bet that old ghost is dancing in his grave, or wherever the Nine Circles are.*

Gliding on the morning breeze, Tharin's faint voice was unmistakable to Ken's ears. "Cor Dreaden Gaeth-le," came the hushed, wind-borne whisper.

Following an unbidden urge, Ken withdrew Stone-grinder from its harness, thrust the blade skyward, and shouted back, "Cor Dreaden Gaeth-le!"

This time, the chorus held more than one voice; the ranks of Tuonim warriors echoed his words. For his part, Garondel Rohr-Kargon found his conjecture confirmed with the uttering of Acadia's ancient blessing in the Old Tongue of the Elder Race, unheard from the lips of man until this day. There could be no coincidence. Nodding to Aristorn, the Rohr-Kargon inwardly acknowledged that the black armor worn by this unusual human was none other than Soulstealer's Doom, whose last resting place had been the lost tomb of Tharin Eberstone, First Kargon of the Morningstars and fallen hero of Acadia. As the company disappeared along Lavlir's Reach, the Rohr-Kargon wondered at the meaning of this rebirth for so dread an heirloom.

CHAPTER 11
LAVLIR'S PASS

With only a few inches of last winter's snow to contend with, Dawn's Aerie disappeared under the shadow of several minor peaks after a day. Walking in his large companions' footsteps, Ken found the pace exhausting. More than once he had expressed internal relief that the magic of Soul-stealer's Doom included its remarkable weightlessness. The knights of old would have given their castles for such armor. Even without that handicap, however, Ken was the weak link in the group. He had considered using the First Mother's Fire to help his body adjust to the altitude, but then he dismissed the temptation. It was a new and dangerous tool, without a manual or teacher to show him its proper use. Smaller steps were warranted; he had been reckless already. How much closer was he to death because he had used it? As Tharin had warned, when he tapped the magic, he was expending precious life energy. There was no way to gauge the extent of the draw.

Nobody to his knowledge had invented a meter to measure life force, but maybe they weren't as far off as he thought. He had once read a magazine article on Kirlian photography, named for a Russian scientist. It was a photographic technique that, by introducing high-frequency electric fields to living matter, produced a visible image of a corona discharge or dynamic bioenergetic field dubbed the Kirlian Aura. The article had stated that the size, shape, and strength of the aura had quantifiable variance depending on a host of conditions. Apart from pressure, temperature, moisture, and the like, the aura had also fluctuated under more intriguing conditions. Plant leaves that were sliced in half had, remarkably, shown an intact aura, though it was weaker around the missing leaf section. Similar observations of this phantom image were also seen in salamanders that dropped their tails as a natural defense mechanism. In humans, the Kirlian Aura could demonstrate the presence of disease. Some people could even manipulate segments of their own auras by channeling focused concentration on the desired area. The day might come, after all, when they could read life energy. For now, however, unable to view his aura, Ken simply intended to use his best judgment and accept the consequences. He was by no means a martyr, yet he meant what he had said to Aldren in the dungeons of Dawn's Aerie; if he had to trade his life to serve a role in preserving all life, then so be it.

Four days had now passed since the group's departure from the Aerie. Ken's system had finally struck a bargain with the lofty heights. By resting for short intervals as the party ascended, he never lagged beyond line of sight of the Tuonim, and during these gaps, Aldren stayed at his side, offering friendly conversation and identifying particular mountains within the panoramic vistas. The breathtaking scenery held no appeal for the Tuonim; neither, apparently, did conversation.

Swayne was preoccupied with covering as much ground as possible under blue sky. Cable and Durn were no different. After traveling together with them, however, Ken knew more about these Falcon Clansmen, despite their reticence to speak. They exhibited similar mannerisms and possessed like features; chestnut-colored hair; strong, chiseled faces with straight noses; and searching blue eyes—they were close in kinship. Cable's respectful deference in the face of Durn's pensive nature marked Durn as the senior. Lean, amply muscled, and constantly scouting the terrain, Cable and Durn showed no sign of fatigue and were ever responsive to Swayne's commands. They moved with the confidence of seasoned veterans and could establish camp in minutes. They were the samurai of imperial Japan, reborn to this world. Ken liked them immensely.

Their journey to the Pass had been hastened by Lavlir's Reach. Where the wind had brushed away drifting snow, easy footing could be gained on the Reach's seamlessly jointed white bedrock. At its widest, Lavlir's Reach permitted the three Tuonim to comfortably walk abreast. Every half mile or so, along its borders, twin stone guardians turned inward upon the path. Each set depicted a signature totem from the Clans: falcons for the Falcon Clan, dragons for the Dragon Clan, and so on. Ken was naturally drawn to their majestic artistry, but his enthusiasm gave way to caution, for each time he came upon the totems, a prickling sensation tickled his exposed skin like static electricity. As far as he could tell, no on else shared his discomfort. Curiosity growing, Ken had finally asked Aldren if he knew more about the Reach's construction.

Surprisingly, it was the reticent Durn who, at hearing the question, had recounted the tale of Lavlir of the Firstborn, the Dawntreader. Ken had enjoyed the story as Durn spoke. "When the Elder Race was newly come to Weir through passage at Windowmere Deep, Lavlir of the Firstborn strode from the rising fortress walls of what would be Dawn's Aerie. His back to the day, Lavlir set forth on a voyage of discovery, seeking that which lay across the Morningstars, for even then, in the Elder Race's youth, old were the mountains. After a great while of scaling insurmountable crags, exploring hidden vales, and charting deep glens and unending caverns, Lavlir's resolve wore thin. He decided to begin the return journey. That evening, as Lavlir lay on his back watching the dusk light of the descending sun give way to brightening stars, he uttered a prayer of thanks to the First Mother for the many wonders he had beheld. As he did so, his eye was drawn to a beam shining hotly against the opposite cliff. How could this be when the mountains shielded the sun?

Marveling at this when all else around was dim, Lavlir did not suspect that he beheld divine intervention. As he navigated loose rock to what he deemed the light's origin, Lavlir rounded a jutting ledge only to come upon a tunnel of pure sunlight. Walking through the slim corridor, Lavlir emerged into open sky and stopped, awestruck. In the distance below, the mighty Gylderhorn roared. Across its shores lay flowing meadow as far as the eye could see—the Kesmark Plains. Later, although it was not said when, Lavlir returned to Dawn's Aerie, telling of his wanderings. Thus it was that Tharin Eberstone, First Kargon of the Morningstars, bestowed the title Dawntreader upon Lavlir and commanded the Reach's fashioning to the Pass so that all within his domain should benefit from Dawntreader's deeds."

Knowing that the Elder Race's history far exceeded that of humanity, Ken wondered how much time had passed since Lavlir had strode the very path on which he now sat. Resting below a pair of Bear Clan totems, Ken removed Stonegrinder's harness and stretched his sword-weary muscles. Last night, as he had every night since leaving the Aerie, Ken had received hours of vigorous sword instruction from Swayne and Aldren. The resulting soreness, though lessening each day, was further aggravated by no more than a blanket separating him from the Reach's cold stone.

Rubbing his lower back, Ken fondly recalled the comfort of his sleeping bag. *Uncle Dale would have given me grief for tossing a perfectly good backpack.... 'Course, Dale also used to say that a man who couldn't survive off the land didn't deserve to leave his living room.*

Handing a water skin to Ken, Swayne said, "You are less talkative today. That is wise, for we shall need to conserve our strength. We are within sight of Lavlir's Pass and should make Delvin's Landing by tomorrow's end."

Looking upward, Ken nodded. "I'm glad to hear you say that, because we're not going to be traveling in ideal conditions. Have you noticed the falling temperature and those clouds? How much snow can we expect for this time of year?"

Cable and Durn frowned, as they and Aldren looked to Swayne for an answer.

"In my days through the Cyclings," said Swayne, "I cannot recall the First Mother permitting the season's first white blessing to fall so early upon the Morningstars."

Under his breath, Cable mumbled, "...not the First Mother's doing."

Swayne heard the comment and countered, "That may be, but we are not unprepared." Digging into his pack, Swayne withdrew a hooded, knee-length winter-gray travel cloak.

Ken and Aldren looked at one another in slight surprise, while Cable produced four additional cloaks from his pack.

As Ken gratefully accepted the insulating garment from Cable, Swayne explained, "A final gift from the Rohr-Kargon and the weavers of Dawn's Aerie. Oath-Companion, Lady Orphiam, too, sends her farewells."

Ken hesitated to cover Stonegrinder, but, taking his cue from Durn, who also favored a back harness, he donned the cloak over the harness, leaving Stonegrinder's pommel freely exposed above his shoulder. Better outfitted, the party resumed the trek.

Hours later, they were enduring blizzard-like punishment in visibility describable only as a whiteout. Ice cube–sized snow was screaming horizontally. Day was replaced with unnerving darkness. A rope was strung among the party, and with the passing hours, movement became a torturous crawl as snow climbed to everyone's thighs.

I've been caught in torrential cloudbursts, thought Ken, *and western snowstorms, and never taken nature's handiwork personally, but this is different. There's an intelligence driving this storm, a focused threat specifically against us, against me. I don't need to invoke the First Mother's Fire to know this, I can feel it. I wonder if the others sense the danger. It seems there are very few rules in a realm where gods appear to mortals and magic is reality.*

Ken shuddered, but not from the cold; power on this scale made his skin crawl.

How do you fight an enemy who can change the elements? Thanks to the First Mother, I can sense good and evil, energy vibrations great and small, but it takes more than that to win a war. And win we must, because living under the Nosferu is not an option. They'll bleed us dry. But first things first...at this rate, we're not going to make it past the Morningstars. We're headed the wrong way.

Ken stood firm. He couldn't see past his hands, but he knew the effect of his action. The chain reaction began. Cable arrived from the rear, Aldren from the front, followed by Durn and Swayne.

Swayne shouted. His words were lost to the storm.

Ken yelled back, to no avail, and thought, *this isn't working, only one way around it. Is this how my life will be parceled away...one seemingly dire situation after another, and another?*

Ken withdrew his mind from the storm and summoned the magic. He thought of the bear hibernating snugly in its den through winter. He would erect a shelter of energy, a bubble of light and calm that would deflect rather than oppose the storm's rage. Maybe this subtlety would leave him less drained than a frontal assault.

And then there was quiet.

Ken opened his eyes to the amazed looks of his companions. They stared first at him and then at the swirling blizzard howling in fury just beyond the party. Cable and Durn were speechless, while Swayne and Aldren quickly adjusted based on previous experience.

Feeling the storm's might pressing on their gossamer-like energy haven, Ken said, "We have precious time before this collapses. Swayne, best guess, how far are we from the Pass?"

"Within," Swayne cleared his throat, "a league."

"Between two and three of your miles," Aldren clarified.

"Yes, that's correct," agreed Swayne, "if we have not strayed from the Reach."

"I know we've diverged from our goal," said Ken.

Aldren replied, "If we have lost the Reach, would it not be prudent to seek shelter from the storm and attempt the Pass after it subsides?"

"Mayhaps," said Swayne, looking up with uncertainty at the storm. "However, if this tempest continues unabated, I am loath to huddle like mice in a snow burrow. That is not how I would choose to enter the Nine Circles. Verily, should we emerge unscathed, I have no doubt our destination will be sealed until the spring thaw. Should that occur, we can yet seek the Valley of Twins, but such can only serve our enemies' plans; much time will be lost, and it is the road they would have us march. He who follows the striking hand should make no outcry when it lands upon his cheek."

As if on cue, the circle of calm shrank in half. With noticeable effort, Ken pushed back, preventing further encroachment.

"Given that information," responded Ken through heavier breathing, "we should head for the Pass now. Follow me. I can sense the Reach." Ken put as much authority as he could muster into that last statement. He was asking Swayne to stake their lives on his instincts.

Swayne hesitated, judging the worth of this human against all that had occurred since their first meeting. And there, protected from the ravaging storm in a circle of calm held alone by, of all things in Weir, a human's will, a turning point occurred.

Swayne's eyes sought Aldren. A scion of Hemdall's Line had freely chosen to stand together in possible death with a mere human, this human—the man who had challenged Mendac's treachery, saved Garondel-Rohr Kargon, and reforged Yoshirim with the First Mother's Fire. True understanding unfolded. In that instant, a bond of trust and respect that would last had ripened.

"Agreed, Oath-Companion," said Swayne. "Now hurry, for we race against the deep snow."

Still shaken by Ken's power, Durn and Cable nodded mutely in agreement. Aldren gave Swayne a friendly slap on the back and quickly readjusted the positions in the rope chain.

Ready to go, Ken released his control, and the weather descended with more ferocity than before.

Now for the hard part, Ken thought.

Gathering his strength, Ken took a tentative first step toward what he believed to be the totems of Lavlir's Reach. The magic had siphoned his energy, but not dramatically so. He took another step. The wet snow gripped his legs like newly poured cement. He persevered.

Time passed slowly.

Ken's world had narrowed to the storm and the Reach. With each stride he felt the Reach's pull increase. It would not be long.

As he urged his leg muscles upward for the next step, Ken's knee connected with an ice wall. *Damn. Where did this come from?*

Reluctantly exposing his numb hands, Ken drew his knife and jammed it into the obstacle. A large fragment chipped away. *Stone underneath. Could it be?* Ken extended his free hand. A blue spark leaped from the stone to his hand. Soothing heat spread along his fingers. He placed his entire hand against the rock.

Ice exploded into the conjured darkness as glorious daylight erupted. Stunned and momentarily blinded, Ken fell backward into Swayne and Aldren, who shielded their eyes.

Twin griffin totems glowed like miniature flaming suns; there were yet wonders in Weir that had not dwindled beyond redemption. The Stonemasons of old had foreseen the need for Lavlir's Reach to guide the lost and had woven potent spells into their work. Like signal towers, each totem set along the entire Reach sent forth a piercing message of hope into the bleak night. Whatever the evil power that had twisted the storm, its intent had been frustrated, for where the light of Lavlir's Reach extended, the wind did not howl so fiercely, nor the snow fall so heavily, nor the cold bite so hard.

Durn was the first to speak. "And the forsaken shall find their way in the arms of the Reach."

Swayne looked surprised.

"Aristorn," said Durn, "is not the only Tuonim to consult the Chronicles of Stone. How is it that we have forgotten so much of the ancient wisdom?"

Aldren shared his insight, saying, "I do not know of the Tuonim's Chronicles of Stone. However, many are the Cyclings during which the First Mother has slumbered, while we, Her children, swelled ever-complacent with no enemy threatening Her domain. The Nosferu have been patient, working their subtle mischief for centuries, weakening the lines and poisoning our land. If we are to survive, the Elder Race must unite to defeat this menace."

"Oath-Companion," Swayne said, "though we do not know the extent of their plans, we owe much to you for revealing this danger. It is an omen beyond good measure to behold the forgotten might of Lavlir's Reach. Let us make advantage of this fortune while we may."

The group approached the griffins, and all knew the moment when they had returned to the Reach. As they progressed, the storm eased into light snow. In no time, they gained the entrance to the Pass. Emerging from the tunnel, they saw lights twinkling far in the distance below.

"Come, Oath-Companion." Swayne pointed. "Delvin's Landing awaits."

CHAPTER 12
DELVIN'S LANDING

Dalia wiped light perspiration from her brow as Delvin loaded the serving tray. Working the taproom was a job for two, but Rachina was pregnant and would not venture to the Landing in such dreadful conditions. Dalia shook her head in dismay. The maiden's reward for a single night's tryst seven months back...if Rachina didn't soon find a man to call husband, it would go hard for her this winter. Even so, she envied the young girl, for her own womb was not so fruitful. Her lineage was a blessing and a curse. She could only imagine what it might be like to have her body swell with new life and unfamiliar awkwardness. Rachina was wise not to imperil herself and her child in such a gale. And then there were also those heeding the recent witch tales.

It had begun as rumor passed among the Gylderhorn villages. Farmers along the North Road had talked of missing sheep and will-o'-the-wisps interrupting the night animals. Of late, the normal comings and goings of the out-villagers had slowed noticeably. Some inexplicable force had stretched an invisible veil of fear across the land, a malignance of such magnitude that even the weather could not escape its influence. Weeks ago, Dalia had wanted to sharpen her sword and investigate the countryside, but Delvin had asked her to stay, saying that he would be marooned with their stablehand, Ned, whose serving skills would drive the customers away. Dalia suspected that her father's motives were other than profit, but she honored his wish; very little occurred in the region without Delvin's knowledge.

So far, Dalia had managed the Landing's storm-weary crowd just fine, despite the sweltering heat radiating from the hearthstone. While her practical side was grateful for its comfort, a more primitive part of her psyche shunned its wrongness. This ill feeling was not hers alone; the storm's timing and ferocity was the center of conversation among the regulars. There was Rusty Tock drinking with his usual cohorts, Hap Musgrave and Lars Amishane. Next to them sat Wil Hammershal. Normally, Wil would be busy preaching the virtues of his tobacco leaf to Badger Furleymoor—Badger had an infallible nose for the finest weed in the Three Corners—but no such banter lightened the mood this night. Further on and in between ales, Dell Westmarch and Trevor Stonehouse were bellowing about this year's crops. The cursed frost had damaged the mid-harvest. And there were many others with complaints owing to the weather. All present, young men and old-timers alike, agreed that none could recall a season when winter's breath had come so soon.

Dalia experienced a twinge of anger at the gathered whitebeards, knowing that they tolerated her only for Delvin's sake. *Old timers, hah!* She thought. *I shall walk with generations of their families, long after their children's children have passed into the Nine Circles.*

She saw Briar Tomassen resting near the hearthstone, prodding young Ned to stoke the logs, hoping to temporarily break time's incessant grip on his rheumatic bones. She was tempted to call Ned over but realized that Briar's pandering gave Ned an excuse to dally by the fire. There was a crockpot dangling on the wrought iron cooking crane, swung out from the mantel so as not to burn the leavings. Ned had supped hours ago. The empty plate at Briar's feet told her that he'd again meted out a portion of his stew to Briar.

Poor Ned, he's a good soul and trying so hard.

The storm meant extra duties both in the stable and main building, and Ned was barely stacking enough wood to keep pace with Delvin's watchful eye. Delvin expected him to fill a man's shoes, no matter when the patrons arrived or in what weather, but she could see that the snowy onslaught and unrelenting service were taking their toll.

I'll have to get Ned a second helping of stew later tonight. And what a night it's been!

Dalia turned her attention from the regulars at the taproom counter exchanging gossip with Delvin and surveyed the motley crowd of humans and Tuonim tucked within the Landing's fold. Even under the bright glare of the hearthstone, the Landing's smoky rafters and shadowed tables only grudgingly revealed their secrets.

The snow has brought many a rat seeking shelter. As ever, father tolerates their presence, both cocky lords from the Undercity and their human rabble.

She met Delvin's knowing look as he firmly planted a fistful of tankards on her tray. Ale splashed onto the countertop but had nothing to do with his missing left forearm, which had been severed above the wrist long ago in the Hinterlands. Despite this physical handicap, Delvin made tasks that required the dexterity of two hands seem easy with only one.

Dalia frowned slightly as she cleaned the spill.

This night, the blizzard is not the only source of tension.

She caught Delvin's eye roaming to the boarshead table as he once again topped off the tankards. The party of Tuonim Lords seated there had been drinking for hours. Delvin had been inclined more than once to silence their raucous behavior, if not for his daughter's sake, then for the peace of the remaining patrons. It was a brazen thought, driven as much by the hostile weather as the nervous crowd, for such action from Delvin, a human, would neither be taken lightly nor preserve the fragile truce that had blessed the Landing with prosperity.

Delvin growled impatiently, "Lass, the customers are waiting."

She smiled and rubbed his grizzled beard. "Those drunkards shall bide a bit longer."

Delvin's face reddened. "Don't provoke them any further. I've no wish for brawling this night. Serve them and be done with it, and watch yer back."

She laughed and said reproachfully, "Father, as if I couldn't handle their ilk." She spun away with the drinks before Delvin could say otherwise. Dalia knew the measure of the heart beating behind that gruff facade. Delvin had never been one for coddling. Since Dalia's mother had died during Dalia's birthing, Delvin had done the best he could to raise her, including imparting what fighting skills he knew. As the half-blood daughter of a Tuonim Clanswoman, Dalia readily took to the rigorous weapons instruction. The years of sparring with Delvin and his occasional friends from the bygone days, however, had come with a price. The training scars scattered about her body were testament to that fact. If her mixed heritage wasn't bane to human and Tuonim alike, the Nobility considered her even less desirable for having such blemishes.

As Dalia delivered the ale, a chill draft swept through the inn. Expecting to see Ned lugging the eve-logs that would last until morning, Dalia paused while a group of snowy strangers seated themselves against the far wall at the bearclaw table. She sought to identify these visitors, but they lay hidden in shadow, and none had removed their ice-crusted cloaks. However, that would soon change.

Other, less-friendly, eyes marked the party's entry into the Landing.

Dalia promptly finished serving the Tuonim Lords and moved to assess these new patrons. Their stature and clothing indicated Tuonim, yet their manner suggested these were not soft-bellied lords from the Undercity.

"What hospitality can Delvin's Landing provide?" she asked.

Swayne's response was crisp. "Hot beef, bread, and five tankards. We also require two rooms for the night." Reaching into his armor, Swayne laid a gold piece onto the table.

Within the folds of his cloak, Ken smiled. He had wondered what, if anything, constituted the currency of the realm. It was comforting, and also puzzling, to see that gold served as a medium of exchange. Had the Elder Race been the ones to engender its value on Earth? Did the Elder Race place independent worth on the metal, or was it merely a means for commerce with humans?

Dalia turned and gestured to her father, who was busy talking at the taproom counter. With a near-imperceptible pause in his conversation, Delvin replied using rapid finger movements. The signals were a practical means of communicating across the oft-crowded taproom, and they afforded privacy from eavesdroppers. As far as Dalia knew, only one or two of Delvin's friends from the Hinterlands could also understand his one-handed code.

Dalia nodded as her father finished. "Gentlemen, food and ale we have a plenty, but the Landing's rooms are claimed."

Swayne slapped another gold piece onto the table.

It was the wrong tactic, for gold, though sought after, held no special power under Delvin's roof. Dalia rolled her eyes and crossed her arms as she mentally grouped this lot with the other Undercity rubbish.

Having received fine lessons in Tuonim manners, Ken intervened before the situation deteriorated. His hand shot out to Dalia's wrist, applying a firm but gentle grip.

In response, Dalia's free hand slid to one of five blades concealed on her person and then stopped short. This stranger's touch was surprisingly pleasant.

Looking at the hand that held her prisoner, Dalia's heart leapt as she recognized the ring of the First Mark. Unmistakable, a powerful and rare token such as this argued for caution; instead, it kindled a wildfire of excitement.

Thinking he might have scared her, and feeling odd himself, Ken released his hold. "Please, we meant no insult. Let's start over. I'm Ken. My friends and I are exhausted from traveling in this weather. We'd be grateful for any accommodations you can arrange." With a quick nod to Swayne, he added, "at a fair price."

Regaining her composure, Dalia introduced herself, "I am Dalia, Delvin One-Arm's daughter," and left to fetch their order.

Ken stared at her retreating figure and alluring curves. It had been a long time since his last night with a woman, and he had discerned a rare connection when he touched Dalia. He had sensed her initial resistance to such closeness and then was stunned as an entirely different feeling washed through that barrier as if it had never been. And though there was an untamed roughness about her and a scarring along her arms, underneath there was no denying her beauty.

As the party waited for Dalia's return, they luxuriated in the Landing's dry, aromatic heat. It presented a stark contrast to the numbing cold endured down the Pass. Cable and Durn slipped their hoods off while Aldren and Ken, despite a disapproving glance from Swayne, removed their wet cloaks entirely and laid their saddlebags on the floor.

From a little-used alcove in the Landing's murky depths, Corin Shadowalker rose in mild amazement and then eased back before any could take notice.

So, human, you have eluded the Master's grasp. Most fascinating. You must indeed have power to have come this far. And you are not alone. Stellrod's chosen accompanies you, along with new friends. No matter. This sanctuary shall prove your undoing.

A brief glow flickered as Shadowalker's hand brushed the crystal dangling from his neck. *And so the trap springs. Farewell, meddler.*

Dalia soon made her way to the bearclaw table, her attention fixed on Ken. She, too, was not uninterested.

Although ample for her needs, Ken was short for a Tuonim Lord. Still, there was something about his ways that made him the equal of any lord she'd known. Her eyes lingered, drifted to his ring, and then studied his face. The mark across his jaw lent a roguish handsomeness, and he had a pleasing manner. There were no Clan markings on his armor, but overall, she judged him a member of the Aerie's Nobility, much more intriguing than the lords of the Undercity. While she had long ago realized that no highborn would tolerate a half-breed for a wife, there were the rare exceptions who had shared her bed. Though they always deserted her come daybreak, she held no regrets for these moments of passion, and always, there was the chance that one would stay.

Smiling seductively, she served the food and ale.

"Delvin is firm on our lack of accommodations and sends his apologies. A party of Tuonim Lords has reserved every bed in the Landing. Verily, he does not wish to leave anyone out in such weather. Delvin hopes that you don't take offense; he welcomes you to bide the night in the stable. 'Tis well built, and the haylofts are clean."

"Thank you. We accept your offer," said Ken.

Swayne pushed the gold forward.

"Delvin is too proud to accept payment for a bed of hay; silver bar will do for the rest."

Swayne removed a gold piece and left the remaining one on the table.

Ken was surprised, but smiled his approval. As Dalia leaned over the table to retrieve the gold piece, she brushed a stray lock of auburn hair from her face. As she did, those forest-green eyes targeted Ken and communicated a most intense invitation. Then she was off, responding to cries for service. While the experience had been barely a moment, the memory would prove enduring.

Aldren cut into the beef while Cable and Durn savored the ale. Swayne broke Ken's reverie by thrusting a tankard into his hand. "Oath-Companion, be careful of what you wish."

"What's that supposed to mean?" Ken retorted.

After taking a drink, Swayne cryptically offered, "The road you admire is not easily traveled."

"How about elaborating on that statement," said Ken. In a more accusatory tone, "What do you know that I don't?"

"Eat," Swayne replied tersely. "The food is hot."

Then, despite Ken's urgings, Swayne refused further comment.

Later, after several more satisfying rounds of ale, Ken pushed away an empty plate. Some time ago, Cable and Durn had excused themselves to mingle at the taproom counter. Ken was reminded of Lord Keshire's request for news. Swayne had relaxed somewhat and was wiping down Yoshirim. Aldren's mood had also lightened. He had produced a pipe from his leather satchel and now sat contently wafting his blend into the inn's thick atmosphere

Dalia had visited their table only briefly for refills, though Ken had followed her movements. Now and again, she bestowed a glance in his direction. More than he wanted to admit, a desire was building within him.

Cable and Durn returned to the table.

"Well?" asked Swayne.

"The villagers," said Cable, "speak of strange happenings along the Gylderhorn, but more so do those from the northern settlements. Nothing specific to glean, but still one may take useful insight from the general. There is fear in the air."

"That is so," added Durn. "The One-Arm has heard of an ancient evil that has arisen in the Hinterlands. He could not name it, but there is no doubt from the description. And he would not lie to the Falcon Clan."

Ken perceived Swayne hardening at the last bit and wondered at its meaning.

"R'Kesh," whispered Swayne.

Durn nodded.

Aldren removed the pipe from his mouth as if to speak and then paused in thought.

Ken was about to query Swayne on R'Kesh, but smashing tankards interrupted.

All eyes turned.

Dalia stood before the Tuonim at the boarshead table as a particularly fat lord, whose fine garments lay drenched with ale, spoke angrily, "Miserable wench, how dare you!"

Dalia retorted, "I am not yours to command, nor would I willingly choose to be with such as you. Take your bribe."

Dalia threw several gold coins at the lord's feet. His drunken companions roared in laughter, increasing his embarrassment and rage. He stepped toward Dalia, and then stopped short as she produced a blade. This changed the situation entirely. Such defiance could not be tolerated, even allowing for the wench's part-Tuonim lineage.

"You will regret this," the fat lord stated. He snapped his fingers, and several figures from his table glided to his side. These Tuonim contrasted sharply with the inebriated lords; they were muscled, dressed in tight-fitting black garments, and purposeful in their manner.

As Ken began to rise, Swayne grabbed his arm. "Leave be, Oath-Companion, they can sort this out without your presence."

Ken shook free. "That's not in the cards."

Aldren joined Ken, ready for action.

Meanwhile, Dalia had produced a second blade. Delvin One-Arm also came to her, swapping ale tankards for a sure grip on the mighty battle-axe that had been hanging above his head in the taproom's rafters.

Ken wondered if the standoff would hold. Within seconds, two of the lords' cohorts split from the main group to circle Delvin and Dalia.

Delvin pivoted to face this threat. He cursed silently as he recognized the identical black-metal forged blades held by each; bad luck, and the more so, because he and Dalia were on their own. His friends from the old days had not visited the Landing in months, for life was harder than usual this season, even for the Hinterlands. The weather was hell-sent, and if the rumors were true, its legions did not trail far behind.

Well, we're not quite alone, he thought as he saw that Ned stood near the great hearthstone, wielding one of the eve logs as a weapon. He gave the kid credit for bravery but knew he wouldn't last a moment against such killers as these.

As the black-garbed Tuonim maneuvered through the Landing, they slowed when they neared Ken and Aldren by the bearclaw table.

Ken made his intent clear as Stonegrinder slid from its scabbard. Caldorsbane followed suit.

Delvin raised an eyebrow at this unexpected aid. He was not the only one surprised. The sneering lord shifted his attention to Ken and Aldren.

In the dark, Corin Shadowalker grinned wickedly.

Foolish human—poking your nose into other people's business is a nasty habit. Your death may be swifter than that contemplated by the hunt this night. Yet, it is of no concern, for with or without you, prey must be culled to satisfy my rapacious friends.

While all this was occurring, Swayne sat considering his options. These were no mere retainers coming to the rescue. The lords of the Undercity were vouchsafed by the Assassin's Guild and did not pass beyond its borders without highly skilled protection. He counted at least one such guardian for each lord, plus the approaching pair. The One-Arm could protect himself; the concern was for the Oath-Companion and their mission. A confrontation would be to nobody's advantage.

"Hold," Swayne's voice reverberated. He rose, still concealed by his cloak, with Durn and Cable on either side.

The fat lord, backed by his assassins, responded haughtily, "Who presumes to command Fortas, Master Trader of the Merchant's Guild? Be silent and do not interfere in this digression. Honor demands satisfaction from the wench."

Honor—I doubt it, Swayne thought. *You seek to avoid your companions' ridicule. Nonetheless, I can provide a face-saving solution, though it has risks. However, I deem the lady's ire not among them.*

Swayne removed his hood and thrust his cloak folds back, revealing his countenance and the Clan-Chief insignia emblazoned on his armor.

Fortas' pudgy fingers rubbed his chest as he choked on his breath. Few within the Undercity could rival his status as Master Trader of the Merchant's Guild, and here, among this churlish humanity, it was seemingly impossible. But the Lord of the Falcon Clan and right hand to Garondel Rohr-Kargon fit the exception.

Through the haze of alcohol and anger, Fortas perceived the abyss over which he teetered. "My Lord Gunderhad," he stammered weakly.

Swayne pointed to Ken and replied, "Mark well my friend here. He had previously requested the pleasure of this lady's presence for the foreseeable future. Your offer has been rejected. The matter will now end. Finish your drinks and depart in peace."

Swayne signaled Cable and Durn, and all three leisurely sat down.

Trembling, Fortas accepted the bone thrown by Swayne. "I was unaware of this *lady's*,"—the word burned—"prior commitment. Please consider this an unfortunate misunderstanding. As my companions and I have sampled quite enough of the Landing's hospitality, we bid you goodeve."

Fortas snapped his fingers. The assassins sheathed their weapons, returned to the table, and began helping their inebriated masters to the door. Though there was understandable grumbling from the other lords, who had not intended to depart the Landing, none challenged Fortas' lead.

Delvin called impatiently, "Ned! Harness the lords' team and bring their carriage forward."

Ned threw his upraised log into the fire and hurried to the stables.

As the last assassin exited the Landing, Delvin emitted a derisive huff and then ambled behind the taproom counter. Conversation among the patrons began only after his battle-axe once again resided in the rafters.

Dalia smiled playfully at Ken before returning her blades to their waiting sheaths and providing service to the Landing's thirsty guests. After such an encounter, several parched mouths among the old timers needed wetting.

Ken and Aldren returned to their seats and Swayne's admonishing glare.

"I appreciate your support," said Ken.

"So noted, Oath-Companion," said Swayne. "Take little comfort, for there will be repercussions to this night's folly."

"Indeed," laughed Dalia as she set five new tankards on their table. "Delvin conveys his gratitude, and as we have lost our lodgers for this night, he wonders if the Lord of the Falcon Clan and his worthy companions would trade the stables for more fitting sleeping quarters as his personal guests. And mine."

Dalia could not resist baiting Ken, "Or have you tired of my company already?"

Ken's face reddened as he searched for the right words. "Swayne did not mean… it merely resolved the situation."

Dalia could hardly contain her desire, for it had been a long time since a Tuonim Lord with such noble qualities had shown any interest in her, and he had called Lord Gunderhad by his familiar name; he might even be Falcon Clan. She managed to feign only slight disappointment as she coyly responded, "If you say so, my Lord…and the rooms?"

"That will be fine," said Swayne. "Now be off. We have events of import to discuss."

Dalia spun away giddily.

Ken rubbed his forehead; the drink and the secondhand smoke were having an effect, or maybe he was enthralled by a more primitive spell, a feminine wile to which he would blissfully succumb. He needed to concentrate and urged Swayne for more, "You were about to explain R'Kesh."

"Can this evil truly have resurfaced?" asked Aldren skeptically. "Their spawn has not been seen during my days upon the land."

"Forgive my ignorance," said Ken, "but as you all know, I am new to Weir. What manner of creature are we talking about?"

Durn whispered a stanza under his breath.

In the blackest night,
from the deepest depths,
come eaters of the flesh.
Long and strong of limb,
pale and hairy skin,
beware of the R'Kesh.

"Oath-Companion," said Swayne, "surely in the realm of Earth, the legends must have survived of subterranean man-like creatures that infect the night, stealing young children and haunting newly turned graves for fresh meat."

"We have stories of trolls and goblins that might fit that description, but no one to my knowledge has ever seen them. They're monsters from folklore."

"That may be," said Swayne. "Is not many a myth rooted in truth? Do you not experience even the slightest trepidation at discovering an underground crevasse? What instinct is it that stirs the heart when all seems harmless?"

Aldren nodded. "Stellrod has studied the Oakenhold's records of R'Kesh sightings and raids since the dawn of the Elder Race. Many times, the Kings have attempted to eradicate this pestilence, delving into the dark places that give this breed succulence. And for a time, all is quiet, yet they return. Little is known of their habits. Some say that not all their victims are devoured, that a worse fate awaits female captives, who are forced to endure their foul touch, birthing one gruesome offspring after another to swell the R'Kesh ranks until death releases them. Many are the abominable forms of this race."

"What about their intelligence?" said Ken.

"Do not underestimate their capabilities," warned Aldren. "Though they have remained hidden for a very long time, even to have avoided the countenance of King Remeth, the records describe them as clever and devious, preferring the tactics of ambush and trap in the deepest night."

"Could the R'Kesh have built up sufficient force since their last appearance to serve as an army for the Nosferu?" asked Ken.

Swayne pondered this. "It is possible, but to successfully challenge Dawn's Aerie and the Oakenhold would require the might of thousands. Such a presence would be difficult to conceal and would speak to a level of organization previously unknown to this marauding race."

Aldren nodded. "It would seem they may have done just that, however."

Ken added, "Probably under the Nosferu's lead. And while we are on the topic, how many Nosferu inhabit Weir?"

The question caught Swayne unprepared.

"Stellrod has pursued this in seeking a cure for the Elder Race," replied Aldren. The Nosferu are seldom encountered, and rarely seen together. No one has witnessed a Nosferu journeying through the Oaken Corridors, yet it is presumed they did so, for their race was newly come to Weir prior to the weakening of the Corridors. Stellrod deems the entire Nosferu presence to be fewer than fifty."

"Fifty may seem like fifty thousand," prompted Ken, "if they are the only ones wielding magic, forbidden or otherwise. Such a group could determine the balance of power in Weir. We may have even less time before they take action than I had thought, especially since they must know by now that Mendac is dead."

"As you say, Oath-Companion," Swayne replied. In the morning, we will see about horses and sending a message to the Rohr-Kargon alerting of the R'Kesh menace. For now, let us retire to regain our strength."

As the group finished their drinks, Swayne motioned to Dalia.

She arrived shortly. "How may I please you, my Lord Gunderhad?"

"Our rooms," said Swayne.

"Certainly." She took a moment to signal Delvin, who, having the patrons well in hand and Ned to pitch in if needed, nodded.

Dalia said, "Kindly follow me upstairs." She led the group, spiraling through the taproom tables, past Briar Tomassen, who was sleeping by the fire, and up a single flight of solid oak stairs to adjacent rooms in the Landing's east wing. The rooms had only the simple comforts of warm hearths, soft beds, and clean blankets. Compared to the frosty stone of Lavlir's Reach, however, they were heavenly to Ken.

Swayne motioned for Cable and Durn to follow him into one room, leaving Aldren and Ken to share the other.

As Aldren entered the room, Dalia grabbed Ken's sleeve.

"My Lord, it may be of interest to know that my room lies yonder at the opposite end of the floor. Delvin beds downstairs in the kitchen behind the taproom."

Before Ken could respond to this invitation, Dalia made her intentions crystal clear. She leaned over and gently kissed him full on the lips. She was warm and tasted of sweet ale, and he returned her passion in kind. His desire was obvious, and although she wanted to savor the moment, there were more subtle preparations to make before his visit to her room.

She pulled away and whispered amorously, "A promise of things to come. I will expect my Lord's company in the next few hours, after the Landing settles for the night."

"Okay," said Ken, smiling. It was all he could manage in the moment. He stared at her departing figure, absorbing the intense feelings and dawning realization that, however unlikely in this strange world of magic and mayhem, his heart had been lost with a single kiss.

He turned from the hallway and entered his room. Aldren was already tucked in cozily, fully dressed, in one of the beds flanking the crackling hearth. The only concessions to decorum were Caldorsbane lying at his side and his waist satchel and saddlebag resting on the floorboards.

Ken put Stonegrinder and his saddlebag on the floor and reclined on the bed cover. After that kiss, the last thing on his mind was sleep, but his body had other plans. Fatigue, assisted by the ale, coaxed a sound slumber in him within minutes.

As the human and his companions left the taproom, Corin Shadowalker slipped out of the Landing unnoticed. Finding his horse in the stable, he led his steed to the Ferry Master's station. After enough pounding to wake the dead, a light winked on inside the Station. The sturdy oak portal cracked ajar.

Otter Thielson was in no mood for visitors. After twenty years' hard ferrying along the Gylderhorn, he knew the value of well-earned rest. And within his memory, including the days spent watching his father ply the family trade, no greater storm surge than this had he seen the mighty river throw against those who would defy its single-minded dominion. The storm system atop the Morningstars had seemingly reached down to plague every member of his crew. More than once, the day's hauling had nearly come to disastrous end.

Otter barked, "What devil comes to m'door at this hour? Begone! You've the word of Otter Thielson that his ferry will be waiting fer ye in the morning."

"I think not," whispered Shadowalker. More loudly, he announced, "I have need for your services. You will be well rewarded."

Otter reconsidered and carefully eyed Shadowalker—not Tuonim, but clearly an Elder Lord from the West. It would not do for any human to insult such as stood before him.

"That may be," said Otter, "but the river demons prowl this night for any mortal so foolish to tempt ye such a fate. Have ye not fathomed the storm up yonder? Th' crossing will be dangerous fer all."

Shadowalker responded sharply, "There are other dangers more perilous than the Gylderhorn."

The veiled threat did not fall on deaf ears. Otter knew that, like it or not, there would be a crossing this night. "What's yer cargo?"

"Only myself."

"And yer beastie?"

"My horse as well."

"Be riskier with th' small load in this chop. Are ye set on this course?"

Shadowalker stewed impetuously.

"Aye, no need to bluster. What say ye to three gold pieces, fer th' lads will not easily rouse."

The fare was outrageous, but Shadowalker paid without further word. In little more than a quarter hour, the Gylderhorn's wet tongue lapped at his boots.

Otter loosed a constant barrage of sharp orders while his tired crew strained on the ferry's icy tug rope.

Midriver, the cold spray stung Shadowalker's face as angry waves crested, fell, and then crashed over the ferry's deck. It was all he could do to keep his horse from being flung into the torrent. Regaining his balance after yet another wild dip, Shadowalker thought, *This river rat did not exaggerate. Human, your capture had better be worth this inconvenience.*

"Captain," yelled Shadowalker, "can you not drive them any faster?"

"Thar doing th' best, m'Lord."

Shadowalker glimpsed Otter's smile in the lamplight.

Laugh now, river rat, but you'll not spend my gold.

Much later, as the ferry docked along the Gylderhorn's western shore, a wet, foul-tempered Shadowalker mounted his equally uncomfortable steed and rode into the wind-whipped grass of the Plains of Kesmark.

"Good riddance," said Otter, crossing his chest and spitting over his shoulder. It was the sailor's charm against evil. Though weary, half-frozen, and scattered along the foredeck, each mate to the last repeated Otter's gesture. Their efforts were futile, for superstition would provide scant protection this night; an evil beyond the river demons was creeping in the stormy darkness.

Within Delvin's Landing, Ken awoke. Was it his nightlight? He shivered momentarily. The dying embers in the hearth held little warmth and signaled that he'd been asleep far too long. The Landing was silent. Sitting up, he sensed a threat. A sweeping malice bore down on Delvin's Landing. It might already be too late. Ken cursed as he realized that there would be no rendezvous with Dalia, assuming that her offer remained open at this late hour.

"Aldren, wake up," said Ken as he strapped Stonegrinder to his back.

"What is it?" sighed Aldren.

"We've got a situation brewing. I can't be specific. Something bad is heading our way fast. Get Swayne and the others up to speed and have them pack the gear. I'm going to warn Dalia and Delvin."

Ken opened the door slightly and peered into the hallway. Heavy shadows on this moonless night blackened the Landing. Seeing no immediate enemy where he stood, Ken glided to the opposite wing. There were three rooms on the

Landing's west wing: two against the outer wall, and another on the interior, above what would be the taproom below. Following Dalia's direction from earlier, he chose the room standing alone and whispered against the wood, "Dalia, wake up. Dalia."

The door opened. She was wrapped sensuously in a soft white comforter amidst the gentle glow of candlelight. Dalia was beautiful. She was also vengeful; her hand whipped across his jaw.

"That's for making me wait so long." Suddenly, she embraced him fiercely.

Ken was keenly aware of the touch of her body as they kissed. Her tongue gently but insistently explored his, while her hands locked around his back. She ground her hips rhythmically against his, unabashedly revealing her desire.

As much as he wanted to abandon himself to love and discover all that Dalia offered, however, now could not be that time. He reluctantly pushed himself away.

"Get dressed. There's real danger coming our way."

She misread his meaning. "If you don't want to be here, just say so, my Lord. You are not the first to do so."

Ken couldn't believe that anyone would refuse the gifts that Dalia sought to share, but he stuck to the subject at hand.

"No, listen. I promise we will continue this… discussion, but right now, we have to warn your father. It's life or death."

These last words energized her. "Stay here." The door closed.

In mere seconds, she reappeared dressed in leathers. A slender sword hung from a scabbard attached to her belt. A longknife rested lightly in each of her delicate hands. Ken stared in genuine amazement at this deadly transformation. If the situation hadn't been so serious, he might have laughed. He had dated women who needed an hour just to do their hair.

Dalia whispered crisply, "Better for close-quarter fighting. Now stop wasting time. Let's get Father."

At the head of the stairs, Ken stopped; he had heard a noise.

Swayne's door opened. "Oath-Companion," whispered Swayne, "what troubles thee?"

"We're about to have company of the worst kind. It's an evil presence. More than that, I can't say. I'd rather not be here when the dam bursts. Come on."

Ken led the group, moving quietly downstairs. Dalia was behind him, pressing on his back, encouraging him onward. Under different circumstances, the close contact would have been pleasant, but now it only heightened his apprehension.

As Ken descended the stairs, he felt, more than saw, that the taproom was empty. The bloodred coals in the great hearthstone could only dispel so much of the Landing's shadows.

Dalia sprinted past Ken to the kitchen storeroom door behind the counter. She knocked twice and then once.

A sleepy but fully clothed Delvin was nearly toppled by Dalia's bear hug.

"Lass, take it easy," urged Delvin. "What mischief is afoot that you saw fit to unbed me at this hour, and bearing such arms? Has Master Fortas returned?"

"I don't have the faintest, Father. Ask them."

Delvin only now noticed Lord Gunderhad's party standing at the stairs. "My Lords?" he asked.

Swayne turned to Ken. "Well?"

Ken said, "Durn, Cable, the dim light shouldn't expose you. Get to the windows and let me know if you can see anything."

Both looked to Swayne, who nodded.

So that's the way it's going to be, Ken thought before shifting his focus.

"Delvin," asked Ken sharply, "is there a back door?"

"No, my Lord, but yon window over there will do."

"Aldren, check it out. And Delvin, my name is Ken. Don't 'my Lord' me again. The novelty has worn thin."

Delvin snorted. "Whatever my Lo… you wish, but—"

Durn's whisper interrupted. "R'Kesh, along the road and by the stables."

"From the woods also," said Cable, "great numbers of their breed."

"What are the chances of fighting our way to the stables?" asked Ken.

Alden, returning from the rear answered, "The horses are likely dead. The back of the Landing is crawling with these abominations."

Dalia gasped. "Father, Ned is in the stables."

"Aye, Lass," replied Delvin sympathetically, "I'm fond of the boy, too. We'll do what we can."

Delvin then secured his great two-handed battle-axe and reached below the taproom counter to produce a back harness with sheath for the axe, thick leather jerkin, assorted knives, and a dinner plate–sized iron shield that strapped onto the stub of his amputated forearm.

Ken did a double take at seeing Delvin's battle garb.

And I was going to rescue him.

Aldren, too, showed surprise at Delvin's armament. Swayne eyed Delvin but gave no other reaction.

Apparently satisfied with his own weapons, Delvin passed a handful of finger-long throwing knives to Dalia.

Ken was amazed to see the blades disappear just as fast. Each of Dalia's boots had special sleeves for several blades; four more slipped neatly into the hollow core of her waist belt; one more under each forearm… Ken lost count and then turned to Swayne. "Any bright ideas?"

"This is no chance encounter," said Swayne. "They've been set on our heels with deadly intent."

Delvin retorted angrily, "The Lord of the Falcon Clan brought this curse upon my house. Hah, I would not have believed it so."

Delvin stepped menacingly toward Swayne.

"You forget yourself," Swayne warned.

"Father." Dalia grabbed his shoulder. "The Lord of the Falcon Clan is not our enemy! Had you known such things did chase him, would you have denied *him* our aid?"

Delvin calmed. "No, lass. You do me proud to have reminded me of such. My Lord, forgive the outburst. What of these beasts? This axe has cleaved the head off many who sought my end."

Swayne nodded and asked, "Durn, how many?"

"No." said Durn.

Too much experience backed that assessment. Swayne mutely withdrew Yoshirim.

Ken interjected, "Even if we fight, we need to have an escape route. The stables are out."

Sharp pounding sounded against the Landing's heavy door. Wood began to groan and crack.

"Oath-Companion," said Swayne, "I see few alternatives. If we are to escape this trap, we will need the First Mother's Fire. Prepare yourself."

"Wait," barked Delvin, who didn't much like the sound of Swayne's option. "We can get to the Ferry Master's station. Let no one say Delvin One-Arm is a fool."

Scuttling sounds and claw scratches reverberated against the Landing's walls.

"This way. Hurry!" yelled Delvin.

Delvin led the party into his sleeping quarters and made straight for his bed. "There's a bolt-hole under the floorboards."

Aldren and Ken easily lifted the loose boards and stared at a dark earthen hole. A wet, musty smell floated upward. Aldren looked to Delvin.

"Should be safe; the trapdoor on the other side is well hidden. It's man-high and runs to the Gylderhorn as the crow flies."

Swayne commanded Cable, "Torches."

Cable disappeared into the taproom.

The door pounding increased, the iron hinges rattling with each impact.

"We can't leave Ned," cried Dalia.

"Daughter, said Delvin, "if he lives, our deaths will not help him. We will do what can be done once we've slipped this noose."

Cable returned with several burning brands. Ken grabbed one and jumped into the hole. He landed with a splash in ankle-deep water. Despite the water, the wood-lined tunnel walls looked solid and widened further on. *I'm beginning to feel like a mole.* "It's wet, but clear. Let's move it, people," he exclaimed.

Dalia followed.

Swayne turned to Cable, took a torch, and said, "Burn it."

Delvin spun to face Swayne. Another challenge seemed imminent. But Delvin had not survived so long by letting emotions rule. He knew a fire would cover their escape—Dalia's escape. It was a fair trade. He nodded.

Swayne disappeared below, with Durn at his back.

Delvin paused at the tunnel entrance and pointed for Cable's benefit "There, against the wall on the lower shelf. Those bottles will see the job properly done."

Cable began hurling the bottles into the taproom and around the storeroom floor.

Amidst the sound of smashing glass, Delvin said, "I swear, old girl, you'll be rebuilt. For now, it's to be the soldier's pyre. It's better than letting these creatures foul your innards. Goodbye." He then dropped into his bolt-hole.

Moments later, Cable returned to the tunnel's opening as the Landing door finally gave way to the onslaught and burst inward with a splintery crash.

Cable leapt downward, flinging his torch into the taproom. It was like he had tossed a burning match into a gas oven.

Boom! The tunnel shook.

Earth rained down onto Cable's head, and heat singed the back of his neck.

Looking up, he beheld a wall of fire and smoke. Piercing guttural wails could be heard above the snapping flames. Satisfied, he moved to overtake the retreating torchlight.

CHAPTER 13
PURSUIT

Ken registered the blast vibration as he hurriedly splashed ahead with Dalia. He could see the tunnel end now. It was cut to form a broad cul-de-sac. A wooden ladder was secured to the far wall and led up to a trapdoor. Throughout the chamber, spacious alcoves with shelving were built perilously close to the water line. They held all manner of jars, bottles, crates and other goods. Dalia began rummaging through their contents.

"If I was a betting man," said Ken, "I'd wager that a tunnel like this would make it easy to smuggle cargo in and out of the Landing under the prying eyes of our Elder friends."

"That's a wager you'd win," replied Dalia as she produced a storm lantern. Ken obliged by lighting the wick, and then he doused his torch in the water.

Swayne, Cable, and Delvin approached, and seeing the lantern, Swayne did likewise with his torch. Thick smoke had settled in the already musty tunnel.

More splashing could be heard in the darkness.

"Cable?" asked Ken.

"Perhaps," answered Swayne.

Durn swung to the rear, weapon drawn. It was unnecessary. Cable materialized, safe and sound.

Durn cracked a grin and sheathed his sword with a satisfied thud.

Cable whispered flatly, "The fire will bar the entrance until daybreak, yet we hide in their element. They will devise another way within."

"Lass," said Delvin, "give the lantern here."

Delvin then pointed to more crates and said, "Gather food rations and clothes for two. We're heading to the Hinterlands to regroup. Favors owed must be called upon."

Durn, ever practical, stocked ample supplies alongside Dalia, refilling his pack and the two saddlebags held by Aldren.

Delvin turned to Swayne. "Lord Gunderhad, yer first duty is to the Aerie, I know. Still, we'd welcome the company. The journey will not be without hazard."

Dalia's eyes shot a piercing message to Ken.

The plea did not go unnoticed.

That woman does more with a glance than most people can with a truckload of words, but I don't have the freedom of choice right now. It's a time for reason, not emotion. Damn, when am I going to catch a break?

Dalia then said, "Father, what about Ned?"

Delvin's response was grim, "Depends upon what's occurring above."

"At least in that respect," said Swayne as he grasped the ladder, "we are in agreement. Shutter that lantern. Let's see what we may."

Once the tunnel was dark, Swayne climbed the ladder and lifted the wooden trapdoor slightly. The greased hinges gave no protest. Leafy shrubbery surrounded the opening and provided adequate concealment. He rose up entirely.

Swayne scouted through parted branches and then receded underground.

Delvin unshuttered the lantern a fraction, preserving their night vision with the survival habit of an old soldier.

"What's our situation?" prompted Ken.

Swayne replied gravely, "Delvin's Landing has passed to the Nine Circles this night. The Ferry Master's station is ablaze. So, too, is the ferry. R'Kesh are herding the living and carrying the dead toward the North Road. And there are yet many R'Kesh storming the woods to our south, furiously beating the undergrowth. They no doubt quest for our nest."

"We can use the confusion to our advantage," offered Aldren, "and slip between their raiders to the south. Should bladework be necessary, their noise will cover our steps. Once free, we can raft across the Gylderhorn."

Swayne nodded.

Dalia's heart sank. Fate, it seemed, had chosen designs for her other than a trip to the Hinterlands.

Swayne continued, "The main R'Kesh host must be found to the northern caverns under the Morningstars' west spur. The depths of Carok Tir have long hosted their evil. The forest would not bear such a presence. As for our escape, it will not be difficult to breach their line. R'Kesh have no stomach for skilled swordplay."

"No," said Ken with quiet finality.

Dalia couldn't believe it. Maybe Ken truly shared her desire.

"What do you mean?" exclaimed Aldren. "What flaw do you suggest in this strategy?"

"Oath-Companion?" said Swayne in bewilderment.

"No flaws, just choices. Those are my people out there, the living and the dead, as you say. I will not abandon them."

In a single breadth, Dalia's passion melted into shock.

His people? She was confused. The door to her dreams was abruptly closing.

"You're human?" stammered Delvin, who had also never suspected Ken's ordinary heritage.

"You better believe it," replied Ken, "one hundred percent, pure grade-A human. That's me. Aldren, we've traveled together now for a while and gotten to know each other. You've got my word that I won't forget about the mission to King Remeth. This has to take priority."

Aldren hesitated.

"Come on," urged Ken, "help me rescue these people."

Aldren relented, "Though I wish another path, it is high time that I repay the burgeoning honor-debt placed by you upon Hemdall's Line."

"Swayne, can I count on you too?"

"You risk the fate of all with this diversion," advised Swayne.

"You may be right, and then again, maybe not. One thing I do know for sure, here and now, I can't sit by and idly watch folks march to their death, or worse, as Aldren mentioned earlier. You don't have to help. The decision is yours."

"I do not refuse. But to achieve the greater victory oftimes requires sacrifice. Do not lose sight of this wisdom in the coming days."

"I'll take that as a yes from the Tuonim," said Ken. "What about you two?"

Dalia seemed in a daze, so Ken repeated his request. "Delvin?"

Finding his tongue, Delvin replied, "You believe these creatures are returning to the northern caverns, to Carok Tir; it is a place not unknown to those who travel the Three Corners, and all avoid its shadow. The Hinterlands also lie northward, far beyond the caverns. I make no promises, for my daughter means the world, and I will not risk her life in any fool's venture. But neither am I made of stone. There are those I would call friends among the prisoners, and we owe it to the boy to try."

"Good to have you aboard," Ken replied. "Now, if no one objects, I suggest we let things briefly settle above. We may have to deal with stray R'Kesh, but I don't want to stumble into a direct confrontation with their full strength… at least not yet. Swayne, what do you think? Half an hour?"

Swayne replied, "Still dangerous, but if you hope to save any of these people, we should not tarry much longer."

Ken weighed the risks and decided quickly. "We'll follow the main horde in half an hour. Feels right. I don't think they'll expect us to chase them, and the unexpected can be fertile ground for opportunity. I've tasted that lesson firsthand." Ken touched the scar on his face.

"And when we overtake them?" asked Swayne.

"Let's cross that bridge when we get to it," answered Ken.

Even in Weir, this phrase was not lost on Swayne, who said, "Very well, Oath-Companion. We shall speak of this anon."

A short while later, Cable took the point position as the party ascended from their hiding place. He guided them safely to the edge of the woods flanking the North Road.

Ken understood this choice. The trees were thinly spaced and would afford easier travel with only modest noise. Although they neither heard nor saw any of the creatures in the immediate vicinity, it would be reckless to pursue the R'Kesh on the open road. Darkness offered only the illusion of cover. As a surface-raiding subterranean race, the R'Kesh would have sharp night vision and superior smell. And there was no telling when the search parties to the south would forsake their task and rejoin their brethren, assuming that they had not already done so.

The group walked in single file. Time blurred as each of them focused on traversing Cable's chosen path from one tree to the next while being careful not to unduly disturb the undergrowth. Steady progress was made, but far more slowly than Ken would have wished. Using the First Mother's gift, Ken sensed their quarry gaining ever-widening distance. This thought caused him much anguish.

About two hours before dawn, Swayne bade Cable halt.

"Sleep now," said Swayne. "I will take first watch. Durn will replace me in two hours. After that, Cable."

Aldren countered, "Cable has kept the path. I will stand his watch. I am not as tired as our human friends."

Swayne nodded.

As Ken lay with his back to a tree, he saw Dalia nestle alongside her father. It was too dark to make eye contact. Instead, Ken hoped that he would find a way into her dreams as she might in his.

Ken was nudged awake from dark dreams. They passed into forgetfulness.

Aldren smiled. "We should get started. Daylight is our greatest weapon."

"I'm awake. Go see to the others."

Ken stood and inhaled deeply. The morning haze on his mind dissipated. He closed his eyes and pushed his senses outward, touching the living web again.

Go farther.

As his energy scoured this field of intangibility for the target, Ken began to understand that the unembodied dimension that he roamed might possibly be infinite. There was so much he didn't know. He put the doubt aside.

Farther still...there, a hovering malignance. How can they be so distant? We were too slow, too cautious. Why have they stopped? Why? See the positive—they're stationary for now. Return. Follow the meridians back.

Ken blinked. He was fully present again. *These mind trips are getting weirder and weirder. On the upside, this isn't the First Mother's Fire; it must be a side effect of the magic or whatever else She granted, so although I'm not spending my old age when I do it, just what sort of risk is it to my life? I keep thinking... man wasn't meant to fly.*

Durn had prepared a cold breakfast by mixing their food with the stores from Delvin's cache. They finished the last of the bread and hard cheese from Dawn's Aerie. The more perishable items had been eaten first. A jar of Delvin's fruit preserves was opened. It helped to wash down the stale bread.

Ken walked over.

Swayne and Cable were already eating light helpings.

Dalia and Delvin were brushing off leaves and stretching.

"They are several hours ahead of us," announced Ken, "and they aren't moving for the time being."

Durn replied, "They must eat. We may have them by late afternoon."

"Durn knows," Swayne continued after finishing a mouthful, "daylight will hinder their movement and speed our pursuit. We no longer need weave between the trees, for there will be no surprises upon the road this day. The sun is no friend to these vermin."

Dalia and Delvin made their way over.

"Morning," greeted Ken. "Durn has seen to our breakfast."

Delvin sat nearby. Dalia ignored Ken as she walked up to Durn.

Durn served a heaping portion on a slab of bread that he put in each of her palms. She then sat next to her father. The two ate without a word.

Ken left it alone. Their livelihood, home, and community had just been obliterated in the space of a single night. He could forgive them a less-than-rosy attitude. Part of him wanted very much to comfort Dalia, to hold her tight and whisper that everything would be okay. The other part recognized that she wasn't the helpless maiden by any stretch of the imagination and that there was no way to predict Delvin's reaction. At this moment, it seemed a much better idea not to incur the wrath of a father who swung a broadaxe like a baseball bat.

A short time later, bellies full and other matters completed, the group resumed pursuit. To make up ground, they alternated hourly between a slow run and a fast walk. There was no chance of losing their quarry; the road's churned-up soil bore testament to the passing of the R'Kesh horde. Other signs were more disturbing.

A wake of assorted items of the mundane lay mutely amidst the dirt. A fallen shoe propped here, Unidentifiable clothing scraps, there. They told a macabre tale in their own right, but it paled in comparison to the group's next discovery.

At noon, they came upon human remains.

In the rush to reach the sanctuary of the northern caverns, the R'Kesh had feasted with raw and savage violence. Bloody bits of flesh were strewn among and attached to bone after shattered bone riddled with teeth marks.

Ken could only count human skulls to determine the dead. He issued a prayer to whatever god was listening that these people had not been eaten alive.

Dalia gasped at one head with the flesh partially intact. Delvin walked over for a closer inspection and then said quietly, "I know, lass, 'tis old Henry Hogswell, a stubborn but likable codger if ever there was. He did not deserve such a fate."

Swayne asked, "Oath-Companion, can you tell how far ahead they lie?"

Ken focused for a few moments, tapping his unseen resources, and then said, "We've halved the distance between us that I sensed this morning. They're on the move. And there's something else. I have the impression of ... well... it's like a cloud that envelopes them."

"How can you," sputtered Delvin distrustfully, "a human, claim to know these things?"

Dalia also stared at Ken.

Ken sighed. It was bad enough having to overcome fear among the Elder Race. It hadn't occurred to him that his own people might hold similar feelings. Was he to be an outcast no matter where he turned?

"Ask me another time, Delvin One-Arm," suggested Ken, "and I promise, you'll get the full explanation. I can't indulge in such conversation now. While we are on the trail of these monsters, every minute that we delay raises the possibility of escape and more unnecessary death. I will not tolerate that."

Ken ran onward, steadfast upon his goal.

Aldren and the Tuonim followed.

Delvin reflected. Dalia also had questions. She had never considered committing to a lifelong relationship with any human, although this one was surrounded by interesting secrets. Who was this man that he commanded power among the Elder Lords, especially someone of Lord Gunderhad's stature? How did he come to wear the ring of the First Mark? And what magic did he possess to spy on these creatures from afar?

"Father, do we continue?" asked Dalia.

Delvin had seen many strange sights in his Hinterland years, and while cautious of this man and his Elder Lords, he had an undeniable respect for the man's purpose. A long time ago, Delvin had also ridden with such conviction for a companion, but that, too, was a tale for another day. Delvin nodded, "Aye, keep pace with me. He can't run that way for long."

And so it went.

The chase continued as the sun drifted across the sky into late afternoon. Still, the gap between the R'Kesh defied Ken's advance and Swayne's predictions, lessening only slightly. At sunset, Ken halted dejectedly. They needed to replenish their strength. While they quickly ate and drank in silence, the R'Kesh pushed ever forward.

In no time at all, so did Ken's group.

As night replaced day, the would-be rescuers continued pursuit. Unlike the prior night, they stayed on the North Road. Ambush was unlikely so long as Ken was willing to trust his gifts to track the R'Kesh.

A few hours before dawn, Aldren tapped Ken on the shoulder. "You must rest for a time."

Ken stopped. The others pulled up. Dalia and Delvin practically collapsed to the ground.

Ken stubbornly replied, "If we do, more lives may end."

Aldren appealed to reason by saying, "The One-Arm and his daughter are very tired. And whether you wish to admit it, so are you. Even we of the Elder Race are not immune to fatigue."

Ken relented. "Four hours only. Swayne, set the watch."

Swayne, who was listening to the exchange, said, "It will be done as you request."

Ken reflected on Swayne's obvious use of the word "request." It was a polite reminder that the pride of Dawn's Aerie did not take lightly to orders. With that, Ken lay down to an uneasy sleep. Pictures kept surfacing in his mind's eye of the horrors that daylight would reveal. He told himself that the R'Kesh would feast on the decaying dead before turning to the living. It provided a dim ray of comfort. He clung to that thought with fierce determination. Nothing good could come of dwelling on the terror of the men, women, and children being driven to their doom by the R'Kesh. And he was right. As he mentally replayed scene after scene of bloody human remains that they had discovered, anger found its way into his being—an anger that rapidly gave way to rage; thus, it came to pass that in this depleted state with powerful emotions holding sway, he was betrayed.

The Dreamers of Soulstealer's Doom had not been over-thrown entirely. Their subjugation was temporary, and the chains that bound them malleable. They sensed the needs of the current host and an opening; in so doing, action was taken. The barest trickle of energy flowed into Soulstealer's Doom, seized from the organisms living in the soil on which Ken slept. The Dreamers would brook no lessening of their power. From the armor, it was exuded into the host. Thus, unwittingly and fast asleep, Ken's body was introduced to the forbidden fruit. There was no resistance. A foothold was achieved without tripping a single alarm. Only time would demonstrate its presence and awful purpose.

Many, many leagues behind, the pursuers were unaware that they, too, were being pursued. The flames swallowing Delvin's Landing had frustrated the R'Kesh. At least, they had for a while. To return to the nest empty-handed would mean death. The Magic Wielders would make a sacrifice of them to their god. And he was a very hungry god. So some of the R'Kesh had stayed, searching even with Her light shining on the land, burning their skin on contact and driving their eyes mad with pain. They were not protected like the horde, and the Green Ones did not shield all Her accursed light.

The wind had finally shifted from the south, carrying away the scent of ash. The manling smell, so potent in fear, was traced to its hidden lair. Were not Gothnu's pack the cleverest hunters in the horde? Her light could not burn away the special manling's scent. And now they also had manling weapons. The Magic Wielders had shown them how to make pokers and jabbers. And some wore pieces of manling clothes and hard skins. Gothnu understood that they would need such things to conquer the manlings, but it was so much more satisfying to rend with arms, tear with claws, and bite with fangs. But the Powerful One was firm in his command. They must bring the special manling back to the nest—alive and whole of limb. The Magic Wielders demanded the pleasure of consuming him themselves. Gothnu wondered how this manling was different from the others. He was stupid to follow the horde; or maybe he was clever and wanted to save himself by pledging his service to the Magic Wielders. The Powerful One had done that. Maybe Gothnu would find out. Maybe Gothnu would eat from this special manling. Surely the Magic Wielders would not begrudge him a finger or toe. Gothnu, the Hunter. Gothnu, the Faithful. Yes, they would reward Gothnu. Drooling, Gothnu pushed the pack faster while the Spirit of Darkness held Her light prisoner. She would soon free Her light to protect the manlings. It was always so. But the Magic Wielders said that such things would not be so for long.

Gothnu thanked the Spirit of Darkness for sending the Magic Wielders.

Just over four and a half hours after stopping, the rescuers once again set forth on their task. Ken had awoken feeling refreshed, unlike his companions. He looked over his shoulder at them now.

I'll give Delvin credit—he's in far better shape than I would have expected for a man his age. And yet, he's slowing us with each hour.

Ken turned his attention to Dalia, who was confidently striding next to her father. She retuned his look with a seething glare. *She's doing great, but she's upset...and justifiably so. I wish I could stop. Not only to let your father regain his strength, but to continue our conversation. I feel you growing distant, and I'm not sure why, although I must admit that present circumstances aren't exactly conducive to romance. Damn. It will have to wait. I hope you'll understand and forgive me.*

Ken strode onward.

Hours passed, and as before, they came upon the R'Kesh's grisly leavings. Ken increased the pace slightly, ignoring the carnage. They were narrowing the R'Kesh lead. Ken estimated that maybe two hours separated the rescuers from the R'Kesh horde. He would do his utmost to close that distance before night descended.

At midafternoon Ken halted the rescuers on the outskirts of a small hamlet. "Can anyone fill me in?" Ken asked. "Where are we?"

Swayne answered, "The village of Karsey, a human settlement. It is the last supply station for the Rheinhold Outpost. It is unusually quiet."

"A trap?" asked Aldren.

"We'll see," replied Swayne, nodding to Cable, who ran ahead to investigate.

Ken said, "I don't think so. The horde is moving away to the north. We've gained another hour on them, though."

"Oath-Companion," began Swayne, "while we wait for Cable, there are matters to be discussed. I have spoken with Durn. We judge the R'Kesh will find the depths of Carok Tir shortly after sunset. The caverns lay a scant few hours' travel through the woods north of the village. Over there. Let your eye wander to the farthest hill in the distance on the left. Beyond that mount, across the gully, and on to the far wall will be found an opening to their foul lair. Many times the Tuonim have sealed that wound, and always, they forge a new orifice."

Ken stared into the north wood. *No more road. It will be tougher terrain, and uphill. How do we make up the difference before nightfall? Even if we run all the way, I need time to fig-ure out a plan of attack, and a little rest wouldn't hurt, either. The Romans marched their foot soldiers all day long only to then engage the enemy in battle. But we're not a legion of Roman soldiers, and this is the third night. The great general, Caesar, might have thought twice about taking his troops into battle under such conditions.*

Swayne saw hesitation. "Oath-Companion, you have led a brave and determined chase, but I do not think we will catch these creatures aboveground. And if we should do so, have you considered how we, who are few and weary, will defeat so many?"

If we could get ahead of them, then we might set an ambush near the lair entrance, just as they're most confident, Ken thought. *We would have surprise on our side, and if we drive a wedge into the R'Kesh line where the captives are thickest, the R'Kesh should lose the numbers advantage, at lease temporarily. It would only work if we somehow keep those inside from joining the fight outside. Hmmm, how to do that?*

Cable was returning from the village.

Delvin, who had caught his breath, added, "Lord Gunderhad makes sense. I told you that I would not risk my daughter needlessly. I share your concerns, but our people might already be dead. Should any yet live, I would not be so foolish as to pick a fight when I'm too tired to lift my axe."

Dalia seemed to want to say something as well, but she held her tongue.

Cable joined them and said, "The village is empty. I deem within the last hour. They did not go without a fight, yet they stood no chance. The tracks of the horde cover the village and regroup heading into the north woods. The animals were left alone. Only humans were taken."

Ken startled. "Animals?"

Delvin said, "These people were mostly farmers. They had chickens, pigs, sheep, and the like. Why wouldn't these R'Kesh have taken them also?"

Aldren replied grimly, "That is not the food these creatures crave, and they were in a hurry."

Ken mused aloud, "For a moment, I thought our problem might have been solved. Horses would have been a godsend."

Cable said, "I did not check, but the supply station usually boards several teams for transporting goods to our Outpost."

"We have no time to spare; show us!" cried Ken.

Cable ushered them to a barn structure on the far end of town. The strong scent of manure drifted heavily. Opening the main doors, Ken nearly screamed. The stalls were full of horses, alive and untouched, and all exhibited Weir heritage in their size. He planted a firm hug around the neck of the nearest mare. The horse nickered happily. Ken was no stranger to horses. He had ridden at Uncle Dale's farm as soon as he had been old enough to tell left from right. Aunt Louise had been nervous, but as Dale had put it, that's the test for any child looking to take a first riding lesson. He had done just fine.

Ken released his hold on the horse before saying, "Well, folks, Problem Number One solved. We've got transportation and a way to rest up before a fight. Can everyone ride?"

Affirmative nods met his inquiry.

"I thought so," said Ken, relieved. "I'm working on a game plan. I won't know for sure how we're going to hit them. I aim to start by overtaking the horde and positioning us near the lair opening. A frontal attack is too risky, so my thought is to stage a guerilla-style ambush when they least expect it."

"It has merit," Aldren said approvingly.

Swayne had his doubts, however. "Let us say that this guerilla attack is successful. What prevents the R'Kesh under Carok Tir from following and retaking us along with the human stragglers?"

"I've an idea, but you'll have to trust me. I won't know for sure until we reach the lair."

Delvin growled, "Did I not say that I would not participate in foolishness?"

Dalia jumped in, surprisingly on Ken's side, "Father, at least hear him out. We can always take the horses and ride on."

"Thanks for the vote of confidence," said Ken with a warm smile. "Look, I'll make a promise to everyone. You all knew there was risk, and you signed up to help anyway. It's the right thing to do. That being said, I don't intend to throw my life away, or yours. If you don't like what I have to say once we reach the lair, you are free to forget I ever mentioned the word rescue. I won't bear any ill will against anyone who chooses to leave then."

"Father, it is a fair bargain. I, for one, will go."

Delvin sighed. "Very well, daughter, until the caverns, then."

Swayne and Aldren nodded likewise.

In short order, the horses were bridled and saddled. Ken had stayed with his first instinct, choosing the mare he had hugged. He mounted and nudged her onto the road with the others following. He directed the horse to the R'Kesh tracks and, before entering the north woods, said, "I'll go as fast as the horses can manage. When we get near the horde, I can guide us around them at a safe distance. Let's ride!"

Ken kicked the horse's side and sped off and heard the others behind him do likewise. It felt great to be on horseback again. The wind blew loudly in his ears as he adjusted to his oversized steed. Within a few minutes, he had found the rhythm. As long as the pace stayed under a gallop, he knew, the trees were not so thick as to pose a danger.

Within the hour, they were gradually ascending the mountainside. Ken focused his senses, and like a beacon on a radar screen he saw the R'Kesh horde in his mind. *They're off to our right, nearing the crest.*

Ken strained his eyes in that direction. Nothing was visible at first. As his glare penetrated deeper and deeper into the woody horizon, shadow eclipsed the light, and the trees faded from sight. It was an artificial fog, a misty dark held together by someone or something's will, and it was moving.

No wonder we haven't caught them. They've been able to move freely in the daytime under that cloud. Let's pull back the curtain and see what's revealed.

Ken gathered his energy and called to mind a few of nature's greatest night hunters—leopards for their sight in near-lightless conditions, and vipers for their heat vision. He felt sure that this overlay of visual and thermal imaging, magically enhanced, would be the right formula to pierce the cloud. The greater mystery behind the magic still eluded him, but he now felt an undeniable self-assurance in wielding the First Mother's Fire.

Releasing his will and power, Ken perceived that which shunned the goodness of light. If the main horde represented the head of the beast, then its tail consisted of human suffering. The refugees were at the rear of the horde, barely keeping pace with their cruel tormentors. Those who hadn't any strength left to stumble under whip and blade were being carried to their doom like potato sacks.

Ken knew he would alter that fate now. He had a plan.

Turning in the saddle to face his companions, he pointed right and made a circling motion with his hand. The others got the message. He routed them left.

At the top of the hill, Ken looked to his side at the declining sun. It was going to be close. The light would be to their advantage.

He pressed the mare downward. Long shadows were taking hold of the bottomland. As the mare navigated the slope, Ken used his power to confirm that they were finally in front of the R'Kesh. He swung the mare back to the right on an intersecting line with the horde's destination.

Ken felt the mare resist. He patted her side and leaned down to whisper in her ear, "I know your horse-sense is telling you to be someplace else. If it makes you feel any better, so is mine. We'll find greener pastures another day, but there's work to be done, and like it or not, we're the ones called to the task. Now giddup!"

It took forever to reach the gully. When they finally did, Ken checked the mare to a walk. The ground had a marsh-like consistency, and the mare's hooves were sinking into its sludge. The sucking pop sound of each footfall was sickening. The woods they encountered had changed for the worse; oppressiveness hung over the forest like an undertaker waiting for the next corpse.

Ken pulled on the rein and dismounted. He tied the mare to the nearest branch. Dalia was right at his heels; her steed, bearing the lightest passenger, had coped better with the terrain. Then came Delvin, squarely at ease on the back of a mount. Aldren and the Tuonim finally drifted in together.

The group stood in the fringe of the tree line that was overshadowed by an imposing escarpment. Falling rock had crushed the trees into submission; their splintery remains were littered amidst loose piles of fragmented stone and massive boulders.

Ken turned to the shrinking sun and then surveyed the destruction along the wall. *So why does the broken woodwork among the stone remind me of crosses in a cemetery? Not the image I was hoping for here.* He shifted his view to the opposite direction, and saw, in a shadowed area about a hundred yards away, a train tunnel–like opening in the cliff. Tons of rubble had been moved aside. *The belly of the beast... don't let it swallow you, too.*

Ken said crisply, "We have maybe twenty minutes until they arrive, so I don't have a lot of time for discussion."

"Oath-Companion," cautioned Swayne, "be brief if you must, but I would hear your battle plan."

"Swayne, it's probably best for you, Durn, and Cable to stay together as a fighting unit. I want you to work your way around to the trees on the far side of the entrance. Stay out of sight until I give the signal. The four of us will spread out on this side. I'll need one of you to remain close to me as a bodyguard. I may not be able to fight for the first few minutes. We'll squeeze them in the middle and have surprise on our side. If we move fast and hit hard, we should be able to save everyone who still lives."

Delvin blurted, "A fool's venture! We few against their numbers? It will never work. Daughter, it's the Hinterlands for us."

"Wait," Ken shot back, "I'm not finished. The reason we haven't been able to catch them before now is that they have been traveling in the daylight."

"Bad sign," Durn pronounced heavily, "if the R'Kesh no longer fear the day."

"I don't think that's the case," replied Ken. "They're cheating, dodging the light, moving under a cloud. It's like a shadowy mist. It's protecting them from the sun and hiding them from curious eyes."

"Not everyone's sight is dimmed," said Aldren.

Ken nodded. "You're getting to know me better, my friend. Earlier, I saw through the mist. The humans are being driven by a small contingent of R'Kesh at the rear of the horde. I'm going to split them from the rest, and then we'll take them out."

Dalia asked, "How are we going to isolate this group of creatures?"

"I didn't say 'we,'" corrected Ken. "I intend to seal the lair entrance after the main horde passes within. I'll wait until the last possible second in order to minimize the number of R'Kesh. The only hitch is that I might not be of much use right away, because the magic is draining."

"Magic? Is he daft?" asked Delvin.

"No," responded Swayne, "he is quite serious. Now, we must hurry into position. First Mother's blessing upon you, Oath-Companion. Remember your training."

Ken had to hand it to Swayne that, though he needed convincing, there was no hesitation in the warrior once the point got home.

The Tuonim disappeared into the undergrowth.

"Which one of you wants to be my bodyguard?" Ken asked his remaining companions.

Delvin took the opening. "Dalia can watch your hide. I don't want her swinging into this melee if I can help it. She's also better with a knife at close quarters."

"Father, I want to go with you."

"Daughter, respect my wishes in this matter."

After a long moment, Dalia nodded and then hugged Delvin.

Ken offered his hand to Aldren and said, "Good hunting."

Aldren and Delvin moved off. In moments, Dalia and Ken were alone.

"Let's get a bit nearer to the entrance," Ken suggested

Dalia positioned them against a fallen tree trunk. Its jutting root bundle provided natural concealment and also permitted a broad lookout. As they lay on their stomachs, side by side, Ken found his attention wandering to Dalia. This was the first private moment he had enjoyed with her since they had left Delvin's Landing, and there was always a chance that one of them might not survive. Ken tapped her shoulder.

"What do you want?" she whispered, her lips mere inches from his.

He leaned in and firmly kissed her.

This time, she was the one to push away, but neither very hard nor very fast.

Ken smiled. "Events haven't really given us a moment to finish our discussion. I know this is poor timing, but things are going to heat up in a few minutes and… well… if something bad happens, to either of us, I wanted to share my feelings."

Dalia hesitated. Ken could see she was at odds with herself. Finally, she said, "You should focus upon your task and not on me. I've never seen anyone perform true magic. I'm sure it must require some level of concentration."

"You're right," said Ken, hiding his disappointment. Her reaction was cold. Had he imagined the connection that they had shared at the Landing? Maybe it was the drink. He would find out one way or the other after this was over.

They waited.

The looming sun burned red above the horizon. Tendrils of mist slithered along the ground. Shadows thickened. Sound dimmed. A black fog arose.

The R'Kesh were coming.

Ken retracted his attention from Dalia and organized his thoughts. Without conjuring a specific image, he began pulling raw energy from his essence. He would need an explosion just inside the tunnel. Flying debris must not cause injury to the captives. He let the magic force build, and as it did, he compressed it into a hovering ball of power. He willed it to the proper position high in the lair opening and waited. Then he called on more energy to once again permit him to see through the darkness. The R'Kesh were passing. They surged into the lair like bees into the hive, eager to return to the depths.

Just a little longer; the prisoners are nearing. Further... further... okay, now let her rip!

Instead of an explosion, Ken suddenly felt a presence. Something deep in the lair had detected him, and it, too, possessed magic. It had just barely thwarted his intent—there was no detonation, but the ball of power remained intact.

Ken acted quickly. The R'Kesh carrying the human bodies were already entering the lair. Like a needle bursting a balloon, he willed a lightning bolt of energy to the ball of power. It did the trick. The explosion was followed by rumbling waves of moving earth and falling rock.

Dalia spoke with new awe in her voice. "I did not think it was possible. How did you come by this power?"

Ken rested against their wood cover. He could hardly speak. That last effort had truly depleted him. "What's happening?"

"The mist has cleared. There are many creatures, maybe three score. But there are more humans. The blast knocked everyone to the ground. Wait. The beasts are stirring. They claw at their skin and shield their eyes."

Howls and screams erupted from the R'Kesh.

"The others are upon them. There is much bloodshed."

"What do you mean? How's our team doing?" asked Ken, worried about the outcome.

"Calm yourself, the blood is neither human nor Tuonim. Even one-handed, father is a tough opponent. The Elder Lords are also very skilled."

Ken breathed a sigh of relief as Dalia continued her narration. "Some R'Kesh are attacking, others are scattering. Hush. Do not speak."

Dalia withdrew two short blades from her boot and pulled herself into a crouch.

Rustling steps approached quickly.

In a single fluid motion, Dalia stood and threw with deadly accuracy.

A R'Kesh fell lifeless.

Ken observed, *There's an edge to her, but she's beautiful.*

Dalia remained upright. More blades appeared.

Ken peered by her waist and cursed.

A contingent of R'Kesh had fled in their direction, five, six, maybe eight of them. The death of their fellow creature had alerted them to Dalia's presence. Women had their use in the lair and were not to be killed outright. They fanned out, surrounding Dalia.

Then they saw Ken. His presence resulted in a flurry of unintelligible speech.

He tried to stand, but his muscles refused to cooperate.

Dalia released one blade, and then another, and another, and another.

R'Kesh howled, but most of these creatures wore crude armor, and though an ape-like stance made them appear smaller, many weighed several hundred pounds. Throwing knives into nonvital regions would only do so much damage. And Dalia was handicapped; she had to keep them from Ken.

Dalia freed her sword from its scabbard. The R'Kesh were preparing to charge.

Ken's mind raced. *No! This can't be happening. Think. The First Mother's Fire...*

Ken reached within, but he was too weak from the last magic he had called forth. *I can't.... I need time to regenerate my strength. Please no, not because of me!*

He looked on in desperation, realizing that he and Dalia had only moments. And then, a picture flashed in his head. The Dreamers of Soulstealer's Doom showed him the way. There was no debate. Ken locked his will onto the nearest

R'Kesh and fed. With surprising ease, the creature's life energy flowed into him. Ken drank voraciously. As the beast's corpse sank to the earth, Ken leapt up and withdrew Stonegrinder. Witchfire danced a brilliant warning across its metal, for the sword had been forged during the days when the Elder Smiths were young and mighty. Within Stonegrinder's heart, the Swordsong remembered well this ancient foe.

The R'Kesh closed upon the pair.

Dalia was her father's daughter—strong, agile, and a hellcat in combat—and she would not go down easily.

Ken was the weaker target, but against these opponents, he might have an advantage. The lead R'Kesh wore only a helmet and no body armor. Ken lanced Stonegrinder into the exposed creature and then ripped the blade free. Another R'Kesh swung a blade down toward Ken, but he blocked high, reversed his grip, and sliced across the beast's metal stomach plating, a basic movement that had been ingrained in him from his practice with Swayne. Ken hadn't expected to find flesh, but Stonegrinder parted the crude armor like a hot knife through butter. Ken realized there was more truth to Stonegrinder's name than he had previously ascribed.

A third R'Kesh was more cautious than its companions and poked a sword toward Ken's chest. Ken deflected the blow to the side. Again and again, the creature jabbed, craftily backing off after each stroke. A fourth R'Kesh charged in, swinging a wooden cudgel thicker than Ken's arm. Stonegrinder met the stroke, sheared the club cleanly in half, and buried itself in the creature's skull. Seeing this, the R'Kesh with the sword darted in to strike Ken.

Plunk.

A throwing knife had pierced the creature's neck.

Plunk.

A second scored the eye. The creature fell dead.

Dalia walked over, and, pinning the R'Kesh down with her boot, retrieved her throwing knives. As she wiped them in the dirt, she said, "Impressive sword. You must learn to guide the stroke better. I might not be here to save your skin next time."

"I can hold my own. Thanks all the same. How are the others doing?"

"I can answer that, my friend," said Aldren, materializing from the dusk. Shadows were losing ground to the encroaching nightfall.

Aldren glanced at the R'Kesh bodies. "I see that you continue to demonstrate a talent for survival."

"How is Father?" asked Dalia.

"Swayne? The humans?" added Ken.

"Your plan was well executed. Among our group, there are only minor scrapes and scratches. The human prisoners are another matter, however. The R'Kesh have been less than merciful. Do not be discouraged; you have much to be proud of, for many of your people will live this day who would have otherwise perished. Follow me."

"One moment," Dalia said as she retrieved the rest of her blades.

Delvin One-Arm was encircled by a crowd of ragged humans. The Tuonim watched from the background. There was no cheering, for these people lacked the energy, but there was gratitude and weeping. Womenfolk and children far outnumbered the men; the R'Kesh had seen to that in choosing their first victims.

As Dalia neared, she saw that Cable had struck a torch. Its orange flicker revealed haunting images. There were villagers from the Landing—Wil Hammershal, bruised and bloody, and Cooter Hollanbeck; old Uriah and his daughter Rachina. Dalia prayed that Rachina's unborn was well. And there were Nell Foxworth, Hilary Wild, Alonna Keys holding Bradson's hand. The fact that her husband Bradson was blind had probably saved him from the slaughter. Mercifully, there were many others—Badger and Marney Furleyman, Martha

Steadwell and her children, and a few from Karsey that she knew—but so many more were either missing or slain. And the Landing was lost. It was almost too much for Dalia to bear. Though she would be unlikely to mourn those who had shunned her as a half-breed, there were others whom she had befriended. It was for them that her heart ached. As she walked among the villagers, she spied Delvin, and her emotions finally gave way. Tears spilled from her eyes as she ran to his side. Delvin's good arm was wrapped protectively around a boy.

"Ned!" Dalia cried.

Hugging her, Ned also wept.

"I never dreamed that anyone would come for us!" exclaimed Ned.

"Aye, Delvin One-Arm," said old Barley Rimmersman, who was as much the leader of these refugees as anyone, "this is a debt that we cannot repay. You and these Elder Lords have our thanks and blessings."

Delvin said, "There is one who most deserves your praise, for it is by his will that we stand together in victory. Here he comes now."

Ken approached with Aldren and Swayne.

Delvin gestured, and before he could get a word in edgewise, Barley had fallen to his knees and said, "We salute the Falcon Clan for this deed."

"Barley, Lord Gunderhad deserves your thanks, but here is the one I meant," Delvin said as he gestured toward Ken.

"Is he not a lord among the Falcon Clan?" asked Barley, somewhat confused.

Delvin shook his head, and said, "I give you Lord… er… I mean…uuhhm…"

"Ken will do just fine," said Ken, striding into the circle.

"Yes, my Lord," said old Barley.

"Stop right there. I am a man like you. No fancy titles, just Ken. At least, that's what my friends call me."

"A man? As you wish, then," was the hesitant, but respectful, reply.

Beside Barley stood a tattered Otter Thielson. His right arm hung in a makeshift sling, and reddish burns colored his cheek and forehead.

Otter asked Ken, "What do ye reckon is to be done? Our homes are gone. Th' countryside is awash with these devils like a flood tide o'er the marshes. Most of m'lads are slain, and there's a gale brewing which few amongst us can weather."

B*rewing in more ways than one,* Ken thought. *It is getting colder. How much more must these people endure?*

"Let's take one issue at a time," offered Ken. "For now, we have food and water to spare for those most in need. For you others, we can hunt game as we go. As for warmth, there are precious few blankets. We can fashion torches, but you're going to have to share resources. Search the R'Kesh. I saw cloth lining inside their armor. It's unpleasant, but better than freezing.

"Laddy, we need t'rest aside a hearty fire and fill our stomachs," said Otter.

"I'm afraid that won't be possible," replied Ken.

The masses cried out in protest.

Ken shouted, "Please. Please, listen. We aren't safe here. There's no telling how long the lair will remain sealed. Eventually, the creatures will give chase, and we're too few to defeat the entire horde. Pass the word. We'll be on the move shortly."

"Where can we go?" cried Barley despairingly.

"Swayne, how about the Rheinhold Outpost?" asked Ken.

"It was not intended to serve as a shelter for humans," enjoined Swayne.

"Look, it's fortified right, and it can't be too far if Karsey was its supply station," Ken reasoned.

"You are correct on both counts, but that doesn't mean these humans should fall under Tuonim protection."

There was grumbling among the refugees.

"Swayne, Aldren, Delvin, step over here for a minute." Ken pulled them aside.

"Look, there's something in the lair besides the R'Kesh. It tried to stop me from blowing the entrance. It might have succeeded, except we had the element of surprise and it was fathoms underground. I think that prevented it from bringing its full power to bear. You can bet that situation won't last long. Whoever, or whatever, it is will use magic and the R'Kesh to either unplug this hole or dig a new one. Get my drift? We've expended effort to rescue these people, and I will not leave them without a measure of safety. As for humans in the Rheinhold Outpost, if you haven't figured it out yet, your world is changing. The First Mother said that the Nosferu would threaten *all* life—animals, plants, my people, your people—it doesn't matter. Like it or not, we're standing on the brink of war and the battle lines are being drawn. I can pretty much guarantee that humanity isn't going to fight alongside the R'Kesh, so why don't you start treating us like the allies that we are?

Delvin nodded and thought, *Guts, wisdom, and the means to back it. A man such as this would rise to command the Dark Riders. I wonder which of the settlements produced his line.... our lot would improve with more men of such caliber.*

"What of our mission to King Remeth?" Aldren asked. "It will be difficult to retrace our path through this danger."

"There is an easier solution," said Swayne reluctantly, "the Ford of Inlahar. It lies northwest of the Outpost. There, the Gylderhorn may be crossed. I would also speak to the Outpost warriors. They must be forewarned of this threat, and a message taken to the Aerie."

"Then we are in agreement," stated Ken. "Delvin, you know these people. Explain the situation. Tell them we will be departing in ten minutes."

"Leave it to me," assured Delvin, who returned to the circle.

"Swayne, you're familiar with the territory. What's our best route?" asked Ken.

"Through the woods and cliff wall on our right shoulder, we shall meet the Cut in a day or so. It's the supply trail from Karsey, no wider than a horse, but preferable to the natural terrain. The Cut ends at the Dragon's Spine - a series of rock stairs and ledges ascending to the Outpost."

"Okay. Have Cable or Durn assemble more torches and distribute them among the humans. I suggest we work out a patrol among our group—one eye scouting ahead and another to watch the rear. I'll leave that to you and Aldren."

Ken turned.

"Where are you going?" asked Aldren.

"I left a friend tied to a branch. Be right back."

As Ken strode to the mare, he passed the R'Kesh that he had slain. Goblins, ghouls, monsters, R'Kesh—whatever the nomenclature, these hideous creatures struck a note of discord in his very being. He had sucked the life energy from one R'Kesh. It had been foul by any manner of description, but it had sustained him. He prayed that he would never again be forced to such an act, but he had gained a unique understanding of the Enemy. The power rush from draining a living entity was fantastic and pleasurable. In that first instant, he could have conquered the world. Then the high had mellowed; he had foreseen the beginnings of addiction. As he untied the mare, Ken vowed to himself, *Never again.*

He led the horse back to the refugees. Swayne had started the procession, moving out the hundred or so refugees in a column. As Ken traveled up the line, he heard them murmur. Hollow eyes followed his every move.

Suspicion, fear... what am I to these people? Too strange to be counted among my fellow humans, and too human to be accepted by the Elder Race.... Am I to be consigned to a seat on the fence? That might not be a bad place to be for the interim while I'm trying to induce new relationship dynamics between the races. Ultimately, though, I'm human, and that's where my allegiance falls.

The mare neighed in protest and stopped even before Ken had had a chance to rein her in. A woman sat rocking feebly back and forth, clutching a young girl. He had missed her in the darkness.

"Aldren," he called.

In moments, Aldren was there, atop his steed. Ken pointed to the woman. "We've lost the light. Do what you can to see that we don't leave anyone else behind. It's a death sentence. I'll take care of these two."

Aldren nodded and turned his horse back to the rear of the refugees.

Ken dismounted.

The woman in front of him wore a mud-stained frock; claws had shredded it, showing a slip underneath in some spots and blood-encrusted wounds in others. A thin kerchief covered the woman's head, and long red hair, knotted and grimy, escaped from its folds. Her face was bruised and haggard but, under better conditions, might be considered pretty. The youngster, who had nestled her face protectively in her mother's arms, had a crude bandage wrapped around her leg.

Physical wounds can heal. What do you do when the monsters in the closet are real? You fight like hell. How do you tell that to a kid? Well, one thing at a time.

"Can I help?" Ken asked softly.

"My Lord, her father is... he's gone," she sobbed. "I can't carry her further. What is to become of us?"

Ken let the title pass uncorrected and asked, "What's her name?"

"Caitlin."

He bent down and lightly touched the girl's cheek. "Well, Caitlin, how would you like to ride on my horse for a while?"

Caitlin peeked out from her mother's breast and stared at Ken. The greatest of all magic occurred—a smile. And instead of fear, her tearing eyes gleamed wide with hope.

Damn, kids are resilient...have to be to survive in any world. He held out his arms.

Caitlin reached for him.

Ever so carefully, he lifted her high into the saddle.

"Hold on tight," he whispered.

Then he helped the woman from the dirt and put her behind her daughter. The woman wanted to speak, but then sought out his hand. She squeezed it hard.

He nodded in understanding and then gently pulled away. He grabbed hold of the mare's rein and began the long trek.

Higher up the line, his small sacrifice did not pass unnoticed. Dalia was at war inside. On the one hand, her attraction was increasing with each moment, but on the other, he was human. Why did he have to be human? It wouldn't work. All her life, she had desired an Elder Lord. She just could not bear to find her true love only to lose him so quickly to old age and death. This was the price of her Tuonim blood.

Dalia nudged her horse forward to find Delvin. Her father's presence had always comforted her. She saw him walking with Martha Steadwell beside his mount. His horse carried her three children, who held a blanket around their shivering bodies.

Dalia looked skyward. A smattering of wet snowflakes rained upon her face. Taking the edge of her travel cloak, she wiped away the moisture and a layer of grit. She laughed momentarily at her vanity.

The snowfall thickened, and the torches fluttered. *Another storm is beginning,* she thought wearily.

Here ends *The First Mother's Fire*, Book One of *The Soulstealer War*.

In *The Splintering Realm*, Book Two of *The Soulstealer War*, to be published soon, Ken and his companions are relentlessly pursued by the Enemy. As open warfare reaps havoc and alliances fail, Ken awakens to the possibility that he may have to endure a fate worse than death....

The Alphabet of the Old Tongue of the Elder Race

a	b	c	d	e	f	g	h	i

j	k	l	m	n	o	p	q	r

s	t	u	v	w	x	y	z

About the Author

W.L. Hoffman was born in 1967 in Atlantic City, New Jersey, and grew up in nearby Margate City. As a resident of a quiet island community, he spent much of his childhood imagining adventures above and below the waves. He worked many summers as a beach lifeguard, where rainy days meant uninterrupted reading and sunny days brought the occasional rescue in riptides best left to the locals.

Hoffman's interest in reading was voracious from an early age, with a keen taste for fantasy and science fiction, and his teachers encouraged him to pursue this passion. He took advanced English curricula through high school and continued this trend in college. He received his BA in English from Duke University and attended English literature classes at New College at Oxford University in England.

Following his introduction to legislative drafting while serving in the Duke University student government, Mr. Hoffman obtained his JD from Cornell Law School. While there, he edited and wrote as an associate on the Cornell International Law Journal and, between legal treatises, continued devouring fantasy and science fiction stories. With his creativity under daily siege from the law professors, his dreams wandered into strange realms as he quested for life's higher meaning. Thus was born the foundation for his first fantasy novel series, *The Soulstealer War*. While the concept for the series lingered for years as he made his way through a legal career, the sleepless nights that come with young children proved to be an apt trigger for putting pen to paper, thereby resulting in Book One, *The First Mother's Fire*.

Hoffman currently resides in central New Jersey with his wife and daughters. When not plying his day job or writing at night, he enjoys spending time with his girls, digging in their organic vegetable garden, exploring the wilds of the nearby Sourland Mountains, and telling tales on the front porch to what he knows will be the next generation of dreamers and writers.

Printed in the United States
201604BV00001B/1-105/A

9 781598 585391